MW00508494

Wm.D. Murphy

# Biographical Sketches of the State Officers and Members of the Legislature of the State of New York in 1861

SALZWASSER
VERLAG

Wm.D. Murphy

# Biographical Sketches of the State Officers and Members of the Legislature of the State of New York in 1861

Reprint of the original, first published in 1861.

1st Edition 2022  |  ISBN: 978-3-37505-537-0

Verlag (Publisher): Salzwasser Verlag GmbH, Zeilweg 44, 60439 Frankfurt, Deutschland
Vertretungsberechtigt (Authorized to represent): E. Roepke, Zeilweg 44, 60439 Frankfurt, Deutschland
Druck (Print): Books on Demand GmbH, In de Tarpen 42, 22848 Norderstedt, Deutschland

# BIOGRAPHICAL SKETCHES

OF THE

## STATE OFFICERS

AND

# Members of the Legislature

OF THE

## STATE OF NEW YORK,

IN 1861.

BY

## WM. D. MURPHY,

AUTHOR OF "BIOGRAPHICAL SKETCHES," ETC., IN 1858, '59, AND '60.

---

NEW YORK:
PRINTED FOR THE AUTHOR,
1861.

# INTRODUCTION.

---

THIS is the fourth of a series of volumes, issued annually, which the author commenced publishing in 1858. Each volume contains an impartial, truthful, and condensed biographical sketch of the Governor, Lieut. Governor, State Officers, and Members of both branches of the Legislature. The author did not design issuing another volume when the first had made its appearance, neither was such his intention when he had completed the second and third volumes; but the work, which is perfectly correct, even as to the most minute and unimportant dates and details, has been found so valuable as a book of reference that he has thought proper to continue the series. Beyond its usefulness as a work of reference, it is, comparatively, of but little interest to the public, and the private details embodied in the sketches are designed only to give it interest as a volume for private circulation, among the friends of those whose lives constitute its pages. If the publication of the series is hereafter continued, the work will doubtless increase in usefulness as the number of volumes increases, and the author is hopeful that some one more competent than himself will succeed him in the enterprise, should he not again find time to continue it.

The alphabetical order in which the Senators and Members of Assembly have been respectively arranged, obviates entirely the necessity of an index to the work.

# BIOGRAPHICAL SKETCHES.

---

## EDWIN D. MORGAN,

### GOVERNOR.

GOVERNOR MORGAN is an instance of the peculiar nature of our institutions, which, while they permit to the poorest man of intellect the opportunity of reaching the highest political positions, at the same time tempt and sanction the choice of those who have nothing but the color of gold and the tinsel of wealth to commend them to popular favor. His political career has always been successful, because he has not often aspired to places of honor; but when he has been a candidate, he has never failed to prompt efforts in his behalf by the most liberal expenditure of the money he has acquired by a shrewdness in trade that is as well a characteristic of his family as of the citizens of the State of his early adoption—Connecticut. The most prominent features in the following résumé of his life, prepared as an electioneering document, during his first canvass for the office of Governor, bring out with vivid distinctness what may be called the *fitness* of his Excellency to cope with the material questions into which our politics have latterly resolved themselves.

Gov. Morgan was born in the town of Washington, Berkshire County, Mass., on the 8th of February, 1811. His father, Jasper Morgan, resided in that town till 1822, when he removed with his family to Windsor, Connecticut, where he is still living at a ripe old age. Until he had reached his seventeenth year, Edwin passed his life very much as the sons of New England farmers generally do—in tilling the soil and going to school. But with his common-school education, a capital of thirty-seven and a half cents, and a firm determination to succeed in life by his industry and integrity, he went forth to seek his fortune, in 1828, in Hartford, Connecticut.

The young men of the present day will doubtless smile at hearing that he bound himself to a Hartford trader, at a salary of $60 for the first year, $75 for the second year, and $100 for the third year. But during his clerkship, and when only nineteen years of age, an incident occurred which exhibits, in a marked degree, his real character. A trip to the great city was not then made with such facility as at this time, but as he had served for two or three years in the store, and acquired the confidence of his employer, he was permitted to go to New York, and, to combine business with pleasure, was intrusted to make sundry purchases of tea, sugar, etc., and also corn, which was then becoming an article of import, instead of export. The visit was made, and Edwin returned in due time, coming home by the old stage route. After being greeted and welcomed, his employer inquired as to the corn. The price was very satisfactory, but his employer doubted if the article would be of very good quality at so low a rate. Edwin immediately drew a handful, first from one pocket and then from another, as samples, and the old gentleman expressed his approbation. It had been usual for the dealers to purchase two or three hundred bushels at a time, and he then inquired of Edwin as to the quantity, but was nonplussed by the answer, that he had bought two cargoes, and that the vessels were probably in the river. "Why, Edwin," said the astonished old gentleman, "what are we to do with two cargoes of corn? Where can we put it? Where can we dispose of it?" "Oh!" replied Edwin, "I have disposed of all that you don't want, at an advance; I have shown the samples to Messrs. A. B., who wish three hundred bushels; C. & Co., three hundred bushels, etc., etc. I could have disposed of three cargoes, if I had had them. I stopped in the stores as I came from the stage office, and made sales."

It was a new phase, and out of the old routine, but the gains and results were not to be questioned. The following morning Edwin was at the store, as always, in season, and had taken the broom to sweep out the counting-room, when his employer entered. "I think," said he, "you had better put aside that broom; we will find some one else to do the sweeping. A man who can go to New York, and on his own responsibility purchase two cargoes, and make sale of them without counselling with his principal, can be otherwise more advantageously employed. It is best that he should become a partner in the firm for which he is doing so much." Although not of age, he was forthwith taken into partnership, and from that day to this, success has marked all his business operations.

Shortly after attaining his majority, Gov. Morgan was elected a member of the City Council of Hartford. In 1833 he was married to Miss Waterman, of that place, by whom he has one surviving child—a son of mature years; and in December, 1836, removed to the city of New York, where he established himself as a wholesale grocer. He was prudent, and used his small capital—$4,000—with sagacity and discretion. He was thus enabled to pass through the trying times of 1837–'42 without disaster, and gradually to increase his fortune, until now he ranks among the richest merchants of the city—the house of E. D. Morgan & Co. standing among the first in New York. He occupied a somewhat prominent position in that city for many years, before he cared about assuming public duties. At length, in 1849, at the request of many gentlemen of his political faith, he became a member of the Board of Assistant Aldermen. In that year, as is well known, the cholera broke out and raged with fearful violence throughout the metropolis. At that time he was one of the Sanatory Committee, and upon him devolved particularly the duty of providing hospitals for the sick; but instead of leaving the city, and seeking safety and repose in the country, he remained at his post, and for nearly four months devoted a large share of each day to administering to the wants of the afflicted.

In 1850, Gov. Morgan was elected to the Senate from the city of New York, and was re-elected in 1852. He at once distinguished himself in that body as a correct business man, speaking rarely, but to the point, and devoting himself assiduously to the less obtrusive but more useful duties of his position. Since the organization of the Republican party, he has been one of its most honored and active members. He was for some years Chairman of the Whig State Central Committee, and was, up to the time of his nomination for Governor, Chairman of the Republican State Central Committee, which position he had occupied since the organization of that party. He was one of the officers of the Pittsburgh National Convention in the winter of 1855, which was the first practical step taken for the establishment of the national organization of the Republican party, and was then chosen Chairman of the National Committee, a post which he still holds. He occupied the position of one of the Commissioners of Emigration some two years, but resigned the place after his election as Governor. Last fall he was re-elected Governor for a second term, though the lowest man on his ticket.

The administration of Gov. Morgan has, thus far, fallen somewhat short of the expectations entertained by his friends at the opening of his official career. His reputation as an eminently successful business man, of positive firmness and great decision of character, had prepared the minds of all for an administration after the style of "Old Hickory"—full of encouragement to the whole people, and the general welfare and prosperity of the entire State; but, strange to say, nothing

1*

has, as yet, transpired in his official conduct to warrant any such distinction, and his course on most of the prominent questions that have come before him, since his advent to Executive honors, has been vacillating, undecided, and, to a greater or less degree, disadvantageous to the best interests of the State. This fact is especially illustrated by his course on the subject of a bill appropriating a certain amount of money to aid the completion of the Albany & Susquehanna Railroad—a measure of conceded merit, and one which cannot fail to prove highly advantageous to the section of the State through which the road is being constructed. After passing both branches of the Legislature, two years ago, his Excellency promptly vetoed the bill, upon constitutional grounds, while in his annual message, a year ago, he took particular pains to inform the Legislature that he would not again withhold his official sanction from a similar measure, if presented to him for that purpose, but which he did not fail to veto again. The same may be said of his course on the subject of the "lobby" —a body which has become second to none other in its influences upon the legislative department of the government. In his first annual message to the Legislature, he impressively warned the representatives of the people, that the legislation of the State had already been too much controlled by the lobby influence, and that he would never sanction any measure which he had the slightest cause to suspect had been passed by such an influence ; and yet, when that portion of his message had been referred to a standing committee in the Senate, with special power, he quietly allowed his political friends in that body to "crush out" all investigation on the subject, and the lobby cormorants, who had wholly deserted the Capitol at the very mention of an investigation, again returned, like the Goths and Vandals of old, with increased numbers and more voracious appetites. Many of his appointments, too, to the various places of public trust under the Executive control, have been made without regard to the fitness of the men named, but at the direction of those whose code of morals justifies the means by the ends attained.

In his Annual Message, at the opening of the last session of the Legislature, Gov. Morgan invited the attention of that body to the necessity of increased railroad facilities in the city of New York, hedging the recommendation with such provisoes and ifs as would commend him and his proposition to popular favor. He knew, probably, how little would be regarded the proposed restrictions by those who had determined to grasp these mines of wealth for their individual benefit. He could not but know that his partisans would conceive their projects in such form as would best answer their ends, carefully keeping in the foreground his recommendations, and as carefully concealing their failure to incorporate in the grants the restrictions shadowed forth in the message. The bills, however, passed the Legislature, and encountered, as it was expected they would, the Governor's veto. But while he thus maintained his character for Jacksonian firmness before the public, he was careful that the greed of his friends should not be disappointed. While, therefore, standing before the public as the opponent of these swindles, he was using his individual efforts to promote their passage over his own vetoes.

This incident is characteristic of Gov. Morgan. The results showed alike his shrewdness and his boldness. Claiming the crown of the martyr, he demanded from the people the reward of honest endeavor. Turning to those who had reaped the spoils of legislation, he demanded their support upon the well-grounded plea of efficient service. Thus was presented the strange spectacle of a candidate nominated for Governor by the honesty of the State, and sustained at the polls by the very knaves who had apparently been cut down by his trenchant sword of integrity. The children have a common saying, "That you cannot eat your cake and have it. too." Gov. Morgan has demonstrated the reverse, for he has been successful in attracting the honest voters of the State to his standard, without alienating the rogues. Few men have so closely veiled their real characteristics behind the cloak of the demagogue. His success in this respect has been a fruitful source of conjecture. How he has escaped, puzzles alike friend and foe, and yet the enigma is not so difficult. In his politics, as in his business, he has been strictly a merchant. He has kept his choicest goods in the front shop—his coarse wares in the rear. While the public have been pleased with the display in the show windows, his retainers have been kept fat with the substantials in the cellar.

# ROBERT CAMPBELL,

## LIEUTENANT-GOVERNOR.

ALTHOUGH too modest for an efficient parliamentarian, Lieut.-Gov. Campbell, as the presiding officer of the Senate, has discharged his duties, during the past two years, with the strictest honesty and fidelity, and has not failed to prove himself a worthy successor, in that position, of such distinguished men as De Witt Clinton, John Taylor, Erastus Root, Edward P. Livingston, Daniel S. Dickinson, Hamilton Fish, Sanford E. Church, Henry J. Raymond, and Henry R. Selden.

Mr. Campbell is a native of the pleasant little village of Bath, Steuben county, New York, where he was born in the year 1809, and where he now resides. He is a son of the late Robert Campbell, Sr., who died in 1849, and who emigrated to this country from Scotland, and settled in the town of Bath, as early as 1794. He followed the honest occupation of a farmer, and was, in every respect, a fair representative of the very best type of Scottish character.

Mr. Campbell was educated chiefly at the Geneva Academy and College. He then received a thorough course of legal training, and at once entered upon the practice of law, in his native village, where he has always since been engaged in his profession, with the exception of a short time, which he passed at Auburn. As a lawyer, he is sagacious and able, and although making no pretensions to forensic display, never fails to express himself with plainness and force. He possesses a clear, strong, logical mind, and is liberal, though tenacious in the maintenance of his own opinions. He is now engaged in farming and in the pursuit of his profession, and has been eminently successful in both. Although not ambitious of political notoriety, he has been an active and very influential politician in the county of Steuben, from his early youth up. He has an unfeigned aversion to office, preferring to devote himself exclusively to the private management of his party, in which he has proven himself an adept, and has almost invariably refused to allow his name to be brought forward in connexion with any public office. He was, however, a member of the Constitutional Convention of 1846, where he took a prominent and influential part in behalf of the notorious " Stop and Tax Law," and is now a Regent of the University. He was always a bold, fearless, and uncompromising member of the Democratic party until the Buffalo schism, when he became identified with the friends of Mr. Van Buren, many of whom have since, like himself, joined the Republican ranks. He was nominated by the Republican State Convention in the fall of 1858, and again in the fall of 1860, with great unanimity for the position he now occupies, and was elected by a large majority in both instances.

Mr. Campbell's personal appearance is that of a man who is in the full enjoyment of matured intellectual powers, and a sound, unimpaired physical constitution. He is rather below the medium size, with dark blue eyes, dark brown hair, head and features finely formed, and has a cool and deliberate, though firm and uncompromising expression of countenance, which at once gives assurance of the man. He is married, and occupies a deservedly high position both in the social and political world. He is unpretending and somewhat reserved in his general deportment ; but his social intercourse is always of the most cordial character ; and the longer he is known, the stronger and more unyielding becomes the attachment of his friends for him. He is, personally, well liked by the people of Albany, among whom he is no longer a stranger, and his re-election to the distinguished post he occupies is a matter of deep gratification to them all. In private, as in public life, he never " carries the war into Africa," being a gentleman of moderate views in everything, and though tenacious of the right, is always conciliatory and compromising, loving peace rather than war.

# STATE OFFICERS.

## DAVID R. FLOYD JONES,

### SECRETARY OF STATE.

THE administration of Mr. Jones, in the distinguished position he occupies, has been eminently successful, during the past year. His courtesy, promptness, and fidelity to the best interests of the people, have secured the approbation of all classes of men, and furnish additional evidence that he has inherited, in no ordinary degree, the high order of ability and capacity for public life which so much distinguished his ancestors.

Mr. Jones was born on the 6th of April, 1813, on the south side of Long Island, at Fort Neck, Queens County, New York. His parents, Thomas Floyd Jones and Cornelia Herring Jones, are both dead, the former having died in August, 1851, at the age of sixty-three, and the latter in December, 1839, at the age of forty-three. His ancestry has been traced as far back as Thomas Jones, who was a major in the army of King James, and who, after being defeated at the battle of the Boyne, emigrated from Strabane, Ireland, to America, as early as 1592. Subsequently, he removed to Rhode Island, and after marrying a daughter of

Thomas Townsend, settled at Fort Neck, where he resided until his death, in 1713. His son, David Jones, to whom his property at that place was devised, was born in September, 1699. In 1737, he was chosen a member of the General Assembly, and continued in that body until 1758, occupying the position of Speaker, during a period of thirteen years. Throughout his whole life, and in every position, he was the unyielding advocate of the rights of the people against every species of royal encroachment, and no man of his day participated more largely in the public confidence and respect. On one occasion, while Speaker, he ordered the doors of the Assembly to be closed against the Governor, until a bill, then under consideration, could be passed, which his Excellency had determined to prevent by an immediate prorogation. In 1758 he was appointed a Judge of the Supreme Court of the Colony, which he resigned in 1773, and died on the 1st of October, 1775.

Thomas Jones, the oldest son of David Jones, was also a Judge of the Supreme Court of the Colony. He married Miss De Lancy, a daughter of Lieut.-Governor James De Lancy, and sister of the father of the Right Rev. Bishop De Lancy, of Western New York, and died in England.

Samuel Jones, the grandson of Major Thomas Jones, and the great-grandfather of the subject of this sketch, was born on the 26th of July, 1734. He was in due time admitted to the bar, and soon found himself in the enjoyment of an extensive and lucrative practice. For his exemplary industry, high attainments, and great purity of character, he was looked upon as a model for

the imitation of all who aimed at distinction in jurisprudence.   His office was eagerly sought by students ; and
besides De Witt Clinton, he instructed many who afterwards rose to much distinction.   He was often in the
General Assembly, and in 1778 was a member of the
Convention that adopted the Constitution of the United
States, of which body his intimate friend, George Clinton, was president.   In 1789, he was associated with
Richard Varick, in revising the Statutes of the State of
New York, which was chiefly executed by Mr. Jones
himself, with uncommon accuracy and expedition.   He
was, in the same year, appointed Recorder of the City
of New York, which position he held until 1797, when
he was succeeded by the Hon. James Kent.   In 1796 he
organized, at the request of Gov. Jay, the office of Comptroller, and was the first comptroller ever appointed
in the State.   He died on the 21st of November,
1819, leaving five sons, the oldest of whom, Samuel
Jones, has been Chancellor of the State of New York,
Chief Justice of the Superior Court of the City of New
York, and a Justice of the Supreme Court of the State.
His second son, Major William Jones, the grandfather
of the subject of this sketch, on his mother's side, was
for eight years a useful and intelligent member of the
Legislature of this State, and died only a few years since,
at an advanced age.   He was greatly esteemed during
life, and left behind him a name of which his surviving
children and grand-children are justly proud.

Mr. Jones received the rudiments of his education at
Christ's Church Academy, Manhasset, Long Island, and
in 1829 entered the Sophomore class of Union College,

at Schenectady, N. Y., from which institution he graduated in 1832. He then studied law with the late Samuel W. Jones, of Schenectady, and in 1836 commenced the practice of his profession in the city of New York, as a partner of the late James P. Howard. He continued the practice of the law until the fall of 1840, when he was chosen a member of the Assembly from the city of New York. He was re-elected in 1841, and again in 1842, and throughout his entire career in that body, showed himself an honest and capable representative. In 1843 he was the successful candidate for a seat in the Senate from the First District, then comprising the counties of New York, Kings, and Richmond, and was a prominent and influential member of the Constitutional Convention of 1846, from the city of New York. Soon after the expiration of his senatorial term, on the 31st of December, 1847, he was, after the death of Jesse Oakley, appointed Clerk of the Superior Court of the City of New York, by Chief Justice Oakley, Judge Sandford, and Judge Vanderpoel. He successfully occupied this position until the spring of 1852, when he resigned it, and returned to his native place, where he now resides, on a portion of the property which has been in the family for more than a century and a half. He has been quite successful in his agricultural pursuits, and during the past two years has been honored with the position of President of the Queens County Agricultural Society.

In 1856, Mr. Jones reluctantly consented to represent his native county once more in the lower branch of the Legislature, and at the session which followed, was the

Democratic candidate for Speaker, and again a useful and industrious member of that body.   He has been Supervisor of his native town, during the past three years, and now holds the position of Chairman of the Board.   His nomination for the distinguished position he now occupies, was made with great unanimity by both wings of the Democracy, at their State Convention, in the fall of 1859; and after receiving the endorsement of the American State Convention, at Utica, with equal unanimity, he was triumphantly elected.   He has, throughout his entire political career, always been a straightforward, consistent, unyielding, and persevering Democrat of the National Conservative or Hard-shell stamp; and, although belonging to the purer class of politicians, has never failed to actively contribute his full share of service to the successful promotion of the principles and policy of that party.

Mr. Jones is a gentleman of prepossessing personal appearance, being tall and elegantly formed, with black, bushy hair, heavy black whiskers, clear black eyes, and a mild, intelligent countenance; and is kind, courteous, and agreeable in his intercourse with all with whom he comes in contact.

## ROBERT DENNISTON,

### COMPTROLLER.

Mr. Denniston is an old-fashioned Democrat of the strictest sect, and was reared in the school of politics to which such men as Silas Wright, A. C. Flagg, and Michael Hoffman belonged. During the Old Hunker and Barnburner schism, he was closely attached to the latter branch of the party; and in the progress of events, by the natural bent of his political education, has become a Republican of the Jeffersonian stamp. He is a gentleman of conceded shrewdness and sagacity; an ardent and zealous politician; and persevering and indomitable in maintaining and defending his principles, and in the pursuit of his political projects. There is nothing brilliant or ostentatious in his manner, and his entire course through life has been simply that of a quiet, straightforward, honest, practical farmer and statesman.

Mr. Denniston was born on the 15th of October, 1800, in the town of Blooming Grove, Orange county, N. Y. His great-grandfather, Alexander Denniston, with his brother-in-law, Charles Clinton, and his friend, John Young, left the county of Longford, Ireland, where they were born, and in the latter part of May, 1729, embarked from Dublin for New York, landing at Cape Cod, in the month of October, after a perilous passage of twenty-one weeks and three days. In the spring of 1731, the three pioneers settled in New Windsor, Orange county, N. Y., and from the top of a high hill in that town, named the country, as far as they could see, Little Britain, which name the neighborhood still retains, while the high hill is known as the Clinton Burying-Ground. The mother of Mr. Denniston, who still survives, was the youngest of a large family by the name of Morrison, all of whom were born at Bellanyhinch, in the county of Down, Ireland, with the exception of herself. They also settled in Little Britain, where many of their descendants still reside. It will thus be perceived that the subject of this sketch is of pure Irish blood, of which he has frequently been known to boast.

Mr. Denniston commenced his education at the Blooming Grove Academy, on the first of January, 1815, under the Rev. Joshua Boyd, who now resides at Newburgh, and in July, 1820, graduated at Union College, Schenectady. Among his classmates were Laurens P. Hickok, present Vice-President of that institution; Tayler Lewis, one of the most accomplished Greek scholars in the United States; William Kent, whose distinguished legal talents have left an everlasting impress upon the jurisprudence of the country; William H. Seward, now representing New York in the United States Senate; John C. Wright, formerly State Comptroller; James G. Hopkins, Alfred E. Campbell, and several others who have held prominent public positions in the country. After leaving college he settled on a farm within one mile and a half of his native place, which he subsequently inherited, and on which he has continued to reside. He soon became a military officer, a Justice of the Peace, and, by the appointment of Gov. Marcy, a County Judge. In 1835 he was an active and prominent member of the Assembly, and successfully held the same position in the years 1839 and '40. The next year he entered the Senate, as one of the Representatives from what was then the second district, and began his labors in that capacity with such men as

Alonzo C. Paige, Gulian C. Verplanck, Alva Hunt, and Erastus Root. The State was then divided into eight Senatorial districts, and each district was entitled to four Senators, who were chosen for four years. He was re-elected to the same position in the fall of 1844, and successfully occupied it until the last of January, 1848. The great question before the people of the State, during his entire term of service in that body, was that of the completion of the public works, and during most of the time he held the responsible post of Chairman of the Standing Committee on Canals. He has always been friendly to the completion of the canals, but, throughout his entire legislative career, acted upon the doctrine, that no work should be undertaken or recognised by the State that will not, when completed, sustain itself, pay the interest on its cost, and contribute something towards a sinking fund to redeem the principal. He made a report in the Senate on the 21st of March, 1844, which contained an extended review of the financial operations of the State, in regard to the public works, and which at once gave him a distinguished reputation as a man of superior ability, and a thorough knowledge of his subject.

After retiring from the Senate, Mr. Denniston remained quietly at home on his farm, until the fall of 1857, when he was nominated by the Republican State Convention, at Syracuse, for the distinguished place he now occupies. Owing to some disaffection, however, in the ranks of his party, he was defeated. Nothing was then again heard of him in the political arena until the fall of 1859, when he was renominated as a candidate for the same office, by the Republicans in State Convention. He was subsequently, likewise, nominated for the same position by the American State Convention at Utica, and was elected by about forty-nine thousand majority. Thus far, he has discharged the duties of the office with efficiency and ability, and bids fair to leave a praiseworthy administration upon the records of the State.

Mr. Denniston was married, in 1824, to Juliana Howell, who, at the end of one year and five months, died, leaving him childless. He was again married, in 1832, to Miss Mary Scott, of Elizabethtown, New Jersey, by whom he has reared eleven children, all now living. In religion he is a New School Presbyterian. He stands well in the social world, being kind and agreeable in his personal intercourse towards all with whom he comes in contact, and enjoys a great degree of personal, as well as political, popularity wherever he is known.

---

# PHILIP DORSHEIMER,

## TREASURER.

Mr. Dorsheimer was born on the 15th of April, 1797, and is, therefore, in the sixty-fourth year of his age. He is a native of Wollstein, in the Canton of Wollstein, Department of Dendersberg, Germany. His father, Wilhelm Dorsheimer, who came to America in 1834, died in Buffalo in 1852, at the good old age of eighty-six, and his mother, whose maiden name was Maria Graemer, died in Germany, at the age of sixty-two. His parents were both distinguished for their persevering industry, integrity, and real moral worth, and died lamented by 'a large circle of sincere and devoted friends.

Mr. Dorsheimer was educated in the common schools of his native place, and came to the United States in 1816. He first settled in Dauphin county, Pennsylvania, where he resided until 1822, when he moved into Wayne county, in this State. In 1836 he removed to the city of Buffalo, where he has always since been a resident. His chief occupation, since arriving at manhood, has been that of milling, though since his residence in Buffalo he has been some years successfully engaged in keeping a hotel. His business qualifications are of a high order, and his reputation in the latter calling is altogether unsurpassed anywhere, as any one who has had occasion to stop at the *Mansion House* in Buffalo can readily testify. The first public position he ever held was that of postmaster, to which he was appointed under the administration of President Van Buren, in 1838, and which he held until 1841. He was re-appointed to the same office in 1845, by Mr. Polk, again holding the position until July, 1847, when he was peremptorily dismissed, in consequence of his Freesoil proclivities. Up to that period he had always been a Democrat, of the old-fashioned school, strenuously advocating the principles and policy of that party under all circumstances; but in the Presidential campaign of the following year he early enlisted in the ranks of the

2

supporters of the Buffalo platform, and has always since then been firm and decided in his adherence to the doctrine of the right and duty of Congress to prohibit slavery in the territories of the United States. In the great contest of 1852, he was found acting with the friends of Mr. Pierce, under the mistaken impression that he was thus favoring the success of that same principle; but after the repeal of the Missouri restriction he was one among the very first to engage in the organization of the Republican party upon that distinctive issue. He remained quietly at home, contenting himself with an honest and industrious pursuit of his own private affairs, after his dismissal from the Post-office department in 1847, until the fall of 1859, when he was nominated by the Republican State Convention, at Syracuse, as a candidate for the distinguished office he now occupies. He was afterwards nominated for the same position by the American State Convention at Utica, and was elected by about fifty thousand majority, as were, also, the rest of his colleagues, with a single exception, on the American ticket.

Mr. Dorsheimer possesses a strong native vigor of intellect, combined with a high degree of general intelligence, and, during the past year, has proven himself qualified to fulfil properly the duties with which the people have intrusted him in the administration of the government. He is a man of liberal views and feelings on all questions of a private or public character, and sustains an enviable reputation, wherever he is known, for his uprightness and integrity of character, his congeniality of temper and disposition, and his unsurpassed combination of all the essential elements of personal popularity. His habits are peculiarly simple and unpretending, whether as a private citizen or a public officer; and his whole appearance is calculated to invite, rather than discourage, the approach of the most humble individual. He devotes himself assiduously and perseveringly to the discharge of the duties of his office, seldom being found absent from his post during the business hours of the day, and never fails to secure the good opinion of all with whom he comes in contact in his official capacity.

Mr. Dorsheimer was married in 1821, in Dauphin county, Pennsylvania, to Miss Sarah, daughter of Joseph Gorgas, an enterprising farmer of that county, and attends the Unitarian Church.

## CHARLES G. MYERS,

### ATTORNEY GENERAL.

Mr. Myers was born in the year 1810, in the town of Madrid, St. Lawrence county, New York. His paternal ancestors were originally from Germany, and, on his maternal side, he is supposed to be of Scotch extraction. His parents, who were also natives of the State of New York, are both dead, and sustained a high reputation for honesty, integrity, and real moral worth, during the entire period of their lives.

Mr. Myers received a classical education, at the St.

Lawrence Academy, at Potsdam, in his native county, an institution from which some of the most talented and distinguished men in the country have graduated. After leaving school, at the age of fifteen, he entered the law office of Governeur Ogden, at Waddington, where, with an interval spent at Rochester, he pursued, for seven successive years, his legal studies, with the most unremitting attention and persevering industry, and was admitted to the bar in 1832. In the year following, he commenced the practice of his profession, in the village of Ogdensburgh, St. Lawrence county, where he has always since been a prominent and successful lawyer. He held the office of Surrogate of that county some years, and was elected District Attorney at the first election under the new Constituiton of 1846. This position he held six years, discharging his duties with considerable credit to himself, as well as entire satisfaction to the great body of the people of the county; and, in the meantime, was also an active, efficient member of the lower branch of the Legislature of 1848. After the expiration of his term of service as District Attorney, he never again occupied any conspicuous public place until the fall of 1859, when he was almost unanimously nominated by the Republican State Convention at Syracuse, as a candidate for the distinguished position of Attorney General of the State. He was, subsequently, likewise, nominated at Utica, by the American State Convention, which made out a ticket composed equally, as near as possible, of the Democratic and Republican State tickets, then already in the field, and was elected by a majority of over forty thousand.

He has been prompt and successful in the discharge of his duties during the past year, and will, doubtless, retire from his position at the expiration of the present year with the approbation of all parties. As a politician, he has never been ambitious, though by no means an indifferent observer of the ordinary course of political events, and has always been reluctantly drawn from the walks of private life and the quiet pursuit of his profession to fill the various public stations to which he has been chosen.

Mr. Myers was formerly a Democrat, of the Silas Wright stamp, from his earliest youth. He remained firmly and of principle attached to that party until 1848, when he had the pleasure of introducing into the Legislature the first resolutions ever presented to the people of the State of New York, in favor of the right and duty of Congress to prohibit the introduction of slavery into the territories of the United States. President Polk, in his Annual Message, at the previous opening of Congress, had asked for an appropriation for the purchase of certain territory, at the close of the Mexican war, and the resolutions in question proposed to instruct the Representatives of this State, in Congress, to oppose any such appropriation, unless the principle of the celebrated Wilmot Proviso was applied to the territorial government of the proposed acquisition. It was a new question, and proved to be the great entering-wedge in the creation of the unhappy division which has always since existed in the Democratic ranks ; but their author urged their passage with vigor and determination, and eventually secured it by an almost unanimous vote in both Houses. Since then Mr. Myers has always been unyieldingly consistent in his support of the great principle involved in his resolutions on that occasion, and when it was more prominently brought before the country by the repeal of the Missouri Compromise, he was one among the very first to engage in the organization of the Republican party, upon the basis of that principle. He looks upon the doctrine of Popular Sovereignty as a " popular humbug," and maintains that Congress has the exclusive and unconditional control of the subject of Slavery in the territories of the United States.

As a lawyer, Mr. Myers occupies a prominent position in his profession. He is a good speaker, combining general coolness with occasional excitability, and whether before the court or a jury, acquits himself in a manner that seldom fails to secure him his point. He is interesting, agreeable, and always full of life and cheerfulness in private conversation, and is affable, gentlemanly, and highly accomplished in his manners. He is a man of family, and in his private and domestic relations is respected and esteemed. In person, he is about medium size, with intelligent grey eyes, bushy grey hair, English side whiskers, a broad, prominent forehead, and a florid complexion, which suggests a keen relish for all the creature comforts of life.

# VAN R. RICHMOND,

## STATE ENGINEER AND SURVEYOR.

MR. RICHMOND is a native of the town of Preston, Chenango county, New York, where he was born in January, 1812. His father, Oliver Richmond, who died, in 1853, at an advanced age, was a successful farmer in that town, and was well and favorably known throughout that section of the State. Mr. Richmond was educated at the Oxford Academy, in his native county, and as early as 1834, when still a mere youth, received from the State the appointment of chainman in the engineering force engaged upon the construction of the Chenango Canal. He occupied this position, gradually rising in point of rank, until 1837, when he received the appointment of Resident Engineer on the Erie Canal, and was located at Lyons, where he has always since resided. In 1842 his location was changed from this place to Syracuse, where he took charge of the entire Middle Division of the New York State Canals, under Jonas Earll and Daniel P. Bissell, as Canal Commissioners. In 1848, he resigned this position, and accepted an appointment on the Oswego Canal. About this time it was decided, by the Whig Canal Board then in power, to run an independent line for the enlarged canal from Jordon to the Cayuga Marshes. There was no one, however, in their employment to whom they felt safe in intrusting the work, and after carefully canvassing the merits of all the engineers of the State, Mr.

Richmond was tendered and accepted an appointment for the execution of the task, in a separate capacity. He immediately submitted a line for the canal, and a plan for the aqueduct across Seneca river, which were adopted, and the work was at once put under contract. This aqueduct is doubtless the most important structure on the Erie Canal, and fittingly attests the skill and ingenuity of its originator.

Having satisfactorily arranged the plan of this noble piece of work across the Seneca river, Mr. Richmond resigned his position, in 1850, to take the appointment of Division Engineer of the Syracuse and Rochester Direct Railroad, occupying the place until 1852, when, at the instance of William C. McAlpine, he was again appointed Division Engineer of the Middle Division of the State Canals. In the fall of 1853, a Whig Canal Board was again elected, including the Hon. John T. Clark, as State Engineer. Mr. Richmond having always been a staunch Democrat, strong efforts were now made to accomplish his removal, but Mr. Clark refused to countenance the measure, and he was retained —a circumstance as creditable to Mr. Clark as it was complimentary to Mr. Richmond. In the winter of 1856, the American party came into power, and he was removed from office for the first and only time in his life. He then lived in the quiet retirement of private life at his home in Lyons, until the fall of 1857, when he was nominated for the distinguished position he now occupies, and was triumphantly elected. About the expiration of his term of office, in 1859, he was renominated for the same position by the Democratic State

Convention at Syracuse, and the American State Convention at Utica, and was again triumphantly elected. It was in this year that the American party placed in the field what was sneeringly termed by their opponents the "Hybrid ticket," composed, as nearly as possible, equally of the Republican and Democratic tickets, previously put in nomination, and Mr. Richmond was among those taken from the latter. During the twenty years he has been in the service of the State as an engineer, he has proven himself equal, if not superior, to any of his predecessors, in industry, integrity, and fidelity to the interests of the people, and there is scarcely any one in the State who can surpass him in the line of his profession. He has seldom participated actively in the political controversies of the day, being constantly absorbed in the ordinary pursuits of engineering, and is wholly indebted to his high standing and ability in his profession for his present prominent position in the administration of the government. He is one of those rare men whom dignity and fortune do not spoil, and enjoys a high degree of personal popularity at the State capital.

Mr. Richmond was married, in 1837, to Miss Anna A. Dennison, who died in the spring of 1854, and by whom he has three children living. He was again married in 1859, and occupies a deservedly high position in all the relations of private life. In person he is somewhat above the medium height, being slender and well formed, and has light hair, light blue eyes, fair complexion, a smooth face, and a quick, active step, denoting a restless, working mind.

2*

# SENATORS.

## DAVID H. ABELL.

FARMER ABELL, as he is popularly known, is the largest, and one of the most attractive men in the Senate. He stands about five feet eight inches in his broad-toed boots, robust and substantial in his general appearance, with dark straight hair, partially mixed with grey, a face suggesting the higher order of conspirator in every lineament, and a general air of deceptive good-nature and shyness, which seems constantly to weigh the weakness of all other men while studiously concealing its own purpose.

Senator Abell is about fifty-four years of age, and was for some years a resident of Genesee county, New York, before removing into Livingston county, where he now resides. He possesses some education, but his character has received its brawn and sinew from practice, and his course through private life has been simply that of a quiet, practical, though not very successful farmer. Although born of wild, strong, determined kindred, who seem from old to have lived a life of " stub and strife," and in a rank just sufficiently high to save him from knowing the pangs of want, the world-oyster was to him firmly closed, and it has been with difficulty only that he has barely succeeded in opening it. He is not averse to the attractions of public office, and always, when his object is attained, consults his personal ease and comfort rather than the arduous duties that have devolved upon him. Thus he sits in his seat in the Senate, " calm as a summer's morning," though all his associates may be immersed in a Senatorial conflict on an exciting topic, and is scarcely ready to give the responsive aye or nay on the final vote. He leaves the toil and trouble of investigation and preparation to others, content that his name is recorded in the vote, so that his constituents may see that he is at his post. He has no personal popularity, and seldom, therefore, has been a candidate for public honors, though his desire for office is unquenchable. His reputation and standing at home would never justify his friends in presenting his name for official distinction with any hope of success, unless some fortunate circumstance placed him in a position to command it. Such an event happened in the fall of 1859, when the merging of Abolitionists and Republicans increased the numerical strength of his party to such a degree that a Senatorial Convention in his district concluded to hazard the experiment, and he was elected.

Senator Abell is not a reliable man. Contrary to the expressed wishes of his constituents, he was a firm supporter of all the schemes of last winter, in which the lobby is reputed to have figured so conspicuously. He regards his personal interest above all other considerations, and will descend to any meanness to gain the object of his ambition. In pursuing his schemes he secured the friendship and confidence of the late Governor Young, succeeded in his purpose, and then betrayed his benefactor. The Governor adhered to his faithless follower until he injured himself by the contact. In 1847 that functionary sent his name to the Senate as a candidate for Canal Appraiser, but that body knowing, and therefore distrusting, the nominee, refused to confirm the appointment. The next year found a more compliant Senate, and, upon the renomination of Governor Young, Mr. Abell was confirmed, and entered upon the duties of his office. No sooner was he fixed in his new position, however, than he forgot his benefactor, and, with characteristic treachery, joined the traducers of Governor Young, and ever after exhibited unwonted hostility towards him.

From that time forward he became identified with the extreme anti-slavery wing of the Whig party, and is now politically associated with such men as William H. Seward, Orsamus B. Matteson, Thurlow Weed, James Watson Webb, William C. Bryant, John Jay, and Hinton R. Helper.

## JAMES A. BELL.

SENATOR BELL was one of the most quiet, yet efficient and industrious men in the last Legislature. His course, both upon the floor of the Senate and as Chairman of the Committee on Manufactures, and a member of the Committee on Canals, was as creditable to himself as it was satisfactory to his constituents. He was always found faithful to whatever was calculated to promote the real interests of the Canals, and the protest, signed by him and Senator Peter P. Murphy, which was presented to the Senate against the New York City Railroads, shows the tenacity with which he opposed the passage of those measures. He proved himself perfectly invulnerable against the attacks of the lobby. His sterling integrity and honesty of purpose would not allow him to support a measure that was even suspected of corruption, and he was the last man to give a vote with a view simply of benefiting his party.

Senator Bell was born of European parentage, in the town of Hebron, Washington county, N. Y., on the 8th of February, 1814. In the spring of 1825 his father, George Bell, removed into Jefferson county, and settled in the town of Brownville, where he resided until his death in December, 1841. He was a farmer by occupation, and a wife and three sons are now the only surviving members of his family.

At the age of seventeen Senator Bell, having received a fair English education, engaged in teaching, as principal of a common district school, assisting his father on his farm during the summer, and teaching during the winter months, and was eminently successful in that capacity. In 1834, when that part of the State of Michigan was yet an unbroken wilderness, he was one of a party who made the United States survey of the shores of Lake Huron, from Fort Gratiot to near Mackinaw. Having returned from the West, in 1836, he engaged in the mercantile business in the village of Brownville; but soon after removed his business to Dexter, a

new village being built up at the mouth of Black river,
and at the head of navigation from Lake Ontario.    To
the business of general merchandising, under the firm
name of J. A. Bell & Co., of which Col. Edmund Kirby
was an equal partner, he added the business of vessel-
building, storage, and forwarding, in which he continued
until the decease of Colonel Kirby in 1849, since which
time his operations have been mainly confined to the
purchase and sale of merchandise, and the disposal of
the vessels and the joint property of the above-men-
tioned firm.

Although not ambitious of political preferment,
choosing rather to devote his time and attention to
business, Senator Bell has held various offices of responsibility and trust. He was Postmaster during the administrations of Presidents Taylor and Fillmore, and held
the position of Supervisor of the town of Brownville
during the years 1857 and 1858.    He was appointed
for two terms, by the Board of Supervisors of his
county, to the post of Inspector of the Poor-House and
Insane Asylum, and, as we see by the official list of the
county, now holds the office of Coroner.    He was
always an ardent and enthusiastic admirer of Henry
Clay, and until after the presidential campaign of 1840,
acted as if he believed the whole salvation of the
country depended upon the success of the old Whig
party.    Subsequent developments, however, greatly
impaired his confidence in the then existing political
organizations, and although not wholly abandoning his
distinctive protective tariff principles, he directed his
energies more particularly to the restriction of the evils

of intemperance, and the further extension of slavery. Impressed with these views, his mind was fully prepared for early and active efforts in the formation of the Republican party, from which he has mainly received all the political distinction he has thus far enjoyed. He received the nomination in the fall of 1859, for the seat he now fills in the Senate, without any effort whatever on his part, by the Senatorial convention at Carthage, composed of delegates from the counties of Lewis and Jefferson, while his competitors for the nomination, the Hon. Calvin Littlefield, of Jefferson, and the Hon. Lyman R. Lyon, of Lewis, had made the most persevering efforts to secure the distinction. The official returns show his election by a majority of more than twenty-two hundred over his opponent, Harrison Blodgett, who, although the Democratic candidate, had Whig and American antecedents.

Senator Bell was married in 1840 to Miss Wood, second daughter of James Wood, who lived only eighteen days after their marriage. He was afterwards married on the 16th day of December, 1841, to his present wife, Miss Rachel P. Smith, a native of Bucks county, Pennsylvania, by whom he has had two children. He united, at an early age, with the Presbyterian church, of which his parents were consistent members; and to establish and sustain this branch of the Christian Church, a Union Sabbath-school, and several other moral and benevolent objects in Dexter, he has been obliged to bear heavy burdens and make great sacrifices of time and money. No doubt, however, these self-denials have qualified him for higher comfort and greater usefulness in the future.

## ISAIAH BLOOD.

SENATOR BLOOD is one of the most substantial old-fashioned Democrats in the Legislature, and although more of a business-man than a politician, has never failed to strenuously advocate the principles and policy of that party. He made his first appearance in public life as a Supervisor of the town in which he resides, and in 1852 was chosen a member of the Assembly, where he discharged his duties with credit to himself and material advantage to his district. In the fall of 1859 he was chosen to his present position by a handsome majority, as the successor of Judge Scott, of Saratoga county; and during the last session of the Legislature was a prominent and influential member of the Committee on Manufactures, Grievances, Militia, and Manufacture of Salt. He is an accurate, industrious business man, of strict integrity, and a high-toned moral character; and fulfils the duties of his position quietly and unostentatiously, though with an eye single to the best interests of every section of the entire State.

Senator Blood was born on the 13th of February, 1810, in the town of Ballston, Saratoga county, N. Y. He is of English descent, and his ancestors emigrated to Massachusetts as far back as the sixteenth century. Both his parents are still living, in Ballston, Saratoga county. His father, Sylvester Blood, was born in 1785, and his mother, Loretta Robertson, in 1787. Hosea Blood, his uncle, was a celebrated surgeon in the United States army, and distinguished himself at Tippecanoe, under General Harrison. He was severely wounded at Hull's disgraceful surrender at Detroit, and died at St. Louis, Missouri, while in the United States service, in 1816.

Having a large family of children, of whom Isaiah was the oldest, Senator Blood's father took him, at the age of twelve, from the district school, which was the only school he ever attended, and educated him for the manufacture of scythes, in which business he had gained no small degree of celebrity. His works being small, however, and his water-power limited, in 1823 he built a new manufactory on the Kayaderosseras creek, in the town of Milton, Saratoga county, and in 1833 associated his son Isaiah with him in business. The Senator then purchased his father's interest in the business in 1836, and having enlarged the work, has continued to enlarge and increase his facilities for the manufacture of scythes. In 1853 he erected an extensive establishment for the manufacture of axes and other edge tools, which, together with his scythe establishment, is now in successful operation, employing a large number of men and master-mechanics. The little settlement in which he now resides bears his own name, Bloodville, and contains several hundred inhabitants.

In person, Senator Blood is a man above the medium size, being somewhat robust and substantially built, and has thin light-grey hair, with intelligent blue eyes, and a good-natured, fresh, smooth face, which indicates permanent good health and a warm-hearted, generous nature. He possesses superior social qualities, and his uniform, genial, frank way never fails to create an attachment for him in the bosoms of all with whom he comes in contact. He is not only the representative, but the gentleman, and the two combined render him especially successful in the discharge of his official duties.

---

## ANDREW J. COLVIN.

SENATOR COLVIN succeeded admirably, during the last session of the Legislature, in making his mark as a representative man. Though strongly averse to the turmoil and strife usually consequent upon the political character of our legislative assemblies, he was always found prompt and efficient in the discharge of the duties pertaining to his position. His speech on the Governor's Message, defending the doctrine of popular sovereignty —the right of the people in the Territories, as in the States, to regulate the domestic institution of slavery in their own good time and way—at once ranked him among the most logical and impressive debaters in the Senate; and the ability, impartiality, and attention exhibited by him in the fulfilment of his obligations as a member of the Judiciary and other Committees, to which he belonged, extorted even the approbation of his most bitter and uncompromising political opponents.

Senator Colvin was born on the 30th of April, 1808, in the town of Coeymans, Albany county, New York. He is the only surviving child of the late James Colvin, an energetic and industrious farmer, who was also a native of that town, and who died in 1846, in the town of Bethlehem, in the same county. His paternal grand-father, John Colvin, who was a member of the lower branch of the New York Legislature in the year 1810, came from Scotland, during the early settlement of this country, and located in the town of Coeymans, where he was an active and successful farmer up to the time of his death. His maternal grandfather, John Ver-planck, who was one of the four original owners 'of Coeyman's Patent, and whose ancestors came from Hol-land, and settled at Verplanck's Point, on the Hudson river, was also born in the town of Coeymans, and lived there during his entire lifetime.

Senator Colvin received a classical education at the Albany Academy, and in 1824 entered the law office of ex-President Van Buren and the Hon. Benjamin F. But-ler, who were then in co-partnership in the city of Albany, although the former had substantially with-drawn from the profession, in consequence of his being then a member of the Senate of the United States. Here he remained, pursuing his legal studies with marked industry and attention, until duly admitted to the bar, when he at once entered upon the practice of the law, with the most flattering indications of future eminent success. During the year 1842, he was Attor-ney for the Corporation of the city of Albany, and was the last District Attorney of Albany county under the old constitution of 1821, having been appointed to that position by the Court of General Sessions, in March, 1846, and holding it until the 1st of January, 1848, when the new constitution of 1846 went into effect.

He was again District Attorney for three years, from the 1st of January, 1851, having succeeded to the position at the election in the fall of the previous year, as the candidate of the Democratic party ; and, during his entire career of official service, discharged all his duties with distinguished ability and success. He occupies a high position as a lawyer throughout Albany and the adjoining counties, and is well and favorably known throughout the entire circle of his associates at the bar, for the untiring industry and superior ability with which he discharges every professional duty devolving upon him. He is a fine speaker, rarely failing to advance directly to the real point in controversy, which he always discusses calmly and dispassionately, though clearly and distinctly, and has been especially successful in the efforts he has made before a jury.

Although always a firm and consistent adherent of the Democratic party, Senator Colvin has never become prominent as a politician, in the ordinary acceptation of that term. He has always been too high-toned in his individual and professional character for this, and has never exhibited any signs of a disposition to excel in anything but the honest and successful pursuit of his profession. He was put forward as the candidate of the Democratic party, for the position he now occupies in the Senate, without any solicitation whatever on his part, and was elected by a handsome majority over the combined forces of almost the entire opposition in his district.

Senator Colvin is the head of an interesting family, and is now living with his second wife, who is the daughter of the late Prudden Alling, of Newark, New Jersey, and who is a sister of his first wife. He is a member of St. Peter's Church, in the city of Albany, and occupies a deservedly high position in all the social and domestic relations of life. In person, he is tall and somewhat slender, with black hair and beard; and has a piercing black eye of unusual force and brilliancy. His complexion is sallow, showing a somewhat disordered state of his physical condition; but his strongly-marked features, and calm, dignified countenance, indicate at once a high order of intellect and an untiring and laborious disposition.

## RICHARD B. CONNOLLY.

Senator Connolly was brought forward with unusual unanimity, in the fall of 1859, by the Democrats of the Seventh Senatorial District for the position he now occupies in the Senate, and was triumphantly elected over Daniel D. Conover, the Republican candidate, by about three thousand majority. During the last session of the Legislature he was a member of the Standing Committees on Canals, Privileges and Elections, and Public Buildings, and was also a member of the special Committee, to which was referred the Pro Rata and Railroad Toll bills, and as a minority of which he made one of the most able and elaborate reports of the session. He is a gentleman of superior intelligence and a high degree of representative ability, and by his course, thus far, in the Senate, has proven himself strictly honest,

straightforward, faithful, and impartial in the discharge
of his legislative duties.   To these qualities are added a
kind, clever, agreeable, and generous disposition, with
a large heart and a cordial grasp of the hand for all his
friends; and there was, perhaps, no one at Albany, last
winter, who enjoyed a higher and more universal degree
of personal popularity than Mr. Connolly.

Senator Connolly is a native of old Ireland—the land
of soldiers, poets, and orators—and is about forty-five
years of age.   He came to the city of New York, where
he has always since resided, in 1826, being then only
about fourteen years of age, with high health and
spirits, and a moderately good education.   In fact, he
was a promising, bright, good-looking boy, with great
quickness and aptitude for study, as well as the acquire-
ment of business knowledge; and soon after his arrival
in America, was taken into the well-known and popular
auction-house of John Haggerty & Sons.   He remained
with this firm some eight or ten years, making rapid
and steady progress in his knowledge of the business
and good opinion of his employers, and at the end of
that time went into the employment of Simeon Draper,
who valued him very highly, and set a great store upon
him.

Long before becoming a voter, Senator Connolly took
a deep interest in politics, and began to play an active
part.   He has always been a straightforward and consistent Democrat, of the Jeffersonian conservative
school, and has thus made his politics as much a matter
of faith as of *profession*, believing that, unless a man's
heart, as well as his head, is in his work, he is very apt

to fly the track now and then, and forsake the long road of principle for some of the short cuts of expediency. He was sent as a delegate to the Young Men's General Committee, and also to several nominating conventions at Tammany Hall, as early as 1836. In 1839 and 1840 he was elected and served as Secretary of the Committee, and in 1846 was made its Chairman. He soon became one of the leading spirits of the " Old Seventh," serving as its constant representative in the party councils and conventions, and in 1845 was rewarded for his exertions. Cornelius W. Lawrence was Collector of the Port at that time, and appointed him to a clerkship in the Custom House. Subsequently he was placed at the head of the statistical bureau in that establishment, and while in that position was one of the three gentlemen chosen by the Collector to make up and revise the tariff of 1846, which was successfully prosecuted under the auspices of the Hon. Robert J. Walker.

In 1849 Senator Connolly left the Nassau street " White House," that plague of Presidents and paradise of disinterested patriots, and through the influence of Mayor Havemeyer, and other influential Democratic friends, was appointed discount clerk in the Bank of North America. He then held this position until the Democracy nominated him for County Clerk in 1852. His opponent in the contest was George W. Riblet ; but although the campaign was spirited, Mr. Connolly was triumphantly elected by over eleven thousand majority. During his term of service in this position he discharged his duties so well and satisfactorily to his party and fellow-citizens generally, that he was renominated by both the *Hard* and *Soft* Conventions in 1855, and elected by an increased majority of over fifteen thousand. A few days before the election the *Sunday Times* spoke of him as follows :

" Mr. Connolly's friends have much reason to feel proud of their nominee, for amid all the storm and whirlwind of public suspicion, the crop of indictments for corruption, and the complaints for inefficiency against public officers, he, almost alone, stands forth untainted by the breath of distrust—the idol and the nominee of every branch of the great Democratic family. Mr. Connolly is one of those warm-hearted, amiable men that everybody admires and everybody loves to honor. He is a ready, prompt, obliging officer. His experience is great, and has only won for him the still greater respect of the public he has so well and so faithfully served. The effort to secure his re-election, therefore, is one of the most honorable kind, and is prompted by the noblest of impulses. That he will succeed is beyond all reasonable doubt. He seems to have no opponents, except a very few verbal ones in the newspapers."

After his retirement from office, the *New York Day Book*, of the 22d December, 1848, spoke of him as follows :

" In a few days our present popular County Clerk will retire from office, and we only give utterance to the general sentiment, when we say that no man has ever left that office with more friends or a wider circle of admirers than he. By his uniform courtesy, and by the strict and careful discharge of all the duties of his office, he made himself universally popular among those who have had occasion to do business with his office. Particularly is this the case among the legal profession, who all unite in ascribing to the County Clerk's office first-rate regulations during Mr. Connolly's *regime*."

Since his first entrance into political life, Senator Connolly has been especially distinguished for his extraordinary vitality and unceasing activity. In the Democratic General Committee he has been among the most active workers, and so also in the Tammany Society, of which he has been twice elected a Sachem. He constantly represented the Seventh Ward in Tammany and at Syracuse, but is now a resident of the Twenty-first Ward, where he exercises his usual ability and influence in everything of a local character. His knowledge of human nature is almost perfect, and but few men have ever been greater favorites with all classes. In enabling him to command this favor, nature has been no stepmother to him, for she has given him a good presence, a handsome, good-natured face, with brown hair and brilliant dark-blue eyes, and a manly air of ease and kindness, which wins him golden opinions among all classes of people, without scarcely any effort on his own part.

Senator Connolly was married, in 1837, to the oldest daughter of John Townsend, Esq., an old merchant of the city of New York, whose ancestors settled on Long Island a century ago, and who, during the Revolutionary War, were true and faithful to the cause of their country. He has an amiable and interesting family, of which he is justly proud. In short, whether

3

as a party man, a business man, a family man, or a
political leader, few men can be found combining so
many qualities of success as Richard B. Connolly.

---

## WILLIAM H. FERRY.

SENATOR FERRY is, perhaps, the finest looking gentleman in the Senate, and never fails to deport himself
with a becoming air of senatorial dignity which con-
trasts favorably with the reckless, ill-bred manner of
some of his legislative compeers. He is rather above
the medium height, with an elegantly-formed body, jet-
black hair and eyes, a face which seems to have always
been unconscious of a razor, and an intelligent expression of countenance which indicates more than ordinary
shrewdness, ability, and legislative tact and ingenuity.
His career in life has been simply that of a plain,
thorough-going, and successful business man, doing well
and earnestly whatever he undertakes; and during the
last session of the Legislature, he gave unmistakable
evidence of more than ordinary capacity for public life.
He was always found prompt and faithful in the discharge of his duties on the floor of the Senate, and stood
prominent in all its deliberations as chairman of the
Committee on Public Expenditures, and a member of
the Committees on Banks and Insurance Companies.

Senator Ferry is a native of the county of Oneida,
N. Y., where he was born in the year 1819. He is of
Dutch, English, and Irish extraction. His father, who

was a gentleman of superior business capacity, died in the city of Utica, in 1856, at the advanced age of sixty-nine, and his mother, a woman beloved by all who knew her, died in Herkimer county, in 1842, at the age of forty-six. His education was received principally in the common schools of his native place, though he passed some time at Amherst College, and was educated chiefly with a view to commercial pursuits. Subsequently he was successfully engaged in the banking and manufacturing business, but is now wholly retired from all active employment. He has held the position of Alderman and Supervisor in the city of Utica, where he now resides, and was elected to the seat he occupies in the Senate by a flattering majority. In politics, he was formerly a Whig, adhering faithfully to that party until it abandoned its organization, when his Freesoil proclivities at once led him into the ranks of the Republican party.

Senator Ferry is the head of a family, having married Miss M. A. Williams some years since, and attends the Presbyterian church. He occupies a high social position in the community in which he lives, and enjoys a high degree of personal popularity.

---

## JOSHUA FIERO, Jr.

Senator Fiero was born on the 4th of May, 1818, in the then town of Broom, now the town of Conesville, Schoharie County, N. Y. He is of unmixed

Knickerbocker stock, though it is supposed that his paternal ancestors, who took an active part in the early settlement of New York, were originally from Italy. When only about nine years of age, he went to Saugerties, Ulster county, N. Y., to live with his uncle, Joshua Fiero, who, having no sons, at once adopted him as his own, and with whom he remained until about the time he had attained his majority. During his younger days he attended a common district school, and in 1838 and '39, was a student at the Academy in Malden, Ulster county, with a view of fitting himself for one of the learned professions. He soon, however, wholly abandoned this idea, and on the 12th of March, 1840, became a clerk in the dry-goods establishment of H. H. Hyde, in the village of Catskill, Greene county, N. Y. Here he remained, fulfilling the duties of his new position with credit to himself and entire satisfaction to his employer, until the 28th of July, 1842; and on the 13th of April, 1843, he embarked, with a small capital, in the mercantile trade, on his own responsibility. From that time to this he has occupied the position of an enterprising and successful merchant in the village of Catskill, and has acquired the reputation of being one of the most accurate, industrious, and successful business men in the county of Greene. Strict integrity and honesty of purpose have always been a marked characteristic of all his business transactions, and it is said, as an evidence of the faithfulness with which he has discharged all his business obligations, that he has never yet, throughout his entire business career, had one of his notes protested. He had, for some time, a branch mercantile establishment in the city of Auburn, and one in the village of Leeds, Greene county; but from 1843 to the present time, he has had an establishment in successful operation in the village of Catskill, where he has always since been a permanent resident.

Senator Fiero may be said to have made his first entrance into public life in 1840, when he occupied the position of Major in the cavalry department of the military force of his native State. He was also Adjutant of the Twenty-eighth Regiment, in 1854, but resigned the place in the following year, and thenceforth devoted his exclusive time and attention to his business, until the fall of 1853, when he was the successful Whig candidate, in his district, for a seat in the lower house of the Legislature. During the session that followed, he was Chairman of the Select Committee appointed to answer the special message of Gov. Seymour to that body, vetoing the Prohibitory Liquor Bill, and was found faithful and conscientious in the discharge of all his legislative duties.

He was unexpectedly chosen to his present position in the Senate in the fall of 1859, from a closely-contested district, and during the last session of the Legislature was Chairman of both the Standing Committees on the Militia and Privileges, and Elections, and was a member of the Committee on Grievances. Politically, he was originally a Whig, claiming to have been of the Henry Clay school, and was one among the first to engage in the Republican movement at the organization of that party. He is not much of a politician, having always been closely confined to business, and is probably as well calculated for the latter as he is for the former.

Senator Fiero was married on the 28th of July, 1842, to Miss Mary F., only daughter of William Pierson, then Clerk of Greene county, and is a member and trustee of the Presbyterian branch of the Church.

Senator Fiero is a man of medium height, and has a stout, muscular body. He has a heavy head of light-brown hair, blue eyes, heavy, light-brown whiskers, and a substantial, business-like face, which indicates great firmness and decision of character.

## THOMAS K. GARDINER.

SENATOR GARDINER was born in the city of New York on the 2d of August, 1832, and is, therefore, one of the youngest men in the Senate. He removed, with his parents, to Brooklyn, in 1840, and has always since resided in that city. His mother was also a native of the city of New York, but his father, George W. Gardiner, who was a New York merchant, and who died in January, 1852, came from Ireland, when quite young.

Senator Gardiner was educated at a private select school in the city of Brooklyn, and has always been chiefly engaged in the manufacturing business. During the great pecuniary panic in 1857, he was connected with the Post-office department in that city, but abandoned the position as soon as business had again revived. His first entrance into public life was in the fall of 1858, when he was brought forward by the Democrats of the Fourth Assembly District of Kings county, as a candidate for the lower branch of the Legislature, and was triumphantly elected by nearly one thousand majority. During his official term of service in that body, he was an influential member of the Standing Committee on Trade and Manufactures, and was industrious, honest, and faithful in the discharge of all his representative duties. So well pleased, indeed, were his political friends and constituents with his legislative career at Albany, that he was placed in the field at the opening of the political campaign, in the fall of 1859, with unusual unanimity, as a candidate for the seat he now holds in the Senate, and his nomination was heartily endorsed by the people of his district at the polls. During the last session of the Legislature he was a member of the Committees on Agriculture and Public Expenditures in the Senate, and was found faithful and honest in the discharge of all his duties.

In politics Senator Gardiner, like his father before him, has always been a Democrat of the old Andrew Jackson style. He has always been active and industrious in his devotion to the principles and policy of that party, and occupies a firm position on the Cincinnati platform. His views on all the great questions of the day are intensely national and conservative, and he regards the doctrine of Congressional sovereignty, as advocated by the Republican party, as a palpable violation of the sovereign rights of the people, whom he considers fully capable, both in the States and Territories, of regulating their domestic institutions in their own way, subject only to the Constitution of the United States.

Senator Gardiner is a member of the Roman Catholic Church, and is still unmarried. He possesses a sound judgment, good temper, great courtesy of manner, and is unsurpassed in his personal popularity among his legislative associates, as well as among the people of his district. There is nothing of the old fogy about him; and although one of the youngest men in the Senate, there are but few members of that body who are more quiet, industrious, and agreeable in the fulfilment of their official duties. In person he is of medium size, with soft blue eyes, light-brown side whiskers and imperial, a thick coat of brown hair, and is altogether personable, not to say prepossessing, in his general appearance.

## EPHRAIM GOSS.

SENATOR Goss is readily recognised, as he calmly sits among his legislative peers, by his somewhat singular personal appearance. He is a man considerably above the medium height, being tall and slender, with an active, wiry frame, and has dark-grey eyes, and straight brown hair, which he keeps carefully combed forward over a forehead made prominent by a partial baldness in front. His face is thin, with sharp, distinct features, and carries upon it the impress of excessive intellectual labor, and great mental energy and activity. During the sittings of the Senate, he is very close in his attention to its proceedings, and is seldom or never out of his seat. He possesses considerable ability as a speaker, usually participating in all the debates of the Senate, and shows a more than ordinary knowledge of the affairs of state and the necessities of the people, and particularly those of his own district. During the last Session of the Legislature he was Chairman of the Committee on Internal Affairs of Towns and Counties—one of the most laborious committees in the Senate—besides being a member of the Committees on Roads and Bridges, Poor Laws, and Expiring Laws.

Senator Goss was born on the 12th of June, 1806, in the then town of Middleburgh, now the town of Fulton, Schoharie county, N. Y. He is of English and Irish descent, and his parents were both born in this country before the Revolution. His grandfather, Ephraim Goss, after whom he was named, served throughout the War of Independence, and was a gallant and successful soldier. His father, John Goss, died on the 17th of June, 1847, at the age of eighty; and his mother, whose maiden name was Mary Lamont, died on the 20th of March, 1844, at the age of seventy-six.

With the exception of some six months in an academical school, Senator Goss received his education in an ordinary district school, and in a law office, where he was compelled to go in consequence of the district school-house in his native place having been burned down. He then, in 1816, removed with his parents to the section of the State in which he now resides, and pursued a classical course, teaching at intervals, until he had attained his twentieth year, when he entered the law office of the late Gen. Ira Bellows, of Pittsford,

3*

N. Y. After a thorough course of legal training, he was admitted to the bar in 1831, and has always since been a successful lawyer, and an industrious practical farmer. Besides holding some minor town offices, he was, in 1828, elected Captain of a company of light infantry, known as the "Washington Phalanx," which position he occupied until 1834, when he was chosen Major of the Fifty-second Regiment. One year afterwards he was promoted to the office of Lieut.-Colonel, and in 1843 became Colonel, which he resigned in 1845. Meanwhile he was elected a Justice of the Peace in 1829, and was re-chosen in 1833, '47, '51, '55, and '59. He was also Supervisor of his town for five years from 1836, holding the position of Chairman of the Board in that year, and in 1848 and in 1837 was chosen County Clerk, which office he held three years.

Senator Goss cast his first vote for Governor for De Witt Clinton, and his first Presidential vote was cast for John Quincy Adams, in 1828. He was always an active and influential Whig, until the Republican movement was inaugurated, when he became a member of that party. At the last election he was brought forward, with flattering unanimity, by the Republicans of his district, for the position he now occupies in the Senate, and was triumphantly elected by a large majority. He is a man of considerable literary talent and ability, and is the author of a work entitled, "Supervisors' Book," containing an abstract of all laws relating to the powers and duties of Supervisors in the State of New York, with suitable forms, notes, and references, together with the parliamentary rules applicable to Boards of Supervisors. The work has been highly recommended by some of the best lawyers in Western New York, and has recently been revised, and the second edition published, containing some eighty pages of new matter, with which nearly one half of the counties in the State have already been supplied.

Senator Goss was married on the 13th of November, 1832, to Miss Margaret Porter, and has been a prominent and influential member of the First Presbyterian Church since 1843.

## ROBERT Y. GRANT.

SENATOR GRANT is a native of the town of Liberty, Sullivan County, N. Y. He is of genuine Scotch descent, and was born on the 22d of November, 1818. Both his parents are still living, his father, Joseph Grant, one of the pioneers of Sullivan county, and a man of prominent influence and distinction, having reached the seventy-third year of his age, and his wife, the mother of the subject of this sketch, having attained her seventy-second.

Senator Grant was educated in the common district schools of his native place, and was brought up a farmer until he had attained the age of his majority. He was then engaged in farming and dealing in cattle, until about ten years ago, since which time he has been successfully engaged in the tanning business. He sustains the reputation of an honest, correct business man, of superior qualifications, wherever he is known, and is well qualified to discharge satisfactorily the duties of the position with which his constituents intrusted him in the Senate. He held the office of Justice of the Peace in the town of Liberty from 1849 until 1855, and was Supervisor during the years 1854 and 1859. He has also held the office of Postmaster during the last six years, and in the fall of 1859 was elected to the seat he now occupies in the Senate by a complimentary vote. He was a member of the Standing Committees on Finance, Charitable and Religious Societies, and Erection and Division of Towns and Counties, during the last session of the Legislature, and was always found prompt and attentive in the discharge of his duties.

Senator Grant has always been a consistent and uncompromising Democrat of the old school. He is a relative of the Hon. David Wilmot, of Pennsylvania, but has no sympathy whatever with the political principles of that gentleman. He has been somewhat active in the local politics of his own and the adjoining counties, but has devoted himself more closely to the discharge of his duties and obligations as a private citizen, than to the observance of the customary routine of latter-day patriots and politicians. He is a good speaker, but prefers talking less and working more than legislators generally, and seldom addresses the Senate at very great length. He is a plain, unostentatious, common-sense man, with a whole-souled, generous disposition ; and whether in the legislative halls of the State, or in the ordinary walks of private life, is still the same unpretending representative of the great mass of the industrious, hard-working, honest portion of the people of his district.

Senator Grant was married on the 4th of September, 1839, to Miss Sarah Smeads, and confines himself to no particular church in his attendance upon religious worship. In person, he is a man of medium height, with broad shoulders, and a substantially-built frame. He has a thin coat of light-grey hair, a broad retreating forehead; intelligent grey eyes, and a smooth, well formed face, which indicates great firmness and decision of character. Although naturally reserved, he possesses in a high degree the elements of sociability, and his warmest and most devoted friends are those who have known him the longest.

## SAMUEL H. HAMMOND.

THE career of Senator Hammond, since assuming the responsibilities of his present position, has been strikingly characteristic of the man—supremely vacillating, inconsistent, and as disreputable to himself as it has been destructive to the best interests of his constituents. His highest ambition seems to have been to, as effectively as possible, belie all the professions upon which he was allowed to take a seat in the Senate, and at no period in his whole history has he apparently been so successful in gratifying such a desire. Before his election, he was, seemingly, at his own solicitation, firmly pledged to the people of his district, in favor of tolling railroads and the measure known last winter as the Pro Rata Freight bill, yet scarcely had he appeared in his place in the Senate before he was found among the most uncompromising opponents of both, and the subtle and pliant tool of the great railroad power of the State. He was, also, an earnest supporter of all the New York city railroad projects, in every one of which there is said to have been a large amount of corruption ; and, perhaps, to his efforts more than to the efforts of any other man in the Senate, did those measures owe their final success. Indeed, there was, perhaps, no man at Albany, last winter, who did more than Mr. Hammond to justify Mr. Greeley, through the *Tribune*, in issuing the following language, apparently harsh :—" It is an undeniable fact that the last Legislature of this State was in part composed of as graceless a set of political demagogues, public plunderers, corrupt place-seekers, and low-bred pot-house politicians, as ever went unwhipped of justice."

The political career of Senator Hammond is strikingly peculiar. He has completely boxed the political compass. He has been a member of every political party that has had a name—a complete political kaleidoscope, through which can be distinguished every shade and color of party change and individual inconsistency. Originally an Abolitionist of the extremest sect, he persistently and resolutely contended that the general government ought to interfere for the abolition of the institution of slavery in the States where it already existed, and was once an unsuccessful candidate of that party for a seat in the body of which he is now a member. He subsequently performed a perfect political somerset, landing square in the Democratic ranks, and was soon among the most ardent and enthusiastic supporters of the principles and measures of that party. He was next found doing service in the ranks of the old Whig party, adhering firmly to the Silver Grey wing of the party until its organization was abandoned, when he became an enthusiastic American. It was during his connexion with this party that he had the control of the *Albany State Register*. In the winter of 1856 he was a member of the American National Council, held at Philadelphia, and was the only supporter in that body, from New York, of the well known " Twelfth Section," which denied the assumed right of Congress to interfere with the subject of slavery in the territories of the United States. He was an ardent outside friend of George Law, as a candidate for the Presidency, at the American National Convention held in that city about the same time, and flew the track after Mr. Fillmore's nomination, by earnestly supporting Col. Fremont. Since then he has kept steady march beneath the colors of modern Republicanism, and since his advent to the Senate has identified himself with the extreme Abolition wing of that party. He is bitterly averse to any compromise or conciliation in the present deplorable condition of the country, and openly proclaims his determination to stand by the Chicago platform, even at the sacrifice of the country, with all the attendant horrors of civil war.

Senator Hammond was born, in 1809, on the banks of the beautiful lake Keuku, in the State of New York, and is therefore in the fifty-second year of his age. He is descended from pure, unmixed Puritanical stock, and both his parents are now dead.  He was educated at the Franklin Academy, at Prattsburgh, Steuben county, and after devoting some time to the study of the law, was admitted to the bar, and entered upon the practice of his profession.  About the year 1844, he removed from the interior of the State, and took up his residence in the city of Albany, still continuing the practice of the law.  At the first election under the new Constitution, in 1847, he was chosen District-Attorney of Albany county, holding the office until 1851, when he was defeated, as a candidate for re-election, by Senator Colvin, the Democratic candidate.  His taste and disposition, however, had never been very well adapted to the pursuit of his profession, he being more naturally inclined to poetry and literature than the abstruse questions of legal jurisprudence, and in 1853 he became the editor of the *Albany State Register*, a paper to which he had been an occasional contributor since its establishment in 1850.  This connexion continued until 1856, when he returned to Steuben county, and resumed the practice of the law.  He had, also, held the office of Loan Commissioner, previous to his becoming District-Attorney, and has recently been a trustee of the village of Bath, where he resides.

Senator Hammond is a good speaker—perfectly self-possessed, and has a habit of thinking on his legs, which furnishes a fine contrast to the studied efforts of some of his legislative associates.  His gestures and manner are rarely inappropriate, and he is always perfectly easy —now turning to the Republican side of the Senate, then towards the Democratic, and always preserving an easy tone of half badinage, half earnestness, which keeps friends and foes in good humor, while at the same time stating his positions with great force, point, and perspicuity. He is equally accomplished as a writer. His style is easy, fluent, clear, and expressive, and adapts itself, like a silken shawl, to every swell and motion and curve of a subject; it has the soft flow and easy cadence which marked the best distinctive styles of the eighteenth century, and is stubborned with something of the sterner music of the nineteenth.

Senator Hammond is one of the portliest and most striking figures on the floor of the Senate, and always attracts the attention of the most casual observer by his singularly imposing personal appearance. He is large-bodied, with a large, round head, covered with a disordered profusion of grey hair, a frontal baldness, showing a broad, full forehead, and a ruddy, good-natured face, illuminated by large dark eyes of an uncertain tinge, deeply set on either side of a short truncated nose, which stands out boldly above a mouth somewhat full and firm in its expression. His features are good, of the mild Roman sort; his eyebrows dark and well arched, and his complexion usually florid, as if he lived chiefly on buckwheat corn, hominy, mush, milk, small tenderloin, fillets of beef, nuts, eggs, apples, raisins, plums, and all other nutriments of a simple and chiefly farinaceous character.

Senator Hammond married a Miss Humphrey, about the year 1830, and attends the Catholic Episcopal Church.

## THOMAS HILLHOUSE.

SENATOR HILLHOUSE was chairman of the Committees on Literature and Grievances in the Senate, during the last session of the Legislature, and was found prompt and faithful in the discharge of his official duties. There is nothing very brilliant or meteoric about him, but his legislative career, thus far, demonstrates that he is simply a plain, unpretending, and successful business man. He makes no pretensions whatever as a speaker, and contents himself with simply a quiet and industrious discharge of his duties.

Senator Hillhouse was born on the 10th of March, 1817, in the town of Watervliet, Albany county, N. Y. His great-grandfather came to America in 1733, from Belfast, Ireland, and settled in Montville, New London county, Connecticut, where he established a Protestant church, and preached the Gospel during the remainder of his life. He had two sons, William and James Abram, the former of whom fell heir to his father's estate at Montville, and the latter of whom removed to New Haven, where he became a distinguished lawyer. William Hillhouse was for forty consecutive years a member of the Governor's Council, and never lost a single year in his attendance upon the meetings of that body. His oldest son was James Hillhouse, of New Haven, for many years a Representative in Congress, and afterwards a United States Senator from Connecticut. His youngest son was Thomas Hillhouse, the father of the subject of this sketch, who, in

1801, removed to the city of Troy, where he remained until 1810, when he purchased and removed upon a farm on the west side of the Hudson river, in the county of Albany. He died in 1834, at the age of sixty-eight ; and his wife, whose maiden name was Anna Ten Broeck, is still living, at an advanced age. Her father was a major in the Revolution, and actively participated in the battles of Monmouth, Yorktown, and Fort Stanwix.

Senator Hillhouse was educated in Columbia county, N. Y., pursuing an academical course with a view of entering college, but abandoned his studies at his father's death, to take charge of the latter's unsettled estate. He was then so engaged, in connexion with farming, until 1851, when he removed to the village of Geneva, Ontario county, where he has always since lived a retired life. He held the position of Treasurer of the New York State Agricultural Society during the administration of Judge Beekman, of Columbia county, as its President. Aside from this, he never occupied any very prominent position in public, until the fall of 1859, when he was brought forward by the Republicans of the twenty-sixth district, with great unanimity, as a candidate for the distinguished position he now holds. The nomination was conferred upon him without his solicitation, he being absent in the territory of Kansas at the time ; but although not ambitious of political preferment, he entered upon the contest, on his return home, with great determination and enthusiasm, and was victoriously elected by nearly one thousand majority. He was originally a Democrat, adhering closely and unyieldingly to the regular organization of that party until 1854, when the repeal of the Missouri Compromise induced him to enlist, among the very first, in the establishment of the Republican movement. Since then he has been active and industrious in the promotion of the interests of that party, and its organization in the county of Ontario.

In his private, as in his public character, Senator Hillhouse is perfectly irreproachable, being distinguished for his integrity, uprightness, and honesty of purpose. Although somewhat reserved in his general habits, his social qualities are of a superior order. He has the happy faculty of making himself agreeable to all with whom he comes in contact, and the longer his friends know him, the stronger becomes their attachment for him. In person, he is somewhat above the medium height; is slender and well formed; has brown hazel eyes, dark-brown hair and whiskers, and a thoughtful, intelligent countenance, which indicates the powers of close application and superior mental force.

Senator Hillhouse was married in December, 1844, to Miss Harriet Pronty, of the village of Geneva, and attends the Dutch Reformed Church, of which his aged mother is an exemplary member.

## BERNARD KELLY.

SENATOR KELLY is a native of the Seventh Ward, in the city of New York, and is thirty-eight years of age. He is of Irish descent, and the son of respectable and intelligent parents. He is a practical mechanic, and eminently a self-made man. Whatever he is, and has, he owes entirely to himself. His education may be pronounced, if not distinctive of the nineteenth century, yet highly characteristic of it. Theoretic education, the education of letters, is in his case rather peculiarly blended with the education of practice. He is one of the strong men, who, amid the sternest toil of mechanical employment, have become acquainted, and that not cursorily and superficially, but systematically and profoundly, with that knowledge of books, which appears almost indispensable, in this age of progress and intelligence, to the man of successful distinction. His business qualifications are of a high order, to which the success he has always met with in his business career bears ample testimony; and his honesty and strict integrity of purpose, have always remained unquestioned in the city of his residence.

Politically Senator Kelly has never wavered in his stern and unyielding devotion to the cause of the Democratic party, having been for many years a representative of his ward in the various prominent Democratic committees in the city of New York, and ranks high among the most distinguished and influential politicians in that section of the State. Notwithstanding his unceasing activity in behalf of the best interests of his party, however, he has always had a strong aversion to holding public office, and with the exception of the position of Superintendent of Wharves, Piers, and Slips, which he held two different terms, he never occupied any prominent public place, until his promotion to the seat he now fills in the Senate. He was brought forward for this position entirely without his solicitation, and against his expressed wishes, at the last election, with entire unanimity, by the united Democratic forces of his district, and was triumphantly elected. Thus far, he has proven himself a safe counsellor and a good representative, and, although the most quiet and unostentatious man in the Senate, has pursued·a straightforward, consistent, and industrious course, which has not failed to have a proper influence upon the deliberations of that body. During the last session of the Legislature, he was an influential member of the Standing Committees on Roads and Bridges, Indian Affairs, and Poor Laws, and was perfectly faithful in the discharge of every duty devolving upon him. He is a man of strong common sense and sound practical judgment, and entitles himself as much by his ability, as by his diligence and industry, to the confidence of the important constituency he represents. His greatest fault is a natural diffidence, which causes him to distrust his own ability, and a degree of modesty that often shuns responsibility. To be fully appreciated, he must be well known; and the more thoroughly he is known, the more will he be esteemed and confided in.

Senator Kelly was married, some years ago, to Miss Hannah A. Doxey, and is of the Roman Catholic persuasion, while his wife is a member of the Methodist Episcopal Church. He is very agreeable and sociable, when once acquainted, and is well constituted to win friends, and keep them, wherever he goes. He is, without doubt, the most popular man in the Eleventh

Ward in New York, where he has resided about twenty-five years, and the same may perhaps be safely said of his standing wherever he is known, throughout the entire city.

---

## JOHN H. KETCHAM.

SENATOR KETCHAM is a native of Dover Plains, Dutchess County, N. Y., where he was born on the 21st of December, 1832, and where he has always resided. He is of pure English extraction. His paternal grandfather, James Ketcham, was a captain in the war of 1812, and in 1819 was a member of the Legislature of the State of New York. His father, John M. Ketcham, who was a member of the Assembly in 1842 and '43, died on the 17th of June, 1853, at the age of forty-seven, and his mother, whose maiden name was Eliza A. Stevens, is still living.

Senator Ketcham was educated at the Worcester Academy, in Massachusetts, and at the Connecticut Literary Institute, at Suffield, Connecticut. After leaving school, he engaged in agricultural pursuits, in which he has always since been successfully employed, besides working one of the most extensive and profitable marble quarries in the State. He has also had the charge of the estate of his father since the latter's death, in 1853, and has acquired the reputation of an industrious, skilful, and correct business man.

Senator Ketcham commenced public life as Supervisor

of the town in which he lives.     He first held the office in 1854, and during that year discharged the duties of the position so satisfactorily, that he was again a member of the Board in 1855.     In the fall of the same year he was elected to the Assembly, and during the session which followed gave considerable evidence of his legislative ability, both on the floor of the House and as a member of the Standing Committee on Agriculture.  He was again a member of that body in 1857, and during the session of that year was chairman of the Standing Committee on Roads and Bridges, and a member of the Sub-committee of the Whole—one of the most important committees in either branch of the Legislature.  He was elected to the seat he now holds in the Senate, in the fall of 1859, by a majority of over fifteen hundred; and during the last session of the Legislature, was chairman of both the committees on Insurance Companies and that on Retrenchment.     As a legislator he is cautious, industrious, and efficient, and as a man occupies a high position among all his legislative associates, as well as among the people of the community in which he resides.     He is naturally a pretty good talker, but is constitutionally quiet, and never makes any efforts at oratorical display in the Senate.     He is utilitarian rather than theoretical in his views on all subjects, and contents himself with pursuing a quiet though eminently practical and efficient legislative course.     His greatest worth consists in his superior business qualifications, and to these same qualities is owing, perhaps, more than to anything else, his signal success as a politician and legislator.

In politics Senator Ketcham was formerly an active Whig, but he was among the very first to embark in the Republican movement at the organization of that party. Since then, he has been unsurpassed by no other member of the party in Dutchess county, in his ceaseless and untiring efforts to promote its interest, and secure its permanent success. He has always been a shrewd, active, and intelligent politician, wielding a strong influence in his own and many of the adjoining connties; and but few men in that section of the State have done as much as he towards the promotion and ultimate triumph of the principles and policy of his party.

Senator Ketcham was married on the 4th of February, 1858, to Miss Augusta A. Belden, a lady of superior female qualities, and belongs to the Baptist Church, as does also his wife. He is a man of medium height, and is somewhat slender, though well formed. He has light-brown hair and beard, blue eyes, light complexion, and a good-natured, clever countenance, which is calculated to make the most favorable impression on all with whom he comes in contact.

# NATHAN LAPHAM.

SENATOR LAPHAM is a native of the town of Collins, Erie County, New York. He was born on the 22d of October, 1820, and is, therefore, forty years of age, although looking nearly ten years younger. He is

descended from good old Quaker stock, and traces his
ancestry as far back as the third generation. His
paternal ancestors were residents of North Adams,
Massachusetts, where they settled about the middle of
the last century, and where his paternal grandfather,
Nathan Lapham, was subsequently born. His father,
• Joseph Lapham, who was a native of Danby, Vermont,
died in 1851, at the age of sixty-five, and his mother,
whose maiden name was Anna Keese, died at a comparatively early age, in 1833.

Senator Lapham removed with his parents, when only
two years of age, to Peru, Clinton County, New York,
where he has always since been a permanent resident.
He was reared on a farm, and received a common-school
and academical education. He was for many years
successfully engaged in farming, and in the mercantile,
lumber, and iron business, and is now pretty extensively
employed in farming and milling. He is a thorough-
going, straightforward, industrious, and energetic business man, and has met with much more than ordinary
success in all the business enterprises in which he has
taken part. The first public position he ever held, was
that of Loan Commissioner, which he occupied for four
years, under the successive administrations of Governor
Clark and Governor King, and acquitted himself with
considerable success in the discharge of all his duties in
that capacity. He then persistently refused to accept
any further public position until the fall of 1859, when,
at the earnest solicitation of many friends, he consented
to become a candidate for the seat he now fills in the
Senate, and was triumphantly elected by a large major-

ity.   During the last session of the Legislature he was
Chairman of both the Standing Committee on Roads
and Bridges, and that on Poor Laws, and was unsurpassed by any of the members of either of those committees in the industry and fidelity with which he
discharged his duties.

Politically he was formerly a Free-soil Whig, of the
Seward school, and was one among the very first to
take an active part in the organization of the Republican
party.   He was a delegate to the first Republican State
Convention ever held in New York, and was also a
representative in the Convention by which Governor
Morgan was nominated for the distinguished position
he now occupies.   As a politician, he is unyielding and
uncompromising in his attachment to principle; inde-
fatigable and very successful in all his efforts; and since
the age of twenty has been working steadily and perseveringly in the harness of Freedom, without ever
exhibiting the slightest disposition to "kick over the
traces."   He maintains a high reputation in the community in which he resides, as a man of capacity and
integrity, and is personally, as well as politically, one
of the most popular men in Clinton county.

Senator Lapham was elected President *pro tem.* of
the Senate, shortly after the opening of the session of
the Legislature, and has shown himself a dignified and
impartial presiding officer of that body.   He possesses
strong common sense, a sound practical judgment, a good
stock of general knowledge, but seldom enters the arena
of debate, and contents himself with being simply a
quiet, industrious, and successful representative.   He is

a gentleman of noble presence, being tall, erect, dignified, and somewhat inclined to corpulency, with dark hair slightly mixed with grey, expressive dark eyes, and a merry, good-natured face, fringed with heavy whiskers. He is seldom absent from his post, and votes and acts on all questions coming before the Senate, as best becomes, in his judgment, not only the interests of his own constituency, but of the people of the entire State.

Senator Lapham was married on the 22d of February, 1842, to Miss Jane R. Barker, and belongs to the Society of Friends, as does also his estimable lady. His social qualities are of a superior order, and he sustains a high reputation in all the private and domestic relations of life.

## EDWARD ARTHUR LAWRENCE.

THERE are, indeed, but few young men in the State who have arisen so rapidly to prominent distinction before the people as Senator Lawrence. He entered public life when only about twenty-one years of age, and whether as a member of the Board of Supervisors of the county in which he resides, or as a member of the lower branch of the Legislature, or as a member of the distinguished body to which he now belongs, his star of progress has always been in the ascendant from that time to this. Seldom, too, has he been surpassed in the promptness, fidelity, and ability with which he has discharged the duties of the various positions to which the people have called him, and his speeches while a member of the Assembly, against the bill for the construction of certain railroads in the city of New York, and the notorious Personal Liberty Bill, will always be read and admired as true specimens of real eloquence and sound logic. The same is true of his speech, delivered in the Senate during the last session of the Legislature, in which he successfully convicted Gov. Morgan of having contributed his private funds to the circulation of "Helper's Impending Crisis," and in which he predicted the present distracted state of the country as the legitimate result of the success of those thus engaged in the circulation of that infamous document.

Senator Lawrence, the seventh son and twelfth child of Judge Effingham Lawrence, of Flushing, Long Island, by his wife, Anne, daughter of Solomon Townsend, of New York, was born at Bay Side, on the estate of his ancestors, on the 3d of November, 1832. He is of unmixed English descent, and his progenitors were, on both sides, among the earliest English settlers of the State of New York. The names of his paternal and maternal ancestors—William Lawrence and John Townsend—are both to be found upon the original patent of Flushing, granted by the Dutch Governor, Kieft, in 1645.

Senator Lawrence's father was first Judge of Queens county for many years. He was one of the earliest importers of merino sheep, and the first President of the Queens County Agricultural Society. His acute perception, solid judgment, and well balanced intellect, rendered him one of the first to seize, and one of the most earnest to develop, every improvement in both the science and practice of agriculture.   A frank, liberal, and hospitable country gentleman, he was, at the same time, eminently a practical farmer, and among the best and most prominent agriculturists of the State of New York.   It is generally conceded that the mantle of the father has worthily descended upon the shoulders of the Senator from the First; for the latter is now President of the Queens County Agricultural Society, having been elected to that position, at the last annual meeting of the Society, as the successor of ex-Gov. King, and he has pursued his profession with such eminent success that more premiums have been awarded him, particularly for stock, than any other man in the county of Queens.

If legislative position could be inherited, Senator Lawrence might naturally claim his present seat.   His maternal grandfather, Solomon Townsend, after serving as a member of the Assembly, from the city of New York, for six years, died in the harness, during the session of 1811.   His great-grandfather, Samuel Townsend, of Oyster Bay, was a member of the New York Provincial Congress, during the Revolution, and of the Convention that established the first Constitution of the State of New York, in 1777.   Under this Constitution he was a member of the State Senate from 1784 till 1790, and one of the Council of Appointment in 1789. He died, in office, in 1790.

Senator Lawrence has been three years Supervisor, his ability, fidelity, and integrity having, during that period, uninterruptedly continued to him the suffrages of the people of Flushing.   In the fall of 1857, he was elected a member of the Assembly, on the same day on which he became twenty-five years of age, from the First District of Queens county, by over five hundred majority; and during the session of the Legislature which followed, gained universal confidence and esteem by his strict attention to business, and straightforward honesty of purpose, both on the floor of the House, and as Chairman of the Standing Committee on Internal Affairs of Towns and Counties, and a member of that on Militia and Public Defence, and other committees; and now these sentiments have been expanded into an affectionate regard, in all cases, where personal intercourse has made apparent his warm heart, cheerful temper, and frank, fearless, and unaffected good nature. He was re-elected, by over six hundred majority, to the Assembly of 1859, where he was again prominent as an industrious and useful member of the Standing Committees on Ways and Means, and Militia, and Public Defence, and where he distinguished himself, not only as a first-class parliamentarian, but as a clear and comprehensive speaker. Politically, he has always been a consistent and straightforward Democrat of the national conservative or Hardshell school, and was the successful candidate for the seat he now occupies in the Senate, by a majority of upwards of sixteen hundred over the combined forces of the Opposition. He is prompt, decided, and industrious in the discharge of the duties of his position, both on the floor of the Senate and as a member of the various committees to which he belongs. He seldom addresses the Senate at any considerable length, save on important occasions, and even then it is only after the most careful and deliberate consideration of the subject-matter in hand.

Senator Lawrence married.Miss Hannah, daughter of the Hon. A. H. Mickle, of New York, formerly Mayor of that city, and in all the social relations of life, stands deservedly high in the community where he resides. In person, he is a large, substantially-built, companionable-looking man, of about medium height, and inclined to corpulency, with a profusion of dark-brown hair, blue eyes, and a fresh, smooth, good-natured face, that seldom fails to attract the attention of the most casual observer on first entering the Senate chamber.

## PERRIN H. McGRAW.

Senator McGraw was born on the 28th of December, 1822, in McGrawville, Cortland county, N. Y. He is the son of the late Hon. Henry McGraw, who emigrated, with his parents, from New Haven, Connecticut, in 1803, at which time there were only three families in that then wilderness. He embarked in the mercantile business in 1818, and was so engaged until the time of his death, in 1849. He died at the age of fifty-two, and was one of the most prominent and influential merchants in the county, having been a man of strict integrity, and upright and honorable in all his transactions through life. He was appointed postmaster in 1827, holding the position up to the time of his death, and represented Cortland county in the Legislature in 1843. He was always an active Whig, and one of the strongest political desires of his life was to live long enough to see Henry Clay chosen President of the United States. He was married, in 1820, to Miss Sally Smith, of Barre, Worcester county, Massachusetts, who is still living, and who is of English descent. Her father was an officer in the Revolutionary war.

Senator McGraw received an academical education. After leaving school, at the age of eighteen, he engaged as a clerk in the mercantile and general produce business, and at the age of twenty-one became interested in business with his father, who was extensively engaged in the mercantile and produce trade. He was then so employed until his father's death in 1849, when he became the leading partner of a firm which existed until 1857, when the mercantile trade was relinquished; the same firm, however, continuing an extensive produce and real estate business. In 1849, he was appointed Postmaster, having been an assistant, under his father, for several years; but his Whig principles were too strong for the administration of President Pierce, and in 1853 he was removed. In the fall of the same year he received an unsolicited nomination for Member of the Assembly, and was elected by the largest majority ever given to a Whig candidate in that county. In the fall of 1859, he was brought forward as a candidate for the seat he now occupies in the Senate, by the people of his county, with an unanimity rarely, if ever, equalled, and received upwards of twelve thousand votes, running far in advance of his ticket, while his opponent, who was supported by the combined Democratic and American vote, received only about eight thousand. The number of votes received by him was the largest given for any Senatorial candidate in the State. He was chairman of the Standing Committee on Charitable and Religious Societies and a member of the Committee on Claims and Literature, during the last session of the Legislature, and was altogether unsurpassed by any of his contemporaries in the faithful discharge of his duties. His career, thus far, in the Senate has been marked by a degree of industry, perseverance, and unpretending quietness that has contrasted favorably with the intolerable talking propensities of some of his legislative peers, and which has not failed to secure him the approbation of the whole Senate. A man of the sternest integrity, he was also found perfectly incorruptible, and was one among the most steadfast and unflinching supporters of the Governor in his vetoes of the New York city railroad projects.

In politics Senator McGraw was formerly a Whig, actively and unyieldingly devoted to the principles and policy of that gallant old party from 1840, until it ceased to exist, and was a delegate to the last Whig State Convention held in the State in 1854. Since then he has been identified with the Republican party, although still entertaining sound conservative views on all the great questions of State or national character. He is a gentleman of superior business qualifications; and although one of the most quiet, unpretending, and unassuming men in the Senate, is eminently well qualified, by his intellectual, social, and moral character, to discharge properly the duties of his official position. He possesses great amiability of temper, being of a conciliatory turn, and is very agreeable in his unreserved intercourse with his personal and political friends. His habits are singularly unostentatious, and he is distinguished for his simple and abstemious manner of life. In person, he is a tall, handsomely formed man, with a broad, retreating forehead, rendered prominent by partial baldness; brilliant, expressive dark eyes, and black hair; features purely and regularly classic in their mould, and a countenance suggesting superior mental and moral worth; while his deportment is at once easy, highbred, and dignified, without a trace of affectation.

Senator McGraw was married in 1848 to Miss Louisa, only daughter of Garret Pritchard, an extensive farmer in Cortland county, and is a member of the Presbyterian Church.

## BENJAMIN F. MANIERRE.

SENATOR MANIERRE is easily distinguished, as he quietly occupies his place in the Senate chamber, by the somewhat peculiar contrast between the personal appearance of him and his legislative associates. He has light hair and whiskers, large blue eyes, a prominent forehead, a smooth, generous-looking face, and a bright, intelligent countenance, which indicates a fine mental and physical organization. He is somewhat below the average size of men, with rather a delicate frame, though he is well-formed, and rather prepossessing in his general appearance.

Senator Manierre is a native of the county of New

London, Connecticut. His father's great-grandfather was a French officer, and his mother's family originally came from Scotland. They were of the somewhat celebrated family of Lees, of revolutionary memory, and locating in New London in the early days of the colony, took an active and prominent part in all the affairs of that province. His father, who was a gentleman of high character and superior ability, died at the age of forty-five; and his mother, whose maiden name was Lee, died at the age of fifty-five, in the city of Chicago, surrounded by her children, for whom she had toiled and suffered, and whom she had the happiness to live long enough to see well settled and respected in life.

All the members of the family to which Senator Manierre belongs, have become more or less distinguished. His oldest brother, John Manierre, was a Commodore in the Buenos Ayres navy, and was lost at sea. Another brother, George, is Circuit Judge of Cook county, Illinois, and his brother, Edward, was for a number of years Treasurer of the city of Chicago. Shortly after his father's death, his mother, deeming it best, with her limited means, to remove to the city of New York with her children, did so in the spring of 1829. The subject of this sketch then received the rudiments of a common English education, in the private and public schools of that city, and at the early age of twelve was placed in a banking and exchange office, commencing with a salary of one dollar and a half per week. Here he remained during an uninterrupted period of twenty-five years, at the end of which time he was chosen President of the Importers' and Traders'

Insurance Company. He has also held the position some time of President of the New York Young Men's Christian Association, and is well known for his active participation in all religious and benevolent enterprises in the city of New York. He never held any prominent official position at the hands of the people, until the fall of 1859, when he was brought forward by the Republicans of the Sixth District for the seat he now fills in the Senate, and was triumphantly elected. He was chairman of the Standing Committee on Cities and Villages, and a member of the Committee on Public Expenditures, in the Senate, during the last session of the Legislature, and was always found at his post in the discharge of his duties. He was originally a Democrat of the Tammany Hall school, and remained closely attached to that party until 1848, when his Freesoil proclivities led him into the ranks of the supporters of Mr. Van Buren for the Presidency. Since then he has been a firm and consistent supporter of the principle of Congressional sovereignty, and was one amongst the first to engage in the inauguration of the Republican movement. Since then he has been second to no one in his efforts to promote the interests and success of that party. During the exciting Presidential contest of 1856 he was President of the Fremont and Dayton Central Union Club, in the city of New York, and during the past three years has been a member of the Republican State Central Committee.

Senator Manierre is a gentleman of sterling honesty and integrity, and labors assiduously and efficiently for the welfare of his constituents, and the general good of the State. He possesses a sound judgment, with a high degree of general intelligence, and has a peculiar faculty of mastering figures and comprehending the most minute details of our financial system. His business habits are eminently correct, which, together with his untiring energy, and other superior qualities, fit him well to discharge properly the functions of a representative position. In his private character he is perfectly unexceptionable, and his excellent qualities as an individual give him far more than ordinary personal as well as political popularity.

Senator Manierre is a man of family, and is a member of the Methodist Episcopal Church, as well as Superintendent of a Mission Sabbath-school.

## CHARLES C. MONTGOMERY.

SENATOR MONTGOMERY was born in the town of Madrid, St. Lawrence county, N. Y., on the 19th of August, 1818. He is descended from New England parents, both of whom were natives of Vermont. His maternal grandfather, Isaac Bartholomew, served three years in the Revolutionary war. His father, John Montgomery, a successful farmer, died on the 5th of May, 1843, at the age of sixty-three, and his mother, whose maiden name was Mary Bartholomew, died on the 7th of June, in the same year, in the fifty-sixth year of her age.

Senator Montgomery was educated at the St. Lawrence Academy, at Potsdam, St. Lawrence county, N. Y., passing through only an English course of study, and, when not engaged on his father's farm, pursued the business of teaching, at intervals, for several years. In February, 1842, he was elected a Justice of the Peace and Inspector of Common Schools in his native place. In 1845 he was chosen Town Superintendent of Common Schools, but resigned the position in October of that year, and went to South Carolina for his health. He passed the winter at Jeffries Creek, Marion district, and returned home in June, 1846, with his health somewhat improved. In 1847 he was re-elected Town Superintendent, and again in 1850, and also Justice of the Peace. He had studied law in the office of James Redington, at Waddington, in Madrid, and in the spring of 1850 removed to Ogdensburgh, and continued the study of the law in the office of the Hon. Charles G. Myers, present Attorney-General of the State of New York. In September of that year he was admitted to the bar, and returning to Waddington, commenced the practice of his profession. In September, 1851, in company with a number of his townsmen, he went to California, arriving there in November following, and remained there about two years and a half, engaged in mining in the vicinity of Sonora, Tuolumne county. He returned home in April, 1854, and in 1855 was re-elected Town Superintendent, holding the office then until abolished in 1856. In 1857 he was elected Supervisor, and was re-elected in 1858, during which year he was Chairman of the Board. In 1859 he was again elected, receiving every vote cast at that election, and was honest and faithful in the fulfilment of his duties throughout his official term of service.

Mr. Montgomery was formerly a Freesoil Democrat, and warmly supported Mr. Van Buren for the Presidency, in 1848. He was one among the very first, after the passage of the Kansas-Nebraska Bill, to engage in the formation of a party to resist the further extension of slavery into the territories of the United States; and is now an enthusiastic and industrious member of the Republican party. He is highly conservative in all his views on all the great questions of a State or National character; and, although acting with his party, never forgets his own individuality by abandoning his own private sentiments and feelings for the sake of preserving peaceable terms with his political friends. He never fails to act in his legislative capacity with the greatest deference to the opinions of his legislative associates; but no party measure can secure his support simply as such; it must first secure something else—the approval of his judgment, and good, sound sense of propriety. He is, without doubt, the most retiring and unpretending man in the Senate, in his general habits and conduct. His qualifications as a speaker are good, when he once becomes thoroughly awakened on his subject; but, unless a matter of necessity, he never indulges in speech-making, and listens with great deference to the opinions of his legislative compeers. Still, his qualities, both of head and of heart, are of a superior character, and he is not only honest and efficient but eminently popular in the discharge of his duties as a legislator.

He was Chairman during the last session of the Legislature, of the Standing Committee on Indian Affairs, and also a prominent and influential member of the Committees on State Prisons, Public Printing, and the Erection and Division of Towns and Counties.

Mr. Montgomery is unmarried, and usually attends the Episcopal Church. In person, he is a large, dignified, substantial-looking man, with light-brown hair, combed back from a prominent forehead; large, blue eyes, of brilliant lustre; a smooth, intelligent, good-natured face, with firmness and decision of character largely developed in its features; and a countenance whose calmness is equal to a summer's eve, and whose expression of dignity and composure no excitement can disturb.

## ALLEN MUNROE.

SENATOR MUNROE has succeeded well in proving himself one of the most quiet, influential, and sensible men on the Republican side of the Senate. Calm, dignified, and dispassionate, he is always for peace rather than war, and while unwilling to make any dishonorable concession in the present distracted state of the country, is ever ready and anxious to lend his might in the restoration of peace and tranquillity to the Confederacy.

Senator Munroe was born on the 10th of March, 1819, in the town of Elbridge, Onondaga county, New York. He is a younger brother of the Hon. James Munroe, who represented the Twenty-second district in the Senate during the four years from 1852 to 1856.

His paternal grandfather, the late Hon. Squire Munroe, was born in the town of Rehoboth, Bristol county, Massachusetts, on the 27th of June, 1757. He was the oldest son of Nathan Munroe, and his grandfather, William Munroe, with his great-grandfather, John Munroe, emigrated from Scotland in the early settlement of America. The grandmother of the Senator was the grand-daughter of Colonel Benjamin Church, a distinguished officer in King Philip's war. At the commencement of the Revolutionary war, he entered the service of his country, at the age of eighteen, and continued in the army some three years, during which time he was continually exposed to dangers and hardships, being located directly on the seaboard. In this school he took so deep an interest in the welfare of his country, that the principles of civil and religious liberty were firmly rooted into his political sentiments at an early period of his life. At the age of twenty-two he married Miss Mary, daughter of John Daggett, by whom he had ten children, five of whom are now living. After various vicissitudes in life, he became possessed of a small farm in Lanesborough, which, in 1794, he exchanged for the farm on which he lived, until his death, in Camillus, now Elbridge, Onondaga county, New York. The country was then new, and land very cheap, the natural increase of which in value at the time of his death in 1835, and his energetic business habits, had made him a very wealthy farmer. He took a deep interest in the benevolent objects of the day, and being a firm Baptist, was considered a pillar in the church to which he belonged. He died at the age of seventy-eight.

Senator Munroe's father, Nathan Munroe, died on the 5th of July, 1839, in the forty-ninth year of his age, and his mother is still living at Syracuse. He was educated at the Munroe Academy, an institution established and endowed by his father, in his native village, fitting himself for the junior class in College, but at the age of eighteen he was placed in charge of an experienced merchant in the city of Auburn, to be taught the mercantile business.

Three years afterwards, in the spring of 1840, he engaged in business on his own responsibility, on the old corner in the village of Elbridge, which had been so long occupied by his father. He then continued the mercantile trade some seven years, when he married Miss Julia, daughter of John Townsend, of Albany, and after an absence of nearly a year in Europe, he returned and settled in Syracuse, where he accepted the agency of the property of the surviving members of the Syracuse Company, and embarked in milling and the manufacture of solar salt. He was elected Mayor of the city of Syracuse, in the spring of 1854, holding the position one year, and is now a Trustee of the Munroe Collegiate Institute, at Elbridge, President of the Onondaga County Savings Bank, a Director in the Bank of Salina, a Trustee of the Asylum for Idiots at Syracuse, a Trustee of the Asylum for Inebriates at Binghamton, a Trustee of the Onondaga County Orphan Asylum, a Trustee of the Oakwood Cemetery at Syracuse, Vice-President of the Oswego and Syracuse Railroad Company, a Director in the Gaslight Company of that city, and occupies various other public positions assigned him by friends. In the fall of 1859 he was brought forward with unusual unanimity as a candidate for the Senate, and was triumphantly elected by a large majority. He was chairman of the Standing Committee on State Prisons, and a member of the Committee on Privileges and Elections, and Joint Library, and was always found diligent and faithful in the fulfilment of his duties.

Senator Munroe was formerly a Whig, but was one among the first to enlist in the Republican enterprise, and has been five years a member of the Whig, and then the Republican State Committee. He is clearly a gentleman of sound common-sense and decisive judgment, and is highly intelligent, cautious, and deliberate, not wishing to give offence, and yet not afraid to express his opinions. His business qualifications are of a superior order, of which his success in life is a striking evidence; and he carries with him into the discharge of his legislative duties the same amount of industry, economy, and systematic arrangement for which he is distinguished in private life. There is method in everything he does, and he engages in everything with a mathematical precision that is always the sure harbinger of unmistakable success.

Senator Munroe attends the First Presbyterian Church, and is a man of great personal popularity. In person, he is tall and rather slender, has clear sky-blue eyes, hair and whiskers of a medium shade between a golden color and the darkest brown, and a pleasant, good-natured face.

# JOHN McLEOD MURPHY.

SENATOR MURPHY is, doubtless, one of the most high-minded, accomplished, and intelligent men in the Senate, and by his career, thus far, in that body, has successfully secured the reputation of a first-class representative. He is one of those men, not very common in public life, whose instincts and education place him far above the ordinary level of modern politicians, and he owes his success, both in public and private, more to his own intrinsic worth than to the power and influence of party machinery, or the customary political tactics of the day. During the last Session of the Legislature he was chairman of the Standing Committee on Joint Library, and a member of the Committees on Literature and Commerce and Navigation, in the Senate, and was always prompt and industrious in the discharge of all his duties.

Senator Murphy is a native of North Castle, Westchester county, New York, where he was born on the 14th of February, 1827. He sprang from genuine Irish and Knickerbocker Dutch ancestry, and is a lineal descendant, on his mother's side, of the celebrated family of Waldegraves, in England. His paternal grandfather, John Murphy, emigrated from Wexford shortly after the Revolution, and settled in the Seventh Ward, in the city of New York, where he established himself as a brewer; and his maternal grandfather, George Warner, the sailmaker, was well and favorably known amongst the old Knickerbocker families of Manhattan Island. His father, Thomas Murphy, who died in New York, on the 15th of July, 1853, at the age of fifty-six, represented Westchester county in the Legislature, in 1831, and was the contemporary of such men as Daniel S. Dickinson, William L. Marcy, John A. Dix, Millard Fillmore, Silas Wright, and others, who have since made their mark in the political records of the State. His mother, whose maiden name was Maria S. Warner, died at Haverstraw, on the 3d of June, 1839, at the comparatively early age of thirty-six. His family were for a long time residents of Westchester county, whence they removed, in 1835, to Rockland county, where they located on a farm near Stony Point.

Senator Murphy was educated in the United States Navy, which he entered in February, 1841. He served four years and eight months in the Mediterranean, under Flag Officer Tatnall, and during that period visited Italy, Greece, France, Spain, Austria, and the Barbary coast. He then passed a short time at the United States Naval Academy, after which he was detailed for the frigate *United States*, and served a year on the west coast of Africa, with the late Dr. Kane. Returning to New York, he commenced the study of the law, but the Mexican war having broken out in the interval of his absence, he abandoned Blackstone and Kent, for the more exciting scenes of the war, and was sent to Vera Cruz. Throughout all the events of that memorable struggle, he bore an active part, and was put in charge of a field-piece, at the capture of Tobasco, under Commodore Perry, whose official reports bear testimony to his services and gallantry. At the close of the war he was again sent to the Naval Academy, where he graduated with distinction, in July, 1848. He shortly afterwards published a work, entitled " Nautical Routine and Stowage," with short rules in navigation, which has become the text-book of the United States Navy, and which exhibits a high degree of literary talent, as well as a thorough knowledge of his subject.

When the Collins steamers were projected, Senator Murphy was detailed by the Administration of President Taylor as a watch officer on board the *Atlantic*, in which vessel he successfully served some eight months. When the expedition for the survey of the Isthmus of Tehuantepec was again organized, in November, 1850, he was engaged as Hydrographic Assistant under Major Barnard, and was confided with the botanical and statistical labors of the expedition. After the lapse of a year in Mexico, he again returned to New York, and resigned from the Navy, with a view of pursuing the open and comprehensive field of civil engineering, for which his experience in Mexico, under the auspices of one of the ablest engineers in the army, had, in a great measure, prepared him. In 1853, however, President Pierce sent him to Mexico on a confidential mission, to aid in the negotiation of the Messilla purchase, and after its successful issue, he again returned to the United States, and renewed the struggle for the mastery of his profession. Mingling occasionally in the political contests of the day, but always clinging to the cause of Democracy, he was an unsuccessful candidate for Congress in the Sixth District, in 1854, and ran unsuccessfully for the State Senate in the following year. His defeat, however, in both instances. was the result of an irreconcilable division in the ranks of the Democratic party.

In 1855, Senator Murphy was appointed a City Surveyor, and was subsequently transferred to the position of Constructing Engineer at the Brooklyn Navy Yard, where he served with credit to himself and satisfaction to the entire party for more than a year. In July, 1858, he was appointed by the Louisiana Tehuantepec Company, of New Orleans, as Superintending Engineer, for the opening of the Tehuantepec route, and succeeded by his unremitting energy and professional skill in the accomplishment of that object. On his return to New York, he delivered a series of important and valuable lectures on Mexican Archæology, and other kindred subjects, which called forth the highest encomiums of the press and the scientific societies. Subsequently he returned to the Isthmus, and conducted the explorations of the Pacific coast of Mexico, the surveys of Guatulco, &c. He was brought forward at the last election, with flattering unanimity, for the seat he fills in the Senate, and was elected by a handsome vote.

Senator Murphy was married in November, 1848, to Miss Mary Teresa Mooney, of the city of New York, and belongs to the Catholic Church. He maintains a high social position throughout the city of his residence, and is altogether unsurpassed in his personal as well as in his political popularity.

# PETER P. MURPHY.

SENATOR MURPHY has, by his course in the Senate, during the last session of the Legislature, proven himself a man of sterling integrity and strong common sense, and an industrious and faithful representative. As Chairman of the Standing Committee on Medical Societies, and a member of the Committee on Railroads, he was always found at his post, honestly engaged in the prompt discharge of all his duties, and was rarely, if ever, absent from his place on the floor of the Senate. He ranked high among the staunchest friends of the Pro Rata Freight Bill, and the bill imposing tolls on railroads, laboring earnestly throughout the session to secure their passage through both branches of the Legislature, and showed himself an uncompromising and persistent opponent of the New York city railroad projects, having joined Senator Bell in a protest against their passage, and supported the Governor in all his vetoes. His presence to the lobby was always exceedingly unpalatable. He was always found setting his face against any measure that was even suspected of corruption, and was not at all long in exhibiting a most supreme contempt for all that class of worthless sovereigns who defile the capital annually with their filthy presence, and are familiarly known as the "Third House."

Senator Murphy is the oldest man in the Senate. He was born on the 18th of July, 1801, in the city of Albany, and is of Irish and German extraction. His paternal grandfather, Patrick Murphy, came to America as early as 1750, and settled in the Mohawk valley, while another portion of the family established themselves south of what is now known as Mason and Dixon's line. He had two sons, who participated in the struggle for American Independence, one of whom was wounded at Johnstown, and the other at the battle of Oriskany. Peter Murphy, the father of the subject of this sketch, who was then too young to participate in the war, died in 1844, at about the age of sixty-five, and his wife, whose maiden name was Catharine O'Connell, died in 1846, at about the same age.

Senator Murphy was educated at the Albany Academy. In 1820 he removed into Herkimer county, where he taught awhile, and then read medicine, in Cherry Valley, with Prof. Joseph White. He graduated in 1826, and entered upon the practice of his profession in the town of Starks, Herkimer county. Here he remained until the fall of 1834, when he was elected to the lower branch of the Legislature, and in the spring of 1835, removed to Niagara county, where his parents had settled in 1828. He took up his residence in Royalton, in that county, where he has always since been successfully engaged in the practice of his profession. Politically he was originally a Democrat of the old Jeffersonian school, and was a delegate to the Democratic State Convention in 1844, which nominated Silas Wright for Governor. In 1848, when the question of the jurisdiction of Congress over slavery in the territories of the United States was first agitated, he took sides with the friends of the Wilmot Proviso, and earnestly supported Mr. Van Buren for the Presidency. He was again true to that principle in 1852, when he advocated the election of John P. Hale as a candidate for the Presidency, and was a prominent and influential delegate in the State Convention, at which the present Republican party was first christened. He has always since then been true and unfaltering in his attachment to the doctrines and policy of that organization, and had the honor of being one of the representatives from the Empire State in the National Convention at Philadelphia, in 1856, which nominated John C. Fremont as a suitable candidate for President of the United States.

Senator Murphy has held the office of Supervisor in the town in which he resides. After the expiration of his term of service in that position, he never occupied any prominent public place until the fall of 1859, when he was brought forward by the Republicans of the Twenty-ninth Senatorial district, as a candidate for the seat he now occupies, and was triumphantly elected. He has always taken a deep interest in politics, participating actively in all the political contests of the day, and exercises a controlling influence over the politics of his own and the adjoining counties. His fund of general knowledge is unusually large; there are but few things of importance that he apparently does not know; and no one in the Senate surpasses him in a thorough and minute knowledge of the political history of the State of New York. His almost unparalleled and intimate acquaintance, too, with the detailed history of all our great men, and the various prominent measures that have agitated the country, during the past three quarters of a century, reminds one very forcibly of John Quincy Adams, and he is equally fortunate in his ability to use that knowledge, both in public and in the private and social circles in which he moves.   He is not a frequent debater, rarely participating at any considerable length in the discussions of the Senate, but is a rigid reasoner —logical, seldom if ever embellishing his speeches; and his arguments are always sound, practical, concise, and convincing.

Senator Murphy was married in December, 1826, to Miss Anna Kayner, and was reared in the old North Dutch Church in the city of Albany.   Physically he is one of the largest men in the Senate, and is unequalled by any of his legislative associates in real dignity of manner, congeniality of temper, and kindness and hospitality of character.

# ERASTUS S. PROSSER.

Senator Prosser is a native of the town of Westerlo, Albany county, N. Y., and is fifty years of age.   He is a self-educated man, having enjoyed only the means of a very limited English education, and, while comparatively young, removed to the city of Albany, where he embarked in the forwarding trade.   After remaining in that place for some time, he located in the city of Buffalo, where he now resides, and where he was extensively and successfully engaged in the forwarding business, till about three years ago, when he retired upon an ample fortune. He possesses fine business capacities, combined with untiring industry and strict integrity, and is wholly indebted to his own unaided exertions and noble aims in life for the eminent and gratifying success with which he has thus far met.

In politics Senator Prosser was formerly a Democrat, till 1848, when his anti-slavery proclivities led him into the support of Mr. Van Buren for the Presidency. He subsequently joined the Republican party, and although elected to his present position by a union of Americans and Republicans, still claims to belong to that party, and acted accordingly during the last session of the Legislature, and thus far during the present session. He never held any public office until his election to the Senate, which first took place in the fall of 1858, when he was chosen as the successor of the Hon. James Wadsworth, who resigned his seat in that body shortly after the adjournment of the Legislature in the spring of that year. During the session of the Legislature in that year, he was Chairman of the Standing Committee on Canals in the Senate, as well as Chairman of the Committee on Manufactures, and rendered the people of the State considerable service in that capacity. He was again brought forward as the American and Republican candidate in 1859, and was again triumphantly elected by a handsome majority. He was again Chairman of the Standing Committee on Canals and a member of the Committee on Commerce and Navigation, in the Senate, during the last session of the Legislature. He has never paid much attention to general politics, in his close confinement to his duties as a strict business man, and outside of the business world has been known in public only as a zealous and consistent friend of the canals. His long experience in the forwarding trade, has long since convinced him of the necessity and advantage of the speedy enlargement and completion of these great channels of commerce, and the deep interest which he has always taken in this great question was probably the only inducement for him to consent to become a candidate for the position he now occupies. He has also been industriously engaged in the enterprise of introducing steam navigation on the Erie Canal, and looks upon it as one of the greatest improvements of the day in canal navigation.

Senator Prosser has a family, and is personally, as well as politically, popular among all who know him. He is rather prepossessing in his personal appearance, being about medium height, with an active frame, sharp, grey eyes, and a bushy, iron-grey beard: and wears a cheerful, good-natured, though dignified and somewhat reserved expression upon his countenance, which at once gives assurance of the real man. He is cordial and unaffected in his social qualities, but is apparently cold and indifferent, and not easily approached.

# JOSEPH R. RAMSEY.

SENATOR RAMSEY is a native of Sharon, Schoharie county, N. Y. He was born on the 29th of January, 1816, and is therefore upwards of forty-five years of age, although he has the appearance of being ten years younger. He is of German and English descent, and is the son of a Methodist clergyman, Frederick Ramsey, who is a man of considerable ability, and who has now attained the ripe old age of seventy-one. Both he and his wife, the mother of the subject of this sketch, are still residing in Cobleskill, Schoharie county.

Senator Ramsey received a good, practical business education, and after spending some time as a clerk in the mercantile trade, removed, at the age of twenty-five, to Lawyersville, in his native county, where he studied law with Jedediah Miller, and where he has always since been engaged in the practice of his profession. He was a member of the Assembly in 1855, and in the fall of the same year was nominated as a candidate for the Senate, by the Republicans of the Fourteenth district, and was elected. During the two succeeding years, he was a member, in that body, of the Railroad and other important committees, and established his reputation as a very industrious and efficient legislator. After the expiration of his services in the Senate, he went back to the practice of his profession, but was soon induced to almost wholly abandon it, for the time being, by the very deep interest he took in the passage of a law appropriating a certain amount of money to the completion of the

Albany and Susquehanna Railroad. His efforts, however, having been temporarily defeated in the matter by the conduct of the Governor in his veto of a bill of that kind, after it had passed both branches of the last Legislature, he appealed to the people, and was triumphantly elected, upon that issue, to the seat he again occupies in the Senate. During the last session of the Legislature he was Chairman of the Standing Committee on the Erection and Division of Towns and Counties, and a member of the Judiciary Committee. A bill, appropriating money towards the completion of the Albany and Susquehanna Railroad, was then passed again, and again encountered the Governor's veto, notwithstanding his pledge in his message at the opening of the Legislature, that he would not withhold his official sanction from the measure again. A similar measure has already been again introduced into the Senate, but with what success remains to be seen.

In politics Senator Ramsey was formerly a Whig of Freesoil tendencies, and at the disorganization of that body became a staunch supporter of the cause of Republicanism. He was a delegate to the first Republican State Convention that ever assembled in New York, and has always since then been active, energetic, and devoted in his advocacy of that party. His ability as a lawyer and as a legislator is far above mediocrity, and he is a fluent and sensible speaker, wielding, at all times, no inconsiderable influence upon the deliberations of the body to which he belongs. He possesses a social temperament; enjoys a large share of personal as well as political popularity; and is a general favorite among all classes of people at Albany.

An old proverb declares that articles of the choicest value are always done up in small packages. So it is with Senator Ramsey, who is the smallest man in the Senate, if not in the entire Legislature. He is only five feet four inches in height, which is precisely the stature of one of the most gifted kings of France; is well proportioned; of active temperament, and wears an amiable and pleasant face, which always kindles with a genial smile when he recognises his friends.

Senator Ramsey was married in March, 1836, to Miss Sarah S. Boyce, a lady of superior intellectual and moral worth, and attends the Reformed Dutch Church.

## VOLNEY RICHMOND.

SENATOR RICHMOND was born in the town of Hoosick, Rensselaer county, New York, on the 23d of June, 1802. He is of English extraction. His great-great-grand-parents came from England, and settled in the colony of Massachusetts. He is the youngest of seven brothers and twelve children. His father, Edward Richmond, who died in Hoosick in the year 1827, at the advanced age of seventy-one, was a Revolutionary soldier, and served in the war, with considerable gallantry and distinction, during a period of five years. His wife, the mother of the subject of this sketch, whose maiden name was Olive Briggs, died about ten years afterwards, at the ripe old age of seventy-nine.

Senator Richmond was brought up on a farm belong-

5*

ing to his father, who was an honest and industrious mechanic, and was educated in the common schools of his native town. At the age of eighteen he went to the wagon and carriage-making trade, and after completing his apprenticeship, engaged in the business on his own responsibility, in his native place. He was then successfully so employed during an uninterrupted period of twelve years, after which he kept a hotel until 1840, when he was elected Sheriff of Rensselaer county, and removed to the city of Troy. He occupied this position during the full term of three years, and during the following three years was engaged as under-sheriff of the county. Meanwhile, he was three years Supervisor, and was a member of the Common Council some four years. In 1857 he was a member of the Assembly, and occupied a prominent position in that body, as a member of the Committee on Banks, and the Sub-Committee of Sixteen.

In 1848 Senator Richmond embarked in the stove foundry business in Troy, which he followed extensively some seven years, and after spending six months in Europe, returned to Hoosick, where he has always since been quietly pursuing his occupation as a farmer. In the fall of 1857, he was brought forward by the Republicans of his district with great unanimity, as a candidate for the position he now holds in the Senate; but through the inactivity of his friends, who were sanguine of his success, he was defeated, by a very small majority, by his opponent, Judge Willard, of Troy. He was again brought forward as a candidate for the Senate at the last election, as the opposing candidate of Judge Willard, who was again placed in the field, and was triumphantly elected by a large majority.

He was a member of the Standing Committees on Railroads, and Cities, and Villages, in the Senate, during the last session of the Legislature, and was seldom absent in the discharge of his duties. He was among those who opposed the passage of the Pro Rata Freight Bill, and the bill tolling railroads, and stands recorded in favor of all the New York City Railroad schemes. In politics, he was formerly a Whig, and a great admirer of the immortal Clay, adhering with unyielding tenacity to the fortunes of that party, until it abandoned its organization, when he became a Republican. He has always sustained the reputation throughout Rensselaer county, of an active, thoroughgoing, and successful politician, and has generally wielded a strong influence among all classes of people, wherever he has been known. In addition to this, he is well known as an enterprising and successful business man, possessing a sound, practical judgment, and a thorough knowledge of human nature, and has never failed to prosecute all his business enterprises with determined vigor and signal success. His chief characteristics are firmness of purpose, and a ceaseless ambition to excel in whatever he undertakes. His general habits are plain, simple, and unpretending. He makes no efforts at speech-making, being a practical working man, but ranks high among the most prominent, industrious, and efficient members of the Senate.

Senator Richmond was married, in 1828, at Hancock, Massachusetts, to Miss Lucy Townsend, who died in

1836, and was again married, in 1838, to Miss Mary
Barnett. He attends the Presbyterian Church, and is
kind and generous in his support of religious objects.
He is a man of medium height, with a comparatively
large, compact, and substantial frame; has light-brown
hair, partially grey, with a slight baldness on the crown
of the head; small hazel eyes; a round, full, fresh face;
and a dignified, calm, though not very good-natured
countenance.

## HEZEKIAH D. ROBERTSON.

SENATOR ROBERTSON is one of the most energetic men
and active politicians in the Senate. He is an earnest
debater and a ready speaker, neither courting nor avoid-
ing a discussion of his views, and no matter what obsta-
cles are cast in his way, never relaxes his efforts in the
accomplishment of whatever he undertakes. During
the past session of the Legislature he was Chairman of
the Committee on Commerce and Navigation, and a
member of the Committee on Manufactures, in the
Senate, and introduced and succeeded in passing many
of the leading bills of the session. Among these was
the Metropolitan Police Bill, whereby the Police Department of the City of New York was remodelled, and by
which Westchester county was exempted from taxation
for Police purposes. The Board of Public Charities
and Corrections in New York, also owes its existence
to his indomitable perseverance and legislative tact—a
measure by which the old Alms-House Governors were

abolished, and the number of members of the Board reduced from ten to four. He likewise introduced the Pilot Bill, and carried it triumphantly over the heads of its opponents, thus securing to the pilots of Long Island Sound the same privileges which are accorded to those at Sandy Hook. The Emigrant Runners' Bill, by which additional safeguards are thrown around the emigrant, was also drafted and introduced to the Senate by him, and he was eminently successful in his support of all local measures calculated to benefit his own immediate district.

Senator Robertson is a native of the town of Bedford, Westchester county, New York, where he was born on the 15th of December, 1828. He is of Scotch and German extraction, and is a cousin of ex-Senator William H. Robertson, the representative of the district now represented by the subject of this sketch, during the years 1854 and '55, and who is at present County Judge of Westchester county. His maternal grandfather, Hezekiah Dykeman, was a Captain in the Revolutionary War, and was distinguished for his courage and patriotism.

Senator Robertson received an academical education in his native place, intending, at the close of a contemplated collegiate course, to enter the legal profession, but the sudden death of both his parents induced him to devote himself to agricultural pursuits. He commenced farming in the town of Poundridge; at the age of twenty-one, was chosen Superintendent of Schools, and at the close of his official term, Supervisor of that town. In 1853 he removed to Bedford, and engaged in the mercantile business with Benjamin I. Ambler, under the firm name of Ambler & Robertson. In 1859, the copartnership was dissolved, Mr. Robertson retiring from the firm. Immediately upon his removal to Bedford, he was chosen Superintendent of Schools in that town, and subsequently, for three years, was elected Supervisor, which position he still holds. Originally a devoted follower of Henry Clay, he became, at the outset of its organization, a prominent member of the American party, to the vital principles of which he still adheres. Always a determined Whig, he has, during his whole political career, illustrated, by his acts, the sincerity of the views he has maintained. It is mainly owing to his efforts, that the Union party, which has been so successful in Westchester county, was formed. As a citizen of the Ninth Congressional District, he advocated and secured, at the hands of the Americans, the renomination and election of the Hon. John B. Haskin, to his seat in the present Congress. His sympathies and proclivities since the campaign of 1858, have been with the Republicans, agreeing with them, substantially, on all questions of national interest.

In 1856, Senator Robertson was the nominee of the Americans of the First Assembly district of Westchester county, for a seat in the Assembly, but, although receiving fifteen hundred votes, was defeated by the Republican candidate. He was elected to his present position by a majority of over eighteen hundred, the Democratic State ticket receiving a majority of two thousand in the district. He was nominated by the Americans, and unanimously endorsed, in Convention, by the Republicans and anti-Lecompton Democrats.

Senator Robertson is still single, and is an attendant upon the services of the Baptist church, in which he was brought up. In person, he is of medium size : has light brown hair and whiskers; intelligent blue eyes, and a good-natured, clever countenance.

## FRANCIS M. ROTCH.

SENATOR ROTCH never occupied any prominent public position until his election to the seat he now fills in the Senate. In 1857, he was unanimously presented, by his own county, as a candidate for the position, but after a contest of twenty-four hours in the Nominating Convention, with the Hon. A. H. Laflin, late Senator from that district, he withdrew, in favor of the latter, who was presented as a candidate with equal unanimity by the delegates from his county, and who was, thereupon, unanimously nominated. After the expiration of Senator Laflin's term of office, however, in the fall of 1859, he received the unanimous nomination of the Republican Senatorial Convention of his district, and was triumphantly elected to his present position by a majority of twenty-five hundred, running far ahead of his ticket in his own county. He was Chairman of the Committee on Agriculture, and a member of the Committees on Indian Affairs and Public Buildings during the last Session of the Legislature, and although evidently not ambitious of any particular distinction, proved himself one of the most faithful and intelligent men upon the floor of the Senate. His most favorite measure appeared to be the bill making an appropriation towards the completion of the Albany and Susquehanna Railroad, which was vetoed by the Governor, and it was owing in a very great degree to his efforts that the passage of the bill through both branches of the Legislature was secured. He is a good speaker and a ready debater; but never participates to any considerable extent in the discussions of the Senate, believing that proper legislation depends more upon enlightened action than useless speech-making.

Senator Rotch is a native of New Bedford, Mass., where he was born on the 20th of February, 1822. His father, Francis Rotch, a gentleman distinguished everywhere for his kindness and benevolence towards the poor, is of English descent, his great-grandfather, Joseph Rotch, having emigrated to this country from Salisbury, England, early in the eighteenth century, and settled in Nantucket. His son was the owner of the ship *Dartmouth*, from which the tea was thrown overboard by the famous " Boston Tea Party ;" and as the consignees refused to give up the bills of lading or pay the freight, the loss fell heavily upon him, thus making him one among the very first to suffer in the great cause of American Independence. The maiden name of the mother of the subject of this sketch was Morgan, and her family were among the earliest residents of the city of Philadelphia.

In 1831 Senator Rotch removed, with his parents, to

the State of New York, and settled in the town where he now resides, in the county of Otsego. He received a thorough collegiate education, having graduated in 1841 at "Old Harvard," but pursued his course chiefly with a view to the pursuit of agriculture, and its kindred sciences of chemistry, botany, &c., which have always been his favorite studies, and to which he has devoted his time, principally, since leaving college. In 1843 he sailed for Europe, and remained abroad some three years, visiting not only the countries in the usual route of tourists, but also Spain, Morocco, Turkey, Greece, and Asia Minor. Since then, he has, likewise, made several brief visits to England and France, chiefly with reference to his favorite pursuit of agriculture. He was for some time President of the Agricultural Society of the town where he resides, and was the first President, under the new organization, of the Agricultural Society of Otsego County, besides occupying, for some years, the position of one of the Vice-Presidents of the New York State Agricultural Society. In politics he was originally a Whig of the Clay and Webster school; but upon the repeal of the Missouri Compromise was one among the first to enlist in the Republican movement. He possesses but little taste for the turmoil and strife usually incident to the party politics of the present day, but has a thorough, comprehensive knowledge of everything pertaining to the character and general history of our State and National Government.

In person Senator Rotch is a gentleman of elegant figure. He is of about medium height, with wavy, dark-brown hair, blue eyes, a light beard, and moustache *à la Française*, and a face whose finely-formed and distinctly-marked features indicate at once a refined and cultivated intellect, and a shrewd, sagacious business-man and politician. He is sociable and frank in his manners; kind-hearted, generous, and hospitable; and is deservedly popular among all his legislative associates.

## WALTER L. SESSIONS.

SENATOR SESSIONS, like some of his Republican colleagues, has clearly demonstrated, by his course since taking his seat in the Senate, that he does not believe in the doctrine that the representative is always bound by the wishes of his constituents, nor that political pledges are ever made to be fully carried out. Although a gentleman of conceded ability, it is generally understood, even among his political friends, that his course at Albany, last winter, was neither very creditable to himself nor his party. As Chairman of the Committee on Finance, in the Senate, he was intrusted with some of the most weighty responsibilities of a representative position, but the fact that he is now excluded from all the important committees in that body is a significant commentary upon the manner in which he discharged his obligations. He came to the Senate pledged to support the Pro Rata Freight bill, and the bill imposing tolls on Railroads, but, for some cause best known, probably, to himself, he very soon proved himself one of their most uncompromising and troublesome opponents. It was for this and similar conduct that the Republicans of Chautauqua county passed the following resolutions after the adjournment of the Legislature, which were published in the New York *Tribune*, with comments of approbation : " Resolved, That we utterly and totally discountenance and condemn the despicable and mercenary course pursued at the last session of our State Legislature by Walter L. Sessions, Senator from this district, and invite him to leave the Republican party."

Senator Sessions is a native of the town of Leister, Addison county, Vermont. He was born on the 4th of October, 1820, and is, therefore, forty years of age. While yet a mere boy, he removed with his parents into Chautauqua County, New York, where he has always since resided. His early educational advantages were not very good, his parents having been poor ; but by industry and perseverance, he succeeded in passing successfully through the course usually prescribed by the academies of the country, and is now a gentleman of considerable literary attainment. He subsequently entered a law office, gaining admission to the bar, after passing through the customary course of legal studies, and has since then been engaged in the practice of his profession. His reputation in the community in which he resides is that of a lawyer of more than ordinary ability, and he is said to have met with more than ordinary success as a practitioner at the bar.

The public career of Senator Sessions may be said to have first commenced in 1853, when he was an active member of the Assembly from Chautauqua county.  He was re-elected to that body in the fall of the same year; and in the Whig caucus, held on the eve of the opening of the following session of the Legislature, was a strong friend of the Hon. Robert H. Pruyn, of Albany, as a candidate for Speaker, against the Hon. De Witt C. Littlejohn, the present incumbent of that position.  The former represented the Freesoil element in the caucus, and the latter the more conservative, or old line portion of the party; but Mr. Pruyn succeeded, and having been chosen Speaker, placed Mr. Sessions at the head of the Standing Committee on Ways and Means, as a reward, doubtless, for his services in the contest.

After the expiration of the legislative term of Senator Sessions, in 1854, he returned to the shades of private life, contenting himself with the quiet pursuit of his profession until the fall of 1859, when he came forward as a candidate in the Republican Senatorial Convention of the Thirty-second district, for the seat he now occupies.  The contest was spirited and protracted, his opponent persistently contesting every prospect of success, however slight; and it was not until after a large number of ballotings had been taken, that Mr. Sessions received the nomination.  The Convention having adjourned, he immediately entered the field, working steadily and perseveringly throughout the entire campaign, and had the gratification of coming out of the struggle with triumphant success.

Politically, as has already been intimated, he began his career as a member of the old Whig party.  His sentiments and feelings have always been thoroughly tinctured with Freesoilism, which naturally enough caused him to identify himself with the extreme anti-slavery branch of that party; and after the passage of the Kansas-Nebraska bill by Congress in 1854, he did not hesitate a moment to take his position on the Republican platform, to the principles of which he has always since firmly adhered. He has always participated actively in the politics of his own and the adjoining counties, and by his industry, and personal popularity, has succeeded in acquiring considerable political influence in the section of the State in which he resides. Although ambitious of worldly fame, he lacks the most essential elements of real greatness, and has, perhaps, now ascended the ladder of political distinction as far as he will ever get. He is a natural talker, an irrepressible speaker—fluent and facile on all subjects, but inclined to remain of his own opinion, notwithstanding any arguments or persuasions, coming from what quarter they may. In temper and disposition he is pyrotechnic, occasionally displaying a blaze of rockets during the debates of the Senate ; and had he been born south of Mason and Dixon's line, would certainly have been inclined to affiliate with the extreme fire-eaters of that section of the Union.

In person, Senator Sessions is of middle height, with a good figure, a square forehead, black hair and beard, shaven on the upper lip, black eyes, and features of the ordinary New England mould, touched with a show of firmness, resolute will, and subtlety.

## FRANCIS B. SPINOLA.

SENATOR SPINOLA is now serving his second term in the Senate, having been first elected to that body in 1857. During the last session of the Legislature he was a member of the standing Committees on Internal Affairs of Towns and Counties, Insurance Companies, Banks, and Public Printing, and during the two preceding sessions served successfully on the Standing Committees on Privileges and Elections, and Internal Affairs of Towns and Counties. His experience as a legislator has been diligently improved, and he is never at loss for a rule by which to support and enforce a point of order. No one in the Senate, perhaps, is more prompt in off-hand, unpremeditated speech, and none more troublesome to the majority when any political party-measure is under consideration ; but his harangues, on all questions, seem an uncorking of all the political cogitations and scrap-readings of his life, rather than any set argument advancing to a particular point in logical expression. He is constantly in his seat, and entitles himself as much by his diligence and industry, as by his abilities, to the confidence of the important constituency he has the distinguished honor to represent.

Senator Spinola was born on the 19th of March, 1821, at Stony Brook, Suffolk county, New York. His father, who came to this country at an early age, to complete his education, and who finally settled here, was a native of the island of Madeira, and his paternal grandfather was an Italian. Both his mother and maternal grand-mother were natives of Long Island, and his maternal grandfather, who served through the Revolutionary war, as an officer, was an Irishman.

In early life Senator Spinola received but very little schooling, and when nearly sixteen years of age, was apprenticed to the trade of a jeweller. He served his time at this business, until he was twenty-one years of age, when he abandoned it, on account of an unusual degree of inactivity in the trade. Being an extremely handy youth, he then turned his attention to blacksmithing, which he followed nearly a year, when he engaged in the grocery business. After pursuing this occupation a short time, he engaged himself to work at the carpenter's trade, which he followed nearly a year, when he was appointed an Assistant to the Clerk of the Common Council of the City of Brooklyn, where he then, and has always since resided. This post he occupied about a year, his engagement having been only for a specific amount of work, which he had completed within that period, and he then became a clerk in the office of the Hon. Cyrus P. Smith, with whom he remained a year. Shortly after, he was appointed Assistant Clerk of the Common Council, which position he filled until he was elected Alderman from the Second Ward, in 1846. He was again the Whig candidate in the following year, and although the ward had always been one of the Democratic strongholds, he was defeated by only one vote. In the following spring, however, he was again elected, and was subsequently re-elected four different times. At the expiration of his term of office as Alderman, he was elected three successive years as Supervisor, and in the fall of 1855 was the successful Democratic candidate, in his district, for the Assembly. In 1857 he was brought forward by the Democrats of the Third District as a candidate for the Senate, and was triumphantly elected to that body, by a large majority, over the combined Republican and American vote. In addition to all these positions, he also held the post of Harbor Master five years, which he received from Governor Young, and has been an active member of the Fire Department for twenty years, filling consecutively all the different offices, save that of Chief Engineer.

Senator Spinola commenced his political career as a zealous and consistent admirer of Henry Clay, and continued to act with the Whig party until it resolved itself out of existence, when his conservative views on the Slavery question led him into the Democratic ranks, where he has always since steadily remained. He was elected a member of the Whig General Committee, before he was twenty-one years of age, in the city of Brooklyn; and was then, as he is now, and as he always has been, one of the most active and influential party men in the district or ward where he resides. He is always on hand on election day, ready to devote one day, at least, to the service of his country, and never fails to contribute his full share of labor to the success of the candidates and measures of the party to which he belongs.

Senator Spinola is married, and was reared in the Episcopal branch of the Church. In person he is somewhat above the medium height ; has a muscular, elastic frame ; dark hair and complexion ; sharp, blue eyes ; smooth face, and a frank, good-natured countenance.

---

## LYMAN TRUMAN.

SENATOR TRUMAN is emphatically one of that class of men whom the world designate "self-made," having arisen, under unusually adverse circumstances, from quite an humble condition in life to his present distinguished public and private position in the State. After receiving a few months' common schooling, he was left alone, at the age of sixteen, with a widowed mother, four brothers, and three sisters, younger than himself, without any means scarcely of a support. His father, who was a farmer, it is true, left them in the possession of the place upon which they were living; but it was so far encumbered as almost to preclude the possibility of their retaining it. Nothing daunted, however, Lyman went to work like a good fellow, and succeeded in supporting the family, sending the children at the same time to school, and in retaining the farm, until all claims against it were fully paid to the very last farthing. In accomplishing this, he employed himself in various ways, until he was twenty-four years of age, when he became a clerk in a store in an adjoining town. Here he remained three years in this capacity, when he embarked with a partner in the mercantile trade for himself, and continued thus engaged for about three years. He then purchased his partner's interest in the establishment, and shortly after took his three younger brothers in with him as partners. About this time he purchased a farm, and presented it to the oldest of his brothers, who had always followed the plough. He was succeeded in the mercantile trade about two years since by his brother-in-law, and has since then been engaged with his younger brothers in various successful enterprises. During the last thirty-five years he has, likewise, been a practical raftsman, and has never failed to make his annual trip down the Susquehanna in this capacity. He is a man of sterling integrity and untiring energy; upright and honorable in all his dealings; and occupies a prominent position among the business men in the section of the State where he resides. A few years since he was elected President of the Bank of Oswego, an institution which had then descended to almost universal discredit; but he succeeded in placing it upon a sure footing, and in successfully carrying it through all the financial troubles of the great panic of 1857. Indeed, there are probably few better business men in the State than Lyman Truman.

Senator Truman is a native of Candor, Tioga County, N. Y., and is of English and Scotch descent. He was born on the 2d of March, 1806, and is therefore now fifty-five years of age. Both his paternal and maternal grandfathers took part in the Revolutionary struggle, and the latter was especially prominent in the troubles at Stonington, Conn., where the General Government contracted a debt with him, which was paid only a few years since. Lyman's father, Aaron Truman, emigrated from Massachusetts to New York, in 1804, and settled in Tioga county, where he died, in 1838, at the age of thirty-eight. His wife, the mother of the subject of this sketch, was a native of Connecticut, and died, in 1844, at the age of sixty.

Senator Truman held various unimportant town offices previous to 1840, when he was elected Supervisor. He was again elected twice to the same position, and in 1847 ran as a stump candidate for the Assembly, in what was then a strong Democratic district, lacking only a few votes of an election. He declined all further nominations from that time until 1857, when the Republicans of the Twenty-fourth District brought him forward for the Senate, and he was triumphantly elected.

During the last session of the Legislature he was Chairman of the Standing Committee on Claims, and a member of the Committee on Finance, and during the two preceding sessions discharged his duties faithfully as Chairman of the Standing Committees on Public Expenditures and Claims. He was re-elected to the Senate in the fall of 1859 by a large majority. In early life he was an advocate of Democratic measures, and cast his first vote for General Jackson. He became a Whig after 1833, and voted with that party until 1848, when his Freesoil proclivities led him into the ranks of the supporters of Mr. Van Buren, for whom he then voted for President. From this time he took no further part in politics, being too much engrossed with his own private affairs, until the repeal of the Missouri Compromise. He immediately then became a zealous advocate of the Republican movement, and has ever since been a warm supporter of the doctrines of that party, taking the stump on all proper occasions in their behalf. He is, also, a strong advocate of the system of free schools, and never fails to exert all his power and influence in support of the great cause of temperance.

Senator Truman was married on the 10th of January, 1838, to Miss Emile M. Goodrich, by whom he has three children, and his family attend the Congregational Church. In person, he is a man about the medium height; is muscular, and tolerably well formed; has blue eyes, a dark complexion, and a profusion of dark-brown hair, with a pleasant, business-like face, whose features are very strongly marked. He is mild, courteous, and unostentatious in his manner; is plainly, though not very well dressed; and never seems to be disengaged. He is a fair, though not very graceful speaker, and a good reasoner, but never troubles the Senate with speech-making, regarding good, sound, safe legislation as more the result of correct thinking and thorough work than long-winded speeches.

## ANDREW S. WARNER.

THE career of Senator Warner thus far through life has been simply that of a quiet, practical, and successful business man, and his official conduct in the Senate is characterized by the same unpretending qualities for which he is distinguished in private life. During the last session of the Legislature, he was Chairman of the Standing Committees on Public Buildings and Engrossed Bills, as well as a member of the Committees on Medical Societies and Charitable and Religious Societies. There is nothing brilliant and imposing about him; his efforts as a debater being more distinguished for their plain, practical common-sense than flights of poetry or the flowers of rhetoric, but he discharges his public duties in a manner that can scarcely fail to command the approbation of his constituency.

Senator Warner is a native of Vernon, Oneida county, N. Y., where he was born on the 12th of January, 1818. He is of English descent, and is a brother of the Rev. W. W. Warner, who is now preaching at Champion, Jefferson county, N. Y. His paternal grandfather, Andrew Warner, who was a gallant soldier in the American Revolution, emigrated to New York from Connecticut, and settled in Oneida county, as did also his maternal grandfather, Israel Young, who came from New Hampshire. His father, Andrew Warner, who was an industrious and enterprising farmer, died at Sandy Creek, Oswego County, in 1843, at the age of fifty-two; and his mother, whose maiden name was Elizabeth C. Young, is still living, at the advanced age of sixty-five.

Senator Warner received an academical education. He has always been successfully engaged in agricultural pursuits, and sustains the reputation of a business man of superior qualifications. He held the position of Superintendent of the Poor in 1848, and was a member of the Assembly during the two successive years of 1855, and '56. The success with which he met in the discharge of his duties in that body was alike creditable to himself and satisfactory to his constituents; but after the expiration of his official term he declined all further political distinction until the fall of 1859, when he consented to become a candidate for the seat he now holds in the Senate, and was victoriously elected. In politics he was originally a strong Freesoiler, persistently opposing everything calculated to further the extension of the institution of slavery, and was a delegate to the Buffalo Convention in 1848, which put forward Mr. Van Buren as a candidate for the presidency. From that time forward, he steadily adhered to the principles of the Buffalo platform, and was early found supporting, with characteristic zeal and determination, the organization and the great cardinal doctrines of the Republican party. He has always been diligent and prompt in the discharge of all his party obligations, working late and early in behalf of the Republican cause, and has succeeded in acquiring a strong political influence in the county of Oswego, where he now resides.

Senator Warner was married on the 19th of October, 1842, and attends the Congregational Church. In person, he is a large, broad-shouldered, substantially built man, with light-blue eyes, black hair and beard; and though somewhat diffident, is kind and sociable towards all with whom he comes in contact, in the fulfilment of his private and public duties.

# ALEXANDER B. WILLIAMS.

SENATOR WILLIAMS was born on the 29th of October, 1815, in Alexandria, District of Columbia, Virginia. His father, John Williams, was of German extraction, but was native-born, as were also his mother's family. He is the second of six sons, three of whom, besides himself, are still living. His father emigrated to New York in the year 1825, and settled in the town of Sodus, Wayne county, on the southern borders of Lake Ontario. He was a successful, practical mechanic, and assisted in the construction of the first packet-boat ever run on the Erie canal. He died at that place, 1843, in a fit of apoplexy, at the advanced age of sixty-seven. His wife, the mother of the hero of this sketch, is still living, and has attained the age of seventy.

Senator Williams had not the advantages of a classical education, having received all the schooling he has before his parents removed to New York, when he was only ten years of age. About this time his father placed him in a dry-goods store in Sodus, as a clerk, and his employer, having no children of his own, adopted him. Here he remained until he was about eighteen years old, when, falling out one day with his employer, he concluded to leave him, and accordingly did so, by hiring himself out to another man, engaged in the same business, at nine dollars per month. He continued in this new position till 1836, when, having become one of the most popular, efficient, and industrious clerks in that section of the country, his employer took him into his establishment as a partner, without any share in the capital, save his qualifications as a merchant. This partnership continued until 1837, when the firm sold out, and he engaged in the same business, with what little capital he had by that time acquired, on his own responsibility. He then continued in the mercantile trade till 1841, when he again sold out. In the summer of the same year he was appointed, under President Harrison, to the post of Deputy Collector and Inspector at Big Sodus Bay, which he held until just previous to the advent of the Administration of Mr. Polk, when he resigned. Then again he embarked in the mercantile business, in which he continued till the fall of 1845, when he finally sold out for the last time. In this same year he was elected County Clerk, and was subsequently elected to the same place, holding the office, in all, about six years. At the expiration of his clerkship he found his health greatly impaired by his too close application to the duties of his office, and from that time until his election to the Senate, he devoted most of his time to travelling in the Western States, where he dealt pretty extensively in the buying and selling of land.

Senator Williams has had considerable experience as a military man, having arisen from a Lieutenancy in a private company, to the position of Lieutenant-Colonel in the 242d Regiment, and has proved himself eminently qualified for every position to which he has been called. In 1841 he was elected a Justice of the Peace in the town in which he resided, by a handsome majority, although the town was strongly Democratic and he was the Whig candidate. In 1845 he was again elected to the same office, and was also at the same time elected Supervisor, by large majorities in both instances. In 1855 he was the unsuccessful Republican candidate for State Treasurer, and in 1857 was nominated for the Senate, with great unanimity, by the Republicans of his district, and was elected by a majority of over three thousand, against a combination of Americans and Democrats. He was renominated in the fall of 1859, and again triumphantly elected by over five thousand majority. During the last session of the Legislature, he was Chairman of the Standing Committee on Banks, and a member of the Committees on Militia Retrenchment, and Engrossed Bills, and as Chairman of the Standing Committee on Roads and Bridges, and a member of the Committees on State Prisons, and Public Printing, during the two preceding sessions, was faithful and industrious in the discharge of his duties.

He has not unfrequently been tendered the nomination of his party for Congress, but has always peremptorily declined.

Senator Williams early espoused the anti-Masonic cause, and was secretary of an anti-Masonic meeting at the age of twelve years. He was a member of the first Whig organization in Wayne county, in 1834, and continued to act with the Whig party until it lost its organization in 1854, when he embarked in the Republican cause. He was a delegate to the first Anti-Nebraska State Convention at Saratoga, in 1854, and was at Auburn when the Republican party was christened at that place.

On his return home last spring, at the adjournment of

6*

the Legislature, he was chosen a delegate to the Chicago Convention, and was among the most ardent friends of Mr. Seward for the nomination for the Presidency. He has a great many personal and political friends in the Senate, and his course in that body has been generally approved by his constituents. He has always been an active, decided party man, and is perfectly booked up in the politics of the State and the Union. He is a man of strong intellectual powers; is a clear and concise reasoner; and in legislation, as in everything else, combines theory with practicability, adopting the former only so far as it conforms to the latter.

In 1832, Senator Williams was married to Miss Sarah M., daughter of John McCarthy, a successful farmer, who died in Wayne county, in 1831. She is a modest, unassuming, sociable woman, and every way calculated for a good wife, a kind mother, and a generous and hospitable friend and neighbor.

# MEMBERS OF THE SENATE.

*Number of their respective Districts, and the Counties and Wards composing the same.*

LIEUT. GOVERNOR ROBERT CAMPBELL, of Bath, President.

| Dist. | Counties and Wards. | Senators. |
|---|---|---|
| 1. | Suffolk, Queens, and Richmond counties | Edward A. Lawrence. |
| 2. | 1st, 2d, 3d, 4th, 5th, 7th, 11th, 13th, and 19th wards of Brooklyn | Thomas A. Gardiner. |
| 3. | 6th, 8th, 9th, 10th, 12th, 14th, 15th, 16th, 17th, and 18th wards of Brooklyn | Francis B. Spinola. |
| 4. | 1st, 2d, 3d, 4th, 5th, 6th, 7th, 8th, and 14th wards of New York | J. McLeod Murphy. |
| 5. | 10th, 11th, 13th, and 17th wards of New York | Bernard Kelly. |
| 6. | 9th, 15th, 16th, and 18th wards of New York | Benjamin F. Manierre. |
| 7. | 12th, 19th, 20th, 21st, and 22d wards of New York | Richard B. Connolly. |
| 8. | Westchester, Putnam, and Rockland counties | Hezekiah D. Robinson. |
| 9. | Orange and Sullivan | Robert Y. Grant, |
| 10. | Ulster and Greene | Joshua Fiero, Jr. |
| 11. | Dutchess and Columbia | John H. Ketcham. |
| 12. | Rensselaer and Washington | Volney Richmond. |
| 13. | Albany | Andrew J. Colvin. |
| 14. | Delaware, Schoharie, and Schenectady | Joseph H. Ramsey. |
| 15. | Montgomery, Fulton, Saratoga, and Hamilton | Isaiah Blood. |

| Dist. | Counties and Wards. | Senators. |
|---|---|---|
| 16. | Warren, Essex, and Franklin | Nathan Lapham. |
| 17. | St. Lawrence and Franklin | Charles C. Montgomery. |
| 18. | Jefferson and Lewis | James A. Bell. |
| 19. | Oneida | Wm. H. Ferry. |
| 20. | Herkimer and Otsego | Francis M. Rotch. |
| 21. | Oswego | Andrew S. Warner. |
| 22. | Onondaga | Allen Munroe. |
| 23. | Madison, Chenango, and Cortland | Perrin H. McGraw. |
| 24. | Tompkins, Tioga, and Broome | Lyman Truman. |
| 25. | Wayne and Cayuga | Alexander B. Williams. |
| 26. | Ontario, Yates, and Seneca | Thomas Hillhouse. |
| 27. | Chemung, Schuyler, and Steuben | Samuel H. Hammond. |
| 28. | Monroe | Ephraim Goss. |
| 29. | Niagara, Orleans, and Genesee | Peter P. Murphy. |
| 30. | Wyoming, Livingston, and Allegany | David H. Abell. |
| 31. | Erie | Erastus S. Prosser. |
| 32. | Chautauqua and Cattaraugus | Walter L. Sessions. |

# ALPHABETICAL LIST OF SENATORS.

*The Counties in which they reside, their Post Office Address, and Politics.*

| Senators. | Counties. | P. O. Address. | Politics. |
|---|---|---|---|
| Edward A. Lawrence | Queens | Flushing | Dem. |
| Thomas A. Gardiner | Kings | Brooklyn | Dem. |
| Francis B. Spinola | Kings | Brooklyn | Dem. |
| J. McLeod Murphy | New York | New York | Dem. |
| Bernard Kelly | New York | New York | Dem. |
| Benjamin F. Manierre | New York | New York | Rep. |
| Richard B. Connolly | New York | New York | Dem. |
| Hezekiah D. Robertson | Westchester | Bedford | Am. |
| Robert Y. Grant | Sullivan | Liberty | Dem. |
| Joshua Fiero, Jr. | Greene | Catskill | Rep. |
| John H. Ketcham | Dutchess | Dover Plains | Rep. |
| Volney Richmond | Rensselaer | Hoosick Falls | Rep. |
| Andrew J. Colvin | Albany | Albany | Dem. |
| Joseph H. Ramsey | Schoharie | Lawyersville | Rep. |
| Isaiah Blood | Saratoga | Ballston Spa | Dem. |
| Nathan Lapham | Clinton | Peru | Rep. |
| Charles C. Montgomery | St. Lawrence | Waddington | Rep. |
| James A. Bell | Jefferson | Dexter | Rep. |
| Wm. H. Ferry | Oneida | Utica | Rep. |
| Francis M. Rotch | Otsego | Morris | Rep. |
| Andrew S. Warner | Oswego | Sandy Creek | Rep. |
| Allen Munroe | Onondaga | Syracuse | Rep. |
| Perrin H. McGraw | Cortland | McGrawville | Rep. |
| Lyman Truman | Tioga | Owego | Rep. |
| Alexander B. Williams | Wayne | Lyons | Rep. |

| Senators. | Counties. | P. O. Address. | Polities. |
|---|---|---|---|
| Thomas Hillhouse | Ontario | Geneva | Rep. |
| Samuel H. Hammond | Steuben | Bath | Rep. |
| Ephraim Goss | Monroe | Pittsford | Rep. |
| Peter P. Murphy | Niagara | Royalton | Rep. |
| David H. Abell | Livingston | Mt. Morris | Rep. |
| Erastus S. Prosser | Erie | Buffalo | Rep. |
| Walter L. Sessions | Chautauqua | Panama | Rep. |

# SENATE STANDING COMMITTEES.

*Claims.*—Truman, P. P. Murphy, Lawrence.

*Finance.*—Hillhouse, Bell, Grant.

*Judiciary.*—Hammond, Ramsey, Colvin.

*Canals.*—Prosser, Bell, Connolly.

*Railroads.*—Abell, Warner, Richmond.

*Charitable and Religious Societies.*—McGraw, Warner, Grant.

*Internal Affairs of Towns and Counties.*—Goss, McGraw, Spinola.

*State Prisons.*—Ketcham, Montgomery, Colvin.

*Poor Laws.*—Lapham, Goss, Kelly.

*Engrossed Bills.*—Warner, Connolly, Montgomery.

*Indian Affairs.*—Montgomery, Rotch, Kelly.

*Commerce and Navigation.*—Robertson, Truman, J. M. Murphy.

*Agriculture.*—Rotch, Abell, Gardiner.

*Literature.*—Sessions, McGraw, J. M. Murphy.

*Militia.*—Fiero, Williams, Blood.

*Roads and Bridges.*—Lapham, Goss, Kelly.

*Grievances.*—Prosser, Fiero, Blood.

*Banks.*—Munroe, Ferry, Spinola.

*Insurance Companies.*—Williams, Ferry, Spinola.

*Privileges and Elections.*—Richmond, Williams, Connolly.

*Manufactures.*—Bell, Robertson, Blood.

*Retrenchment.*—Ketcham, Williams, Kelly.

*Public Buildings.*—Warner, Rotch, Connolly.

*Erection and Division of Towns and Counties.*—Ramsey, Montgomery, Blood.

*Cities and Villages.*—Manierre, P. P. Murphy, Lawrence.

*Public Expenditures.*—Ferry, Manierre, Gardiner.

*Expiring Laws.*—Lawrence, Sessions, Gross.
*Medical Societies.*—P. P. Murphy, Warner, Colvin.
*Public Printing.*—Richmond, Montgomery, Spinola.
*Manufacture of Salt.*—Hillhouse, Munroe, Grant.
*Joint Library.*—J. M. Murphy, Munroe, Abell.

## SELECT COMMITTEES.

*On Rules of the Senate.*—Fiero, Ramsey, Spinola.
*On Petitions for aid to Albany and Susquehanna Railroad.*—Ramsey, Hillhouse, Connolly.
*On so much of the Governor's Message as relates to Federal Relations.*—Hillhouse, Colvin, Spinola, Manierre, Goss, J. M. Murphy, P. P. Murphy.

# MEMBERS OF ASSEMBLY.

## DEWITT C. LITTLEJOHN,

### SPEAKER.

MR. LITTLEJOHN belongs to that class of public men, in this country, whose success in life is more the result of fortuitous circumstances than the force of their own individual worth. Since his advent to public notice, scarcely a hobby has appeared in the political arena, to which he has not firmly adhered until he found himself safely astride of something better calculated to gratify his aims. His greatest fault is an over-stock of ambition, aspiring high in the scale of political distinction; and to this feature in his character, may, perhaps, be safely ascribed most of the apparent inconsistencies and acts of treachery by which his political career is prominently marked.

As a presiding officer, however, he is remarkably ready and decided, and possesses a calm dignity which scarcely any confusion or excitement can disturb. This is the fifth time he has been Speaker of the House, having previously held the position during the years 1855, '57, '59, and '60, and it is but just to accord him the praise of having discharged his duties with signal success.

Mr. Littlejohn was born in 1818, in Oneida county,
N. Y., and while yet young, removed with his parents
to Albany, where his mother, a good-natured, clever,
sprightly old lady, of some sixty years, still resides.
Having received a complete academical education in
that city, he removed to Oswego in 1839, where he became a clerk in the commission and forwarding business,
in which he became a partner with his employer in 1842,
and in which he is still engaged. His first prominent
appearance in public life was in 1853, when he was an
active member of the lower branch of the Legislature,
and during the years 1854, '55, '57, '59, and '60, he
successfully occupied the same position in that body.
As a member of the Standing Committee on Canals, he
distinguished himself somewhat during the session of
1853, by his efforts to procure the amendment to the
Constitution for the speedy enlargement of the canals,
and took a very active part, in the winter of 1854, in
the enactment of a law changing the mode of awarding
contracts on the public works. He was the candidate
for Speaker, at the opening of that session, of the old
line national conservative branch of the Whig party,
but was defeated in the caucus by the Hon. Robt. H.
Pruyn, of Albany, who represented the Freesoil portion
of the party, and who was the successful candidate for
that position. In 1855 he was chosen Speaker of the
House, as the American candidate, and during that
session, signalized himself by the prominent part he
enacted in the movement that resulted in the re-election
of Mr. Seward to the Senate of the United States. It
has always since been charged that his support of Mr.

Seward, on that occasion, contrary to the wishes of the American party, was in consequence of an understanding with the friends of Mr. Seward, that if he would support the latter, they would make him Speaker. But although his course on that occasion was bitterly repudiated and denounced by many, in consequence of his having been among the first to enlist in the American movement, yet he was triumphantly elected Mayor of the city of Oswego, in the spring of that year, which his friends claimed to have been an endorsement, by his constituents, of the prominent part he took in Mr. Seward's success. In the fall of 1856 he was re-elected to the Assembly, as the Republican candidate of the district, and has always since then been the candidate of that party.

Mr. Littlejohn's early political tendencies led him into the Whig ranks, where he remained, a great admirer of Henry Clay, till the disorganization of that party, when he became an American, subsequently a Republican, and since Mr. Seward's return to the Senate of the United States, has been one of the most prominent and zealous members of that organization. As a politician he is somewhat cautious in reaching conclusions, but when once determined upon a course, is bold, positive, and straightforward in action. He can scarcely be called a representative man, lacking sufficient originality for that; and lacks, in a great degree, that discipline of mind and judgment, which enables one to recognise reason and truth, and detect fraud or fallacy.

Although calm and dispassionate as a presiding officer, his whole manner, in speaking, is changed. He becomes nervous, impassioned, and not unfrequently vehement; and even the most feeble thought goes from his lips with the most forcible enunciation and energetic delivery. He seldom holds out long, however, and apparently lacks the ability to make an extended and logical argument, his speeches being always brief and impromptu.

Mr. Littlejohn is married, and attends the Episcopal Church. He is personally, as well as politically, a somewhat popular representative, and has a genial suavity of manner which seldom or never varies.

---

## STEPHEN H. AINSWORTH.

Mr. Ainsworth is one of that class of men, not very common in American politics, whose modesty is more of a damage to them than a credit, and who pass quietly through life without receiving that degree of reward to which their real merits, perhaps, entitle them. He is a gentleman now in the prime of life, being about forty years of age, and is a successful practical farmer, residing at West Bloomfield, in Ontario county. This is his first appearance in public life, but his prominence even now is more the result of the numerical strength of his party, than any particular fitness on his part for a representative position.

In politics, Mr. Ainsworth is a Republican of the most extreme stamp; and possessing a degree of firmness which amounts to downright stubbornness, is always ready to indulge in the passage of Personal Liberty Bills, Gunpowder Resolutions, Military Supply Bills, and all other extravagant measures, calculated to show to the world that we are determined to wage an exterminating war upon the institution of slavery— even at the point of the bayonet, and with fire and sword. It was generally thought in the beginning of the session, that his vote for Mr. Robinson for Speaker, in the Republican caucus, was an indication of a more conservative view of our present national difficulties; but not so, because his hostility to the compromise submitted to the House by Mr. Robinson, is understood now to be of the most intense character.

## LUCIUS C. ANDRUS.

MR. ANDRUS was a member of the Assembly in 1859, and has been again elected, by a handsome majority, from the district which he then represented. He was quite an active and prominent member during the session of that year, and, both on the floor of the House, and as a member of the Committee on Internal Affairs of Towns and Counties, was prompt and faithful in the discharge of all his duties. He is a gentleman of deservedly high standing wherever he is known, and wields no ordinary influence in the deliberations of the body of which he is a member.

Mr. Andrus is the son of the Hon. Cone Andrus, of Malone, Franklin county, N. Y., who died in December, 1821. He was born at that place in March, 1809, although looking ten years younger, and sprung from genuine English stock. After receiving a good business education in his native place, he engaged in the mercantile trade, and remained so employed, in Wheatland, Monroe county, till 1852, when he retired from business, and removed to the city of Brooklyn, where he now resides. He held various town offices previous to his going to Kings county, in every one of which he was found honest and efficient in the discharge of his duties. He was originally a Whig, clinging to that party as long as it had an organization, when he became a staunch and unyielding Republican.

Mr. Andrus was married, in 1836, to Miss Mary Ann Savage, of Upper Middletown, Connecticut, and is a leading member of the Clinton Avenue Congregational Society, in the city of Brooklyn.

---

# WILLIAM ANDRUS.

Mr. Andrus is an elder brother of the Hon. Lucius C. Andrus, the representative in the Assembly from the Fifth District of Kings county, and holds a high position among the Republicans of both branches of the Legislature.

Mr. Andrus is a native of Malone, Franklin county, N. Y., where he was born on the 27th of September, 1806. He is of English extraction. His father, Cone Andrus, died on the 10th of December, 1821, at the age of forty-seven; and his mother, whose maiden name was Melinda House, died in 1809, at the age of thirty-two. Both his parents came to New York, from Vermont, as early as 1804, and were among the pioneer settlers of the northern section of the State. Mr. Andrus received a common school and academical education, and was reared a farmer, in which occupation he has always since been engaged. He held the office of Sheriff in his native county from 183– until 1842, and was Supervisor of the town of Malone, where he still resides, from 1847 until 1852, and again from 1857 until 1860. In politics, he was originally a Whig of the conservative stamp; subsequently became an American, and now comes to the Legislature as an exponent of the principles and measures of modern Republicanism. He stands firm upon the Chicago platform, and is unwilling to strike a single plank from it in the present distracted state of the country.

Mr. Andrus was married on the 28th of February, 1832, to Miss Susan Roberts, and is a member of the Protestant Episcopal Church.

## WILKES ANGEL.

Mr. Angel was born on the 26th of February, 1815, in Exeter, Otsego county, N.Y. He is of fine Anglo-Saxon stock. His father, the Hon. William G. Angel, who died at Angelica, Allegany county, N.Y., on the 13th of October, 1858, at the age of sixty-eight, was distinguished for his sound judgment, strong common-sense, and incorruptible integrity. He was two years a prominent member of Congress, under the Administration of John Quincy Adams, and was a member of that body during the whole of General Jackson's first Administration. He was, also, a representative from Allegany county in the last Constitutional Convention of this State, and was always found honest and capable in the discharge of the duties of every position to which the people called him. His wife, the mother of the subject of this sketch, whose maiden name was Emily P. English, died at Burlington, Otsego county, on the 11th of May, 1822, at the age of thirty-two.

Mr. Angel received a common school and academical education, and studied law. He was subsequently admitted to the bar, and has since then been successfully engaged in practice. He held the office of District Attorney of Allegany county from 1840 until 1844, and was Master in Chancery under the appointment of Silas Wright. Like many others of his Republican associates in the House, he was formerly a firm and unyielding Democrat of the Barnburner school. Upon the repeal of the Missouri Compromise, however, he was one among the foremost in the inauguration of the Republican movement, and is now a strong believer in the right and duty of Congress to prohibit slavery in all the territories of the United States. He is one of the leading men of his party in the House, and unlike a few of his Republican associates in that body, never speaks upon a subject without some advantage either to himself or those who hear him.

Mr. Angel was married, on the 23d of December, 1841, to Miss Hannah Marble, and attends no particular church.

---

## SMITH ANTHONY.

MR. ANTHONY is one of the quiet men of the House, and unless privately interrogated, his position on a question is seldom known until the ayes and nays are called.

Mr. Anthony was born on the 18th of April, 1813, in Greenfield, Saratoga county, N.Y., and sprang from English stock. Both his parents, John Anthony and Susannah Allen, are still living, the former having attained the age of eighty-two and the latter seventy-seven. His educational advantages were wholly confined to a common district school, and he has always been engaged in farming. He settled in Ledyard, Cayuga county, in 1822, and in 1843 removed into the town of Fleming, in the same county, where he held the office of Supervisor during the years 1846, '47, '49, '57, '58, and '60. He also held the office of a Justice of the Peace in 1852. In politics, he was formerly a Whig, and is now an unswerving Republican, being strongly opposed to the further extension of slavery.

Mr. Anthony was married, in 1837, to Miss Mary Gray, and entertains liberal views on the subject of religion.

## HENRY ARCULARIUS.

MR. ARCULARIUS ranks high among the most practical, common-sense, and valuable men at Albany. His career, during the last session of the Legislature, was unusually modest and unpretending, but he exhibited qualities both upon the floor of the House, and as a member of the committees to which he belonged, which render him peculiarly fitted for a representative position in a Democratic government. He belongs to that class of energetic, practical, incorruptible, progressive, self-made men of whom Brother Jonathan is constantly boasting, and whose history should be carefully studied by every American boy in the country, whether born abroad or on the soil. It is, indeed, rarely the case that we find any one whose life illustrates in a higher or more striking degree what may be accomplished under our system of government by industry, perseverance, and self-reliance, than that of Mr. Arcularius. Born of poor, though honest and respectable, parents, he had but little encouragement on entering upon life's active career; yet with a heart buoyant with hope, and an honest, enthusiastic desire to succeed, he fearlessly and resolutely launched forth his little bark upon the troubled waters of active life, and by his firmness and integrity of character, and his energy and stability of purpose, has succeeded, thus far, in successfully riding, in triumph, the storm of human strife and activity.

Mr. Arcularius was born on the 8th of February, 1814, in the city of New York, where he has always resided. He is of German extraction, and his paternal grandfather, George Arcularius, came to America in 1784, shortly after the treaty of peace between Great Britain and the United States. His father, Henry Arcularius, who died about three years ago, at the age of sixty-seven, held the office of Commissary-General during two terms, and was a man of high standing and influence during his lifetime, and an accomplished military officer.

Mr. Arcularius never attended school after attaining the tenth year of his age, when he engaged in the baking business with his father, in whose establishment he became foreman when only seventeen years of age, and continued to follow that business until 1840. In 1848 he was nominated by acclamation, at Tammany Hall, as a candidate for Register, but owing to the division then existing in the Democratic party, the Free-soilers running a candidate against him, he was defeated, although running nearly four hundred votes in advance of Gen. Cass, the regular nominee of the Democracy for the Presidency. In 1849, after the Democratic Convention in the city of New York had unsuccessfully balloted five successive nights for a candidate for Sheriff, he was nominated unanimously as a candidate for County Clerk, but was again defeated in consequence of the same distracting causes still existing in the Democratic ranks. In 1850 he was nominated, on the first ballot, as a candidate for Congress, in the Fifth District, then comprising the Eighth, Ninth, and Fourteenth Wards, and was defeated by a very small majority, by the Hon. George Briggs, now in Congress.

In 1851 he was triumphantly elected Commissioner of Streets and Lamps, in the city of New York, for a term of three years, but, becoming dissatisfied with the position, resigned at the expiration of two years. He then wholly retired from public life until 1857, when he became a member of the Common Council, where he held the position of Chairman of the Finance Committee, and was one of the Commissioners of the Sinking Fund. He was brought forward, in the fall of 1859, with entire unanimity, as a candidate of the Mozart Hall Democracy, for the seat he now occupies, and was triumphantly elected over both the Tammany Hall and Republican candidates. He has always been a staunch, fearless, uncompromising, and consistent Democrat, of the genuine National conservative stamp, and is the only Hard-shell Democrat in the House elected exclusively by that branch of the Democracy. He possesses a large share of sound, practical, common sense, and although always cool, calm, civil, and friendly to all, is obstinately firm in the right. He is a good speaker, using the purest and strongest Anglo-Saxon, and always advances in a straight geometrical line right to the real point in controversy, with a directness that there is no mistaking.

Mr. Arcularius has no *fixed* religious views, but is liberal in all such matters, carrying out, as his motto, to the fullest possible extent, in his every-day action, the beautiful expression of the Holy Book, " *Do to others as you wish to be done by.*"

# HENRY BAILEY.

THIS is Mr. Bailey's first appearance in public life. With the exception of the office of Justice of the Peace, which he held in Orleans, Jefferson county, from 1848 till '52, he never held any public position until he took his seat in the present Legislature. Still he has already proven himself a faithful representative.

Mr. Bailey was born on the 13th of October, 1818, in Lorraine, Jefferson county, N. Y. He is of pure English descent. His father, George Bailey, died in that town in June, 1838, at the age of fifty-four, and his mother, whose maiden name was Olive Kasson, is still living at the advanced age of seventy-two. Mr. Bailey was educated in the common schools of his native county, and has always been engaged in the business of harness-making. In politics, he was always closely attached to the old Whig party, until the inauguration of the Republican movement, when he, at once, became a staunch and zealous member of that organization. He is a quiet, unpretending gentleman, and enjoys a high degree of personal popularity wherever he is known.

Mr. Bailey was married to Miss Laura Ann Wright, in 1836, and attends the Union Church.

## EDMUND BALDWIN.

MR. BALDWIN is a native of the town of Turin, Lewis county, N. Y., and is of pure English descent. He is one of the oldest men in the House. His father, Ebenezer Baldwin, died on the 3d of November, 1834, at the age of sixty-six, and his mother, on the 1st of February, 1813, at the age of forty-one.

Mr. Baldwin received a common school and academical education in his native county, where he has always resided. He has always been engaged in agricultural pursuits, having been reared upon a farm, and possesses a superior business capacity. He held the office of Supervisor during the years 1841, '42, and '50, besides other town offices, and has always been found prompt and faithful in the discharge of his public duties. Politically he was originally a Democrat until 1856, since which time he has been a faithful Republican. He was chosen to his present position by over eight hundred majority, and has already proven himself a very quiet, unpretending, though efficient representative.

Mr. Baldwin was married on the 20th of May, 1832, to Miss Minerva H. Scovill, and attends the Presbyterian Church.

## L. CHANDLER BALL.

MR. BALL was born on the 25th of February, 1809, at Wilmington, Vermont. He is of English extraction. His father, Samuel Ball, died some years ago, at the age of eighty-seven, and his mother, whose maiden name was Lucina Chandler, died on the 17th of January, 1851, at the age of eighty-three.

Mr. Ball was educated in the common schools of his native place. He was brought up on a farm, and has always been employed in agricultural pursuits. In 1836 he held the office of Justice of the Peace, and in 1840 was Judge of the Court of Common Pleas in Rensselaer county, where he now resides. Politically he was always a staunch Whig until the dismemberment of that party, when, upon the repeal of the Missouri Compromise, he became identified with the Republican movement. He is one of the quiet men of the House, but is nevertheless a capable representative, and is perfectly true to the interests of his constituents, whose confidence he appears to enjoy to the very highest degree. He is a gentleman of good impulses, high-minded, honorable, and strictly honest, and is industrious and faithful in the discharge of all his duties.

Mr. Ball was married on the 21st of September, 1833, to Miss Marcia Ann Parsons, and attends the Episcopal Church. He is personally as well as politically popular wherever he is known.

## CERO F. BARBER.

MR. BARBER belongs to that class of Republicans who were formerly Democrats, and supported Mr. Van Buren for the Presidency in 1848. He is a native of Colebrook, Littlefield county, Connecticut, where he was born on the 19th of April, 1822, and claims to be of genuine Yankee descent. His education is such as was usually received by New-England boys in those days, and he has always been engaged in the cultivation of the soil. He came to the State of New York in September, 1853, and located in the town of Spencer, Tioga county, where he now resides. With the exception of the office of Justice of the Peace, which he held one year, this is the first public position he ever occupied, although always more or less active in the politics of the community in which he lives. He is attentive in the discharge of his duties in the House, but seldom participates to any extent in the debates of that body.

Mr. Barber was married on the 17th of September, 1853, and attends the Universalist Church. He is regarded with respect wherever he is known, and stands high in the opinion of his intimate personal friends.

## MILTON BARNES.

Mr. Barnes is a native of the town of Warwick, Orange county, N. Y. He was born on the 8th of April, 1808, and is, therefore, nearly fifty-three years of age. He is of English and Dutch descent. His father, John Barnes, died in 1851, at the advanced age of eighty-four; and his mother, whose maiden name was Milicent Edsall, died in 1857, at the age of eighty-one.

Mr. Barnes received a common school education. He was reared a farmer, and with the exception of some twelve years, which he spent at the carpenter and joiner's trade, he has always been principally engaged in farming. He held the office of Justice of the Peace from 1845 until '57, and is now serving his second term in the Assembly, having been a member of that body in 1851. Politically he has always been an old-fashioned Democrat of the Jeffersonian Republican school, and firmly believes that the principles of that party can alone save the country from the evils of dissolution by which she is now so seriously threatened. He is not a noticeable member of the House, but always discharges his duties quietly, though satisfactorily and efficiently.

Mr. Barnes is unmarried, and although a believer in the Christian religion, confines himself to no particular church in his attendance upon divine worship.

## GILBERT BEDELL.

MR. BEDELL is a native of the town of New Baltimore, Greene county, N. Y., where he was born on the 27th February, 1821. He is descended from Quaker stock, of the Hicksite school, and his ancestors, who were early settlers in Greene County, came direct from Long Island. His paternal great-grandfather had two brothers who were said to have been killed in the Revolution at the battle of Kingsbridge, and all his ancestors were staunch Whigs throughout the Revolutionary struggle. His father, Gilbert Bedell, a thrifty and industrious farmer, died on the 6th of December, 1857, at the age of sixty-seven, and his mother, whose maiden name was Zillah Sarles, died on the 14th of July, 1844, at the age of fifty-five.

Mr. Bedell was reared on his father's farm, and received a common English education. At the age of twenty-two he became engaged on the Hudson river, where he remained seventeen years, gradually rising in point of rank, until he was largely engaged in the freighting and produce business on his own responsibility. Since then he has been engaged in the cultivation of his farm on the banks of the Hudson, in the town of Coxsackie, where he now resides. He has always been a staunch line Democrat of the olden school, and is a strong advocate of compromise and conciliation in the present lamentable state of public affairs. He is a man of great personal popularity throughout the community in which he lives, and was chosen to his present position by a greatly increased Democratic majority. This is his first appearance in public life, but his strong common sense and superior business capacity have already rendered him one of the most substantial and useful men in the House.

Mr. Bedell was married on the 7th of February, 1849, to Miss Jane Maria Hollenbeck, and usually attends the Methodist Church.

## LEWIS BENEDICT, Jr.

Mr. Benedict is a bachelor, and is one of the finest-looking men in the Legislature. He is a native of the city of Albany, N. Y., where he has always resided, and is about thirty-seven years of age. He is of English and Holland extraction. Both his parents are still living, his father, Lewis Benedict, being now seventy-five years of age, and his mother, whose maiden name was Susan Stafford, having attained the age of sixty-nine.

Mr. Benedict was educated at the Albany Academy, and at Williams College, Massachusetts. After leaving school he studied law, and since his admission to the bar has been engaged in the practice of his profession in his native city. He has held the offices of City Attorney and Surrogate, and was Judge Advocate General of the State of New York, under Governor Young and Governor Field; besides being a commissioner, under the law of 1854, to examine into the condition of the States Prisons, &c. In politics, he was formerly a Whig, of the Seward school, and has always been an active Republican since

the organization of that party. He possesses considerable personal popularity, but has never been very successful as a candidate for office. He is a gentleman of
considerable ability. He is a fair speaker, participating
constantly in the discussions of the House, and wields
no inconsiderable influence among his immediate Republican associates. In all prominent points of character,
he is perhaps a fair representative of the party to which
he belongs.

## HEMAN BENTON.

Mr. Benton is a native of the town of Ira, Cayuga
county, N. Y., where he now resides. He was born on
the 18th of September, 1820, and is of English and
Scotch descent. His father, Allen Benton, and his
mother—whose name was Deborah Willey—are both
still living.

Mr. Benton was educated in the common schools of
his native place, and the Academy at Fulton, Oswego
county. He remained on his father's farm until he had
attained the age of twenty-one, when he engaged in the
construction of mills. At the age of twenty he went
to Canada, where he followed the same business some
five years, when he returned to this State and located
in Sodus, Wayne county. After remaining here about
five years, engaged in the running and construction of
mills, he returned to his native town, where he has
always since been engaged in farming. He was formerly
a member of the old Whig party, and held the office of

Supervisor during the years 1857 and '59. He is a man of strong common sense and good judgment, with strong natural mechanical ability, and although quiet and unostentatious in the discharge of his duties, has shown himself well qualified for a representative position. When properly known, he is kind, clever, and agreeable in the social circle, and is a gentleman of considerable personal as well as political popularity.

Mr. Benton was married on the 17th of October, 1849, to Catharine L. Smith, of Sodus, Wayne County, and belongs to the Disciple Church.

## ALEXANDER J. BERGEN.

Mr. Bergen is an old-fashioned Democrat, of the Silas Wright school, and is one of the most substantial and popular men in Kings county. He was nominated for the seat he now occupies in the Legislature without any solicitation on his part, and in the contest which followed, ran upwards of five hundred votes ahead of his ticket. He is too modest and unpretending ever to make a brilliant display in public life, but possesses a native vigor of intellect, and a faculty of correctly weighing men and things, which render his counsels more frequently sought after than are those of some of his more boisterous legislative associates.

Mr. Bergen was born in Kings county, New York, in 1813, and is of Dutch and Scotch descent. His maternal grandfather was a distinguished colonel in the

British army, and came to this country with Cornwallis during the struggle for American Independence. His father, John T. Bergen, was a member of Congress in 1831 and 1832, and died only a few years since, at an advanced age.

Mr. Bergen was educated in his native place, with a view to mercantile pursuits, in which he was successfully engaged, in the city of New York, until about six years ago. Since then he has occupied an extensive farm at Islip, Kings county, where he lives a retired life. His business capacities are of a high order, with which are combined all the elements of personal popularity, and to these qualities are doubtless more attributable than to anything else the gratifying success with which his efforts in life have thus far been crowned. The associations of his friends, whether personal or political, are always cordial and hospitable, and when thoroughly acquainted, he is looked upon as one of the most sociable, clever, and kind-hearted gentlemen at Albany.

## ANSON BINGHAM.

MR. BINGHAM was a member of the Assembly in 1859, and again in 1860, and during both of those years was a prominent member of the Judiciary Committee, having been chairman during the session of 1860. He possesses much more than ordinary legislative and legal ability, but is generally quiet in the discharge of his duties, and is held in the highest esteem by his legislative companions.

Mr. Bingham is a native of the good old State of Connecticut, and is about forty years of age. He removed from his native place to New York, when comparatively young, and settled in the village of Nassau, Rensselaer county, where he studied law and practised his profession until about two years since. He then came to the city of Albany, although still claiming Nassau as his place of residence, and formed a copartnership in the law with his brother-in-law, Hugh W. McClennan and the Hon. Andrew J. Colvin, present Senator from the Albany district. He has been Supervisor of the town of Nassau, and District Attorney of Rensselaer county, and has always been elected to the Assembly by an increased majority. Politically, he was formerly a Whig, and became a Republican at the first organization of that party. He was formerly quite Conservative, but has now become so extreme in his views on the subject of slavery, that he is usually pronounced an Abolitionist. He has never paid much attention to politics, and has devoted himself chiefly to his profession, in which he has acquired some notoriety by his efforts in behalf of the cause of the anti-renters in Rensselaer county. He was chairman of the Republican Caucus at the opening of the present session of the Legislature, and when the contest for the Speakership between Messrs. Littlejohn and Robinson had become close and protracted, he was offered the nomination, on the motion of the latter, but at once declined it on personal considerations.

Mr. Bingham was married some years ago to a daughter of the late Dr. Samuel McClellan, of Nassau, and attends the Presbyterian Church, of which his wife is a member. He is a brother-in-law of Robert McClellan, late Surrogate of Rensselaer county, and of Judge T. Hogeboom, of Columbia county, who was a member of the Assembly in 1857.

## CHARLES E. BIRDSALL.

MR. BIRDSALL is a native of Pittsfield, Massachusetts, where he was born on the 3d of February, 1831. His ancestors emigrated to this country from Yorkshire, England, about two hundred years ago, and settled in New England. His father, Col. Elbert Birdsall, late Assistant Commissary General of the State of New York, who is a native of Brooklyn, is a relative of Major Birdsall, of Revolutionary distinction, and a cousin of Elias Hicks, the leader of the Hicksite Quakers. His mother, whose maiden name was Lucretia M. Beebe, and who is a sister of Judge W. R. Beebe, of New York city, is a native of Columbia county, New York, and was born in 1810.

Mr. Birdsall received an ordinary English education, and passed a couple of years at the grammar-school of Professor Webb, at Pittsfield. He also previously passed a short time at the Academy at Danbury, Connecticut, and after leaving school commenced the study of theology. He was then, at the very early age of twelve, licensed to preach the gospel in Connecticut. In the spring of 1848 he removed to the city of New

York, where he has always since permanently resided. In the fall of 1849 he began the study of the law in the office of his uncle, Judge Beebe, and in 1852 was admitted to practice. In February, 1855, he was appointed by Gov. Clark to fill a vacancy in the bench of the Marine Court, in the City of New York, and held the office until January following, when he was succeeded by Judge Maynard. He has since then been successfully engaged in the practice of the law. Politically he was formerly a Whig, and is now ranked among the most ardent and uncompromising Republicans, among whom he is one of the leaders in the House.

Mr. Birdsall was married some six years ago to Miss Whitehouse, of Boston, a relative of ex-President Pierce, and attends no particular church.

## FREDERICK A. BOLLES.

Mr. Bolles was born on the 5th of February, 1811, at Vernon, Oneida county, New York. He is of English descent. His father, Elias Bolles, who was born at Chatham, Connecticut, on the 27th of January, 1785, and who was a soldier in the war of 1812, died at Buffalo, on the 16th of September, 1856, having fallen dead in the street, with a disease of the heart, on his return home from a visit to Wisconsin. His mother, whose maiden name was Nancy Taylor, and who was born on the 21st of September, 1790, in the city of Albany, died at Utica on the 5th of November, 1857.

Mr. Bolles was educated in the common schools of his native place, and is a carpenter and joiner by trade, having always worked at the business until the establishment of his connexion in the hardware business with L. G. Cone & Co., at Unadilla, where he now resides. At the time of the anti-rent insurrection, in Delaware county, some years since, he received a Captain's commission from Gov. Wright, accompanied by an order from Thomas Farrington, Adjutant General, requiring his company to be recruited to a hundred men, and repair forthwith to Delhi. On the third day from the receipt of the commission, he had recruited nearly that many men, and was in Delhi, ready for duty. He was discharged on the 24th of December, 1845. In 1850 he was elected Town Clerk where he now resides, and in 1851 was chosen Supervisor; also, Assessor in 1854. He has always been a Republican since the organization of that party, previous to which he had always been a faithful and uncompromising , Whig. His majority for the position he now holds in the Assembly was the largest ever given in the district, he being one of the most popular men in Otsego county, and he is one of the most unassuming men in the House.

Mr. Bolles was married in June, 1839, to Miss Julia, daughter of Dr. N. Cone, of Unadilla, and attends the Episcopal Church, of which his wife is a member.

## CHARLES T. BREWSTER.

MR. BREWSTER was born on the 15th of November, 1814, in Putnam county, N. Y. He is of English stock, and a lineal descendant of Brewster who came to America in the Mayflower. His father, William Brewster, is still living, at the ripe old age of seventy, but his mother died on the 25th of January, 1855, in Philipstown, Putnam county, at the age of sixty-two.

Mr. Brewster was educated in the common schools of his native place, and has always been engaged in farming, merchandizing, and boating. He was Superintendent of the Poor in Putnam county, from 1853 until 1856, when he was chosen Sheriff of the County, which office he held until 1859. He has occupied various town offices since 1842, and during the past two years has been Supervisor of the town in which he resides. He has always been a member of the Republican party since its organization, previous to which he was a Whig, of the Seward school. He stands upon "irrepressible" ground on the slavery question, and by his course since assuming his duties as a legislator, has exhibited a strong determination to resist the further extension of the institution in this country.

Mr. Brewster was married on the 15th of November, 1841, to Miss Mary Ann Van Winkle, and attends the Methodist Episcopal Church.

## DANIEL B. BRYAN.

MR. BRYAN belongs to the radical wing of the Republican party, having originally been a faithful Democrat, and believes in the right and duty of Congress to prohibit slavery in the Territories of the United States. He is a plain, substantial farmer, of considerable business experience, and never attempts to make any display whatever in the House, contenting himself with a quiet and attentive discharge of his official duties.

Mr. Bryan is a native of Ovid, Seneca county, N. Y., and is of English, Dutch, French, and Irish descent. His father, George Bryan, died on the 11th of August, 1853, at the age of seventy-seven, and his mother, whose maiden name was Jane Covert, is still living, at the age of seventy-six. He was educated in a common district school, and was reared on a farm. He has been Postmaster some twelve years at Sonora, Steuben county, where he now resides, and comes to the Legislature by a large majority. His position in the community in which he lives is highly respectable and influential, and he wields a strong personal strength wherever he is known.

Mr. Bryan was married, in 1838, to Miss Elizabeth B. Hallett, and attends the Methodist Episcopal Church.

## JOSEPH BUCKBEE.

MR. BUCKBEE is one of the most whole-souled, good-natured, and substantial men in either branch of the Legislature. He is a large, healthy, companionable looking man, with a large heart and a cordial grasp of the hand depicted in his very countenance, who always listens with pleased attention to a good story, bartering back another quite as good in return, and who would be a capital fellow to sit opposite to in a railway car from Albany to New York, with his remarks on men and things.

Mr. Buckbee is a native of the city of Albany, New York, where he was born on the 1st of March, 1818. He is of pure Scotch descent. His father, Joseph Buckbee, died in 1849, at the age of seventy-two, in Schoharie county, where the subject of this sketch now resides; and his mother, whose maiden name was Susan Beetes, died in Albany, in 1851, at the age of seventy-two. Mr. Buckbee received a common English education, and while yet a boy, became engaged on the Hudson river, where he remained some twenty years, gradually rising to the position of captain. He then had charge of a steamer some two years in California, and was the first steamboat inspector appointed in that State after her admission into the Union. He was subsequently engaged in running between New York and Panama, in the employment of the Panama Railroad Company, and afterwards passed a year in making through trips from New York to San Francisco. In politics he was formerly an old line Whig, of the Clay and Webster school, and, after the dissolution of that organization, became an American, to the principles of which party he still adheres. He was triumphantly elected to his present position by a large majority, being, both personally and politically, one of the most popular men in Schoharie county ; and, as against the Republicans, is now co-operating with the Democratic party. His conduct in the House is modest and unassuming, but his good judgment and sound common-sense render him one of the most reliable men in that body.

Mr. Buckbee was married, in 1836, to Miss Catharine Davis, of Albany, and usually attends the Presbyterian Church.

## JAMES H. BURR.

MR. BURR was born on the 9th of May, 1816, in Gloversville, Fulton county, New York. He is descended from Puritan stock, and both his paternal and maternal grandparents came from Connecticut. His father, James Burr, who was a relative of Aaron Burr, died on the 28th of September, 1853, at the age of seventy-four; and his mother, whose maiden name was Amarillis Mills, died on the 27th of February, 1856, at the age of seventy-three.

Mr. Burr received a common school and academical education. He was brought up to the manufacture of buckskin mittens and gloves, and the dressing of deerskin, and is still engaged in the same pursuit. When the business was first started some years ago it amounted to only a few hundred dollars a year, but it now reaches the sum of nearly a half million of dollars annually, at Gloversville, where he resides. He never had any prominent public position until his election to the present House, and has always been simply a business man. He was formerly a Whig, and at the dissolution of that party became a zealous Republican. He is a quiet, substantial man, and has already shown considerable representative ability.

Mr. Burr was married on the 29th of September, 1841, to Miss Azubah Warner, of Troy, and is a member of the Baptist Church. He stands high in the community in which he lives, and enjoys great personal popularity.

## FRIEND H. BURT.

MR. BURT, who was named after the late Friend Humphrey, of the city of Albany, was born on the 8th of January, 1808, in Berkshire county, Mass. He is a descendant of one of two brothers, by the name of Burt, who came from England and settled on the Connecticut river, near Springfield, and who were the first of the family in America. He is a brother of Orlo Burt, a member of the Massachusetts Legislature, and a relative of Judge Burt, late of Orange county, and Mr. Burt of South Carolina, formerly a Member of Congress from that state. His father, Caleb Burt, died in 1846, at the age of eighty-four, and his mother, whose maiden name was Anna Merry, died at the age of seventy-five.

Mr. Burt was educated chiefly in the common schools of his native state. He came to New York in 1854, and settled in Corbettsville, Broome county, where he now resides. He was bred a tanner. During the past fifteen years he has been very extensively engaged in that business, and is now writing a work, setting forth much valuable information which has hitherto been overlooked in the trade. He was a member of the Massachusetts Legislature in 1842, where he exhibited considerable legislative ability, and was chosen a member of the body to which he now belongs by a handsome vote. Politically he always acted with the Democratic party until 1852, and from that time he was like "a sheep without a shepherd" in politics until the inauguration of the Republican movement, when he attached himself to that party. He believes in the principles of the Chicago Platform; and in our present national difficulties, is always ready to sustain the honor and glory of the American flag.

Mr. Burt was married in 1840 to Miss Maria Hodges, of Connecticut, and is a member of the Presbyterian Church.

## JOHN CALLAHAN

Mr. CALLAHAN is a native of the city of Cork, Ireland, where he was born in 1836. He is descended from unmixed Irish stock. He came to the United States in 1843, and took up his residence in the city of New

York, where he is still living. His education is simply of a business character, and his occupation is that of a plumber. In politics, he has always been a staunch Democrat of the National Conservative stamp, but, although always actively engaged in politics, he never held any prominent official position until his election to the present Legislature.

Mr. Callahan is one of the quiet men of the House. He looks upon the incessant speech-making which not unfrequently turns the Assembly Chamber into a mere recitation room as a most consummate bore. He is a man of action rather than words. Nevertheless he wields no inconsiderable influence on the Democratic side of the House, and is well liked by all with whom he comes in contact. He is always at his post, and has always given evidence, in the discharge of his duties, of a degree of legislative ability which conclusively shows that his constituents have not misplaced their confidence in entrusting him with the responsibilities of his present position.

## BENJAMIN F. CAMP.

Mr. Camp is a native of the city of Baltimore, and is a brother of Gen. William Camp, who still resides on the eastern shore of Maryland. He was born on the 26th of April, 1816, and is, therefore, forty-four years of age, although looking nearly ten years younger. He is of Scotch and French descent. His father, William Camp, who was a gallant soldier in the war of 1812,

8

died in 1822, at the age of forty-eight, and his mother, whose maiden name was Mary Reynolds, is still living, at the advanced age of seventy-six.

Mr. Camp was educated in the city of Philadelphia, where he resided from 1824 until 1835, when he removed to the city of New York. He has since been engaged in building in the latter place until recently, and is now residing in the town of Somers, Westchester county, where he is engaged in operating an extensive farm. This is his first appearance in public life, though he has already exhibited the necessary qualifications of an industrious and successful legislator. He is a gentleman of superior personal popularity, and was elected to his present position, in a closely contested district, by nearly seven hundred majority, running far in advance of his ticket. Politically he was formerly a Whig, but was one among the first to engage in the inauguration of the Republican movement, having signed the call, with such men as John May and Horace Greeley, for the first Republican meeting ever held in the city of New York. In social, as in public life, he is kind and agreeable, and is well liked by all his legislative associates at Albany.

Mr. Camp was married, on the 8th of January, 1839, to a daughter of William Smith, of New York, and has been a member of the Methodist Church since 1842.

# THOMAS CARTER.

MR. CARTER was born in Franklin county, Massachusetts, and is one of the oldest men in the House. He is of pure English descent. His father, John Carter, and his mother, whose maiden name was Nichols, both died in his native place many years ago, the former having attained the age of forty-five, and the latter sixty-five.

Mr. Carter was educated in the common schools of Massachusetts. He came to New York thirty-four years ago, and settled in Chenango county, where he now resides. His occupation through life has been that of blacksmithing, and he has always sustained the reputation, wherever he is known, of a hard-working, honest, and industrious mechanic—one of those who constitute the very bone and sinew of the American people. He was formerly a Whig of the old school, but since the organization of the Republican party, has ranked high in the community in which he lives as one of its most earnest and faithful supporters. With the exception of some military distinction, he never occupied any prominent public position until his election to the present House. Nevertheless he has shown himself well qualified in every essential particular, for a proper discharge of the duties with which his constituents have entrusted him.

Mr. Carter was married, in 1824, to Miss Susan Lyman, of Franklin county, Mass., and belongs to the Congregational Church.

## NICHOLAS M. CATLIN.

THE subject of this sketch is a descendant of the family of Catlins who have been located at Newington, near Rochester, in the county of Kent, in England, ever since the Norman Conquest. He is a relative of Judge Phineas Catlin, of Tompkins county, N. Y., and is a brother of Pope Catlin, of the New York Corn Exchange. His immediate ancestors came from Connecticut. He was born in 1814, in Kingsbury, Washington county, N. Y., where he now resides, and is the youngest of nineteen children. His father, Asa Catlin, died in Kingsbury, on the 28th of August, 1855, at the advanced age of ninety-five; and his mother, whose maiden name was Sarah Lane, died in the same town, on the 3d of October, 1853, at the age of eighty-two.

Mr. Catlin received a common English education in his native town, and has devoted most of his life to agricultural pursuits. He has been a Justice of the Peace and Notary Public since 1859, and is said to have been honest and faithful in the discharge of all his public duties. Politically he was always a Whig before becoming a Republican, and has never failed to closely adhere to the principles and policy of his party. He is not one of the noisy members of the House, being naturally averse to anything like parade or ostentation; but he attends to his duties faithfully and honestly, and will no doubt leave a clean record behind him at the expiration of his Legislative career at Albany.

Mr. Catlin was married, in September, 1844, to Miss

Helen A. Mears, of Franklin county, N. Y. In religion, he was formerly a Baptist, but is now associated with Jacob Blain, George Stores, Dr. Thomas, and others, known as "Destructionists."

## ABNER CHAPMAN.

MR. CHAPMAN is one of the oldest and most influential gentlemen in either branch of the Legislature. He was born on the 30th of September, 1798, in the town of Ashford, Windham county, Connecticut, and is of Irish and French descent. His father, Amasa Chapman, who was one of the pioneer settlers in Central New York, having located in Marcellus, Onondaga county, as early as 1799, died on the 1st of April, 1855, in the city of Syracuse, at the advanced age of eighty; and his mother, whose maiden name was Hannah Amidon, died on the 14th of April, 1851, in the town of Onondaga, at the age of seventy-two.

Mr. Chapman was educated in an old log schoolhouse in the wilderness, and subsequently passed several winters in teaching. He is a practical mechanic, having spent most of his time at the mason trade and at brickmaking; but, in consequence of ill health, has not been actively engaged in any business during the past four or five years. When quite young he removed, with his parents, into the town of Onondaga, Onondaga county, N. Y., where he has always since resided. He has held various offices in that town, from time to time, including that of Justice of the Peace, which he occupied some twenty years. He was, also, for several years, a Justice of the Sessions; and has had more or less military experience, having held a commission under Gov. Troop as far back as 1828. Being a strong temperance man, however, there was no office ever held by him in which he felt so much pride as that of President of the South Onondaga Temperance Society, and as that of one of the Vice-Presidents of the New York Temperance Alliance. In politics, he was always an unyielding Whig, of the Adams, Clay, and Fillmore stamp, until the repeal of the Missouri Compromise, when he became a Republican.

Mr. Chapman was married, in 1821, to Miss Eliza Mirick, and attends the Congregational and Methodist Church.

## CLARK S. CHITTENDEN.

Mr. CHITTENDEN was born on the 16th of May, 1803, in Benson, Rutland county, Vermont. He is supposed to be of Welsh descent, and is a brother of the Hon. Joseph Chittenden, of Vermont, who has been a prominent and influential member of both branches of the Legislature in that State. His father, Solomon Chittenden, who died on the 9th of February, 1855, at the advanced age of ninety-three, was a Revolutionary soldier, a true patriot, and an upright citizen, and lived in happy wedlock with Susannah Sanford, the mother of the subject of this sketch, over seventy years. She survived her husband until August, 1855, when she died, at the age of ninety.

Mr. Chittenden received a common-school education, and came from his native State to New York, in 1822. He was always an enterprising and eminently successful merchant, until April, 1858, when he retired from business, and was succeeded by his sons, K. S. & V. A. Chittenden, in the same business. Since then, he has devoted his time chiefly to his farm. In politics, he was formerly a Whig, zealously defending the principles and policy of that party, but was one among the first to engage in the Republican movement. He has been a Justice of the Peace some twenty years in the town where he resides, and was Supervisor some eight years. In addition to these he was also Postmaster for some twelve years. His position in the last House, to which he was chosen by a handsome majority, was prominent and influential, and he was seldom absent from his post as a member of the Committee on Expenditures of the Executive Department. His position throughout the community in which he is best known, is that of a man of influence, character, and real moral worth, and he discharges the duties of his position at Albany with a degree of honesty and intelligence of which his constituents may well feel proud. He never makes any unusual display in the House at speechmaking or otherwise, and is only known by his sterling good sense, sound judgment, and diligent attention to the business of legislation.

Mr. Chittenden was married in January, 1827, to Miss Julia A. Sheldon, and is an active and consistent member of the Congregational Church.

# NORTON S. COLLIN.

MR. COLLIN was born in 1812, in Hillsdale, Columbia county, N. Y. He is of French descent. His paternal grandfather was an active soldier in the war of the Revolution, and was long a distinguished Whig in Dutchess county. His father, David Collin, died in 1845, in Onondaga county, at the age of seventy-seven, and his mother, whose maiden name was Lucy Bingham, died in 1855, at the age of seventy-seven.

Mr. Collin was educated in the common schools of his native place, and subsequently passed some time at the Hudson Academy. From 1853 until 1858, he lived in the city of Brooklyn, and with the exception of that period, has always been actively engaged in farming in his native county. He was recently elected President of the Columbia County Agricultural Society, but never held any prominent public position until his election, by an unusually large majority, to his present office. He was formerly, in politics, a Freesoil Whig, and subsequently very naturally became a Republican on the first organization of that party. Although always an active politician, he has never cherished any special desire for official distinction, and holds his present position by the choice of his constituents rather than at his own solicitation. Mr. Collin was married some years since to Miss Eliza, sister of Avery Park, President of Racine College, Wisconsin, and attends the Presbyterian Church with his family.

## NATHAN COMSTOCK.

MR. COMSTOCK is a native of the city of New York, and is descended from genuine Quaker stock. He is about thirty-three years of age, and ranks high among the most quiet men of the House. His father, Nathan Comstock, who came to the city of New York about forty-five years ago, from Rhode Island, where his family had lived for many generations, died in January, 1859, at the age of eighty-two; and his mother, whose maiden name was Ann Merritt, and who belonged to a Quaker family in Westchester county, died in Sept. 1860, at the age of seventy-four.

Mr. Comstock received a common English education in his native city, and until 1846, was engaged in a counting-house. He then commenced the study of the law, in the practice of which he is now successfully engaged. This is the first public position he ever occupied, and it is doubtless gratifying to his constituents to know that he has thus far proved himself faithful to the representative trust with which they have clothed him. In politics he was formerly a Whig, of the Seward or Freesoil school, and is now among the most faithful in the Republican ranks. His abilities are above mediocrity; but his unassuming and retiring disposition seldom allows him to appear to the best advantage.

Mr. Comstock was married in 1853, to Miss Cromwell, of Orange Co., N. Y., and still retains his birthright in the Quaker Church.

8*

## JOSEPH W. CORNING.

MR. CORNING is a native of Yarmouth, Nova Scotia, where he was born on the 4th of November, 1814. He sprang from English stock. His immediate paternal ancestors were natives of Massachusetts, and descendants of the Corning and Walker families. His maternal ancestors were descended from the Strickland and Sanders families, residing in the vicinity of Stonington, Connecticut. Soon after England took Nova Scotia from the French, and about the close of the old French war, a number of families from what was then the New England provinces, removed to and settled at Yarmouth, and among these were his grandparents. His father, John Corning, died in 1850, at Palmyra, Wayne county, N. Y., at the age of seventy-two, and his mother, whose maiden name was Olive Strickland, died in the same year, and at the same age and place.

Mr. Corning's father removed, with his family, to the State of New York in 1823, and located at Rochester, where the subject of this sketch received an academical education. From the age of ten until fourteen, Mr. Corning worked in a cotton factory at that place. He then worked most of his time in a tobacco factory until the age of twenty. During the next four years he worked at farming in the summer, and taught school during the winter. He was afterwards engaged in the mercantile trade a few years at Palmyra, and then spent some three years in California, and at the Sandwich Islands. On his return, in 1853, he completed the study of the law, and has since then been engaged in the practice of his profession. He has been a resident of Palmyra, Wayne county, since 1837.

Mr. Corning was chosen a Justice of the Peace at the age of twenty-three in the town of Ontario, Wayne county, and has held that office several terms. He was elected to his present position by a large majority, and is regarded by all as a valuable man in the House. Politically he was originally a Whig, with strong Free-soil proclivities, and since 1856, when he was an American, he has been a firm and consistent Republican.

Mr. Corning was married in Seneca county, in 1838, to Miss Julia W. Jones, and is a consistent member of the Episcopal Church.

## LUKE F. COZANS.

MR. COZANS is one of the youngest men in the House, and is, perhaps, the most fluent, eloquent, and intelligent impromptu speaker in either branch of the Legislature. This is his first prominent appearance in public life; but he evidently possesses qualities which befit him well for a representative position, and if life and health are spared him he is doubtless destined, with proper care and prudence, to live a career of usefulness and honor.

Mr. Cozans is a native of the island of Prince Edward, where he was born on the 15th of March, 1836. He is of pure Irish descent. His father, John Cozans, is still living, at an advanced age; and his mother, whose maiden name was Mary Comerford, died in January, 1860, at the age of sixty-three. Mr. Cozans came to the city of New York, where he was educated, when only three years of age, and studied law with Ogden Hoffman, the senior partner of the firm of Hoffman, Cutter & Flanders. He was admitted to the bar in May, 1857, and since then has been successfully engaged in the practice of his profession, in the city of New York, as one of the firm of Cozans & Tracy, at 41 Ann street. In politics he has always been a staunch, unyielding Democrat, of the Jeffersonian and State Rights' school, and was supported by the united Democracy of his district for the seat he now holds in the Assembly. His views on the present distracted state of public affairs are intensely conservative; and since the opening of the present session of the Legislature, he has exhibited a strong desire to do whatever is best calculated to restore peace and harmony between all sections of our common country.

Mr. Cozans is still single, and belongs to the Catholic Church.

## ANDREW CRAFT.

Mr. Craft is a native of Westchester county, N. Y., where he was born on the 14th of October, 1808. His ancestors came to America from Holland, over two hundred years ago, and both his fraternal and maternal grandfathers were soldiers in the Revolution. His parents were also both natives of Westchester county, where his father, James Craft, who died in 1823, at the age of fifty-six, was for many years a successful farmer. His mother, whose maiden name was Hannah Cypher, died in 1857, at the advanced age of ninety-one.

Mr. Craft removed, with his parents, when only ten years of age, to the city of New York, where he has since been a resident. He received a common schooling, and in 1825 was bound out to a ship-carpenter, with whom he served an apprenticeship, and then worked at the trade until September, 1849. He was afterwards appointed to a position in the New York Custom-house, where he remained until 1854, when he was removed on political grounds. He was then employed again at his trade until 1857, when he was appointed agent of the Pilot Commissioners, which office he still occupies. In 1856 he was chosen one of the New York Fire Commissioners, holding the position until 1858, when he was elected Councilman from the Fifth District. He was named again for Councilman in 1860, but declined the nomination. He was elected to his present position in the House by the largest vote ever before given to a Republican in his district, and has proven himself a capable representative. Politically he was formerly a Whig, and is now a Republican.

Mr. Craft was married in 1832 to Miss Mary Moore, of New York, and attends the Universalist Church.

## JAMES DARCY.

Mr. Darcy was born in the city of Buffalo, on the 12th of November, 1834, and is a descendant of pure Irish stock. His father, Daniel Darcy, a prominent and influential man, is still living in that city, and his mother, whose maiden name was Eliza Devenport, died in 1848, at the age of thirty-two.

Mr. Darcy was educated in the public schools of his native city, and after removing, in January, 1851, to the city of Brooklyn, where he now resides, served his time as a house-carpenter, which has always since been his chief occupation. He was elected to the Assembly, which is the first public position he ever held, in the fall of 1859, by a majority of upwards of six hundred, over the combined American and Republican parties in his district, and during the last session of the Legislature was a member of the Standing Committee on Internal Affairs of Towns and Counties. He introduced the bill, last winter, establishing a public market in the city of Brooklyn, and also the Brooklyn Ferry Bill, and has again introduced them this session, with the determination, if possible, to secure their success. At the last election he received the unanimous nomination of both the Douglas and Breckenridge branches of the Democratic party, and was again triumphantly elected to the position he now occupies. His legislative career has, thus far, been quiet and unpretending; but he has shown himself an honest, capable, industrious, and intelligent representative. He has, like his father, been a Democrat of the old-fashioned conservative stamp, and has never faltered in his devotion to the real interests and policy of that party.

Mr. Darcy is married. He is a young man of more than ordinary promise; has a fine, prepossessing personal appearance; and enjoys a high degree of personal as well as political popularity wherever he is known.

# REDMAN S. DAVIS.

Mr. Davis is a native of the town of Charlton, Worcester county, Mass., and is of Welsh extraction. His father, Levi Davis, is still living at the good old age of seventy-nine; and his mother, whose maiden name was Mary Spurr, died on the 12th of July, 1855, at the age of seventy-two.

Mr. Davis came to New York, with his parents, in 1815, and after living a year in Chenango county, settled in Dryden, Tompkins county, where he remained some nine years. In 1825 he removed into Steuben county, where he has always since been living. He received a common school education, and has never been engaged in anything but an honest and industrious cultivation of the soil. He has held several unimportant town offices from time to time, but has never been much of a politician, preferring to attend to his own private business. He was originally a Whig, of the Adams school, and subsequently became a Democrat, voting with that party until the passage of the Kansas-Nebraska Act in 1854, when he became a Republican. His course in the House is that of a quiet and useful member, and he sustains a very high standing among men of all parties in both branches of the Legislature.

Mr. Davis was married, on the 14th of June, 1829, to . Miss Jane A. Porter, and attends the Universalist Church.

## JOHN J. DOOLITTLE.

MR. DOOLITTLE is one of the most finished and best educated men in the House, and brings with him to the discharge of his official duties the experience of a successful business man—always an essential quality in a good representative.

Mr. Doolittle was born on the 5th of February, 1825, at Wetherfield Springs, Wyoming county, N. Y., where he now resides. He is a descendant of genuine Yankee stock, and is a cousin of the U. S. Senator Doolittle, of Wisconsin. His father, Ormus Doolittle, is still living, at the age of seventy-two, as is also his mother, who has now attained the age of seventy-five. Mr. Doolittle is a graduate of Hobart College, at Geneva, and has been engaged in the mercantile trade. He held the office of Supervisor in 1851, and was chosen a member of the present House by a large majority. He was formerly a Democrat until 1856, when he became a Republican. His attachment for his party is strong, being bitterly opposed to the further extension of slavery, but nevertheless he is strongly attached to the Union of the

States, and is one of those who would cheerfully sacrifice mere party, if by so doing he could preserve the peace and prosperity of our entire common country.

Mr. Doolittle was married on the 9th of October, 1849, to Miss Jane Agnes Thompson, and is a member of the Episcopal Church.

## JOHN B. DUTCHER.

Mr. Dutcher is a native of the town of Dover, Dutchess county, N. Y., where he was born on the 13th of February, 1830, and has always lived upon the farm on which he was born. He is of genuine English descent. His father, David Dutcher, died on the 9th of June, 1853, at the age of fifty-six; and his mother, whose maiden name was Amy Bordish, is still living at the advanced age of sixty.

With the exception of one term, passed at a select school in Litchfield county, Connecticut, Mr. Dutcher was educated in the common schools of his native place. He is a gentleman of good business capacities, and has always been successfully engaged in the cultivation of the soil. In March, 1857, he was elected Supervisor of his native town, holding the position one term, and in March, 1858, was chosen a Justice of the Peace, which office, contrary to his wishes, he still holds. Politically he was formerly a Whig, but, since the repeal of the Missouri Compromise, has been closely attached to the principles and policy of the Republican party. He is one of the quiet men at Albany this winter, being in no wise afflicted with the talking propensities usually common to new beginners in public life, and entitles himself to the respect and confidence of his Republican associates more by his unobtrusive attention to the discharge of his duties than any figure that he makes upon the floor of the House.

Mr. Dutcher was married on the 22d of May, 1860, to Miss Christina, daughter of Daniel Dodge, of Dutchess county, and attends the Baptist and Methodist Churches, though belonging to neither.

---

## JEREMIAH W. DWIGHT.

THIS is Mr. Dwight's second term in the Assembly, having been a member of that body a year ago. He was renominated without his solicitation, at the last election, with unusual unanimity, and was again triumphant by a majority larger than the average majority of the Republican ticket in his county. His course during the last session was perfectly satisfactory to his constituents, and it is generally conceded that the appropriation of $30,000 for draining the Cayuga Marshes, was obtained almost solely by his influence.

Mr. Dwight was born about the year 1820, at Cincinnatus, Cortland county, N. Y., being only about forty years of age. He is of English descent. His father, Elijah Dwight, is still living, as is also his mother, whose maiden name was Olive Standish. He attended a village high school for a time, but was chiefly educated in an ordinary district school. When about the age of eighteen, he entered a dry-goods store as a clerk, and was employed in that capacity some four or five years, when he engaged in the mercantile trade on his own responsibility. He has always, since then, been successfully engaged in that business, and has also dealt considerably in real estate. He was elected Supervisor of the town of Dryden, where he resides, in 1857; was re-elected in 1858, and was unanimously chosen Chairman of the Board during both years. He was always a Freesoil Democrat, until the establishment of the Republican party, and has always, since then, been an active supporter of the principles and policy of that organization. He is a gentleman of capacity, shrewdness, and energy, and is governed in all his public and private acts by a sense of justice, and a strict regard for the interests of the whole State. His sound sense and good judgment seldom mislead him as to the merits of any question, and no one is more faithful and industrious in the discharge of their representative duties.

Mr. Dwight was married, in 1846, to Miss Rebecca A., daughter of the Hon. Elias W. Cady, and attends the Presbyterian Church.

# H. DANE ELLINGWOOD.

MR. ELLINGWOOD is a native of the City of New York, and is of English descent. He is a relative of Nathan Dane, the celebrated author of the Ordinance of 1787, and a nephew of Thomas H. Smith, who was for many years successfully engaged in the East India trade. Both his parents are now dead, his mother, Mary Smith, having died when only twenty-five years of age.

Mr. Ellingwood was classically educated in New Jersey, and was a successful practitioner in the law about thirty years, in the city of New York, where he is well and favorably known among gentlemen of eminent distinction in the legal profession. He is now a resident of Staten Island, to which place he retired from the cares of active life some fifteen years ago, and where he sustains a high standing among all classes of people with whom he comes in contact. Although not an inattentive observer of the ordinary course of political events, he has never participated actively in politics, never having claimed a very strong allegiance to any party, and was elected to his present position entirely without his solicitation. He has always, however, belonged to the Democratic party, and considers the principles and policy of that organization as the only remedy for the country in its present distracted condition. He is a gentleman of superior ability, both as a lawyer and , a legislator, although never having before appeared in public life, and belongs to that class of high-minded, honorable, and intelligent men, who, unfortunately for the State, but seldom find their way into the legislative halls of the State.

Mr. Ellingwood is unmarried, and attends the English Church.

---

## JEREMIAH EMERICK.

MR. EMERICK was born in Ghent, Columbia county, N. Y., and is sixty-two years of age. He is of German and Holland descent. He resides at Baldwinsville, Onondaga county, and was a member of the last Legislature, where he occupied a position upon the Standing Committee on Claims and on the Select Committees on Petitions asking for the passage of a Pro Rata Freight Law, to be applied to railroads. He was re-elected to the Assembly at the last election by an increased majority—more, however, in consequence of the numerical strength of his party, than any specific merit of his own.

In politics Mr. Emerick is a bitter Republican, of the strictest sect, and is brimful of all manner of horrible apprehensions, lest the slaveholding States, as well as the common Territories of the United States, may have the privilege of disposing of their own domestic affairs, in their own way. He is a gentleman of some ability, occupying a respectable position in the community in which he resides, but is not particularly remarkable in anything, and will, in all probability, be no better off, in point of reputation, as to his legislative ability, at the end of his representative career, than he was at the beginning.

## SAMUEL J. FARNUM.

MR. FARNUM is a native of the town of Uxbridge, Worcester county, Mass., where he was born in the year 1806. He came to the State of New York in 1816, and settled in the town of Poughkeepsie, where he served his time at the tanning business. He subsequently removed to Newburgh, Orange county, where he engaged in tanning until some years since, when he returned to Poughkeepsie, where he now resides. He was quite a prominent and influential man in the village of Newburgh, having held the position of President and Supervisor, and in 1852 ran unsuccessfully in that district for Congress.

Mr. Farnum was a member of the Assembly in 1859, and during that session was Chairman of the Standing Committee on Trade and Manufactures, and a member of the Committee on Expenditures of the House. He was renominated at the ensuing election for the same place, but was defeated in consequence of the hostility exhibited by him while in the House towards an appropriation to the Troy University—an institution towards which he had always before been understood to be very friendly. He is a gentleman of very little personal popularity in the immediate community in which he lives, and although representing a strong Republican district, was chosen to his present position, at the last election, by only one majority. In politics he was originally a Seward Whig, and was one among the first to enlist in the Republican movement. As a business man he has been successful, but has never yet, and probably never will, distinguish himself in the capacity of a public servant, being evidently no better qualified for such a position than the great mass of his fellow citizens.

Mr. Farnum was married, in 1829, to Miss Sarah Ann Swartout, and is a member of the Methodist Church.

## ·WALTER A. FAXON.

Mr. Faxon was born in Kingsbury, Washington county, N. Y., and is in the prime of life. He is of American descent. His father, the Rev. Henry Faxon, a Baptist clergyman, died on the 3d of February, 1829, at the age of forty-six, and his mother died on the 10th of August, 1857, at the advanced age of seventy-eight. His parents were both natives of the State of New York.

Mr. Faxon received a common school education, and has always been engaged in the honest occupation of farming. During the years 1858 and '59 he held the office of Supervisor in the town of Chester, Warren county, where he now resides, and was chosen to the seat he now occupies in the House by a very handsome majority. Originally, until 1855, he was always a Democrat; but since the repeal of the Missouri Compromise he has been unyieldingly attached to the principles and policy of the Republican party. He is a man of quiet, unpretending manners, and makes a good representative, attending closely to his duties, both upon the floor of the House and as a member of the several committees to which he belongs.

Mr. Faxon was married on the 28th of August, 1831, to Miss Mary Foster, and is a member of the Baptist Church.

---

## ELIJAH E. FERREY.

Mr. Ferrey is a native of Otsego, Otsego county, N. Y. He was born on the 28th of February, 1812, and is of English descent. Both his parents are dead, his father, Elijah Ferrey, having died in 1814, at Philadelphia at about the age of fifty, and his mother about the year 1845, at the good old age of about seventy-five.

Mr. Ferrey received a common school and academical education. He was originally a mechanic, having worked some time at the harness-making trade; was subsequently engaged in farming, and is now a practising lawyer. Politically, he was always a Democrat until the organization of the Republican movement, since which time he has been an ardent and enthusiastic supporter of the principles and measures of that party. He is one of the most active men in the House, and usually wields considerable influence in the deliberations of that body.

Mr. Ferrey was married, in 1838, to Miss Sarah Stever, who died in March, 1855, and was again married on the 18th of December, 1856, to Miss Emily A. Brown, who died in April, 1860. He usually attends the Methodist Church.

## ZEBULON FERRIS.

MR. FERRIS is a native of Kingsbury, Washington county, N. Y., where he was born on the 8th of May, 1816. His father, Warren Ferris, who died in September, 1828, in Saratoga county, was a minister of the Society of Friends, among whom he was quite distinguished, and his mother was Ruth Curtiss, the daughter of a respectable family of Friends in Queensbury.

Mr. Ferris received a common school education, and after his father's death went to Washington, Dutchess county, where he served an apprenticeship at the saddle and harness trade. Some five years afterwards he removed to the city of Buffalo, where he resided until 1839, when he commenced business at East Hamburg, in Erie county, where he now resides. He has now added agricultural pursuits to his other business, and is also proprietor of a line of stages. He has been a Justice of the Peace during the past twelve years, and has been twice elected Justice of the Sessions, besides holding various other positions of public trust. Politically, he was formerly a Democrat, but, in 1844, when the Democracy adopted resolutions in favor of the annexation of Texas, he abandoned the party and supported

Henry Clay for the Presidency. He was a Free Soil Democrat in 1848, and voted for Gen. Scott in 1852. He then, in 1854, aided in the formation of the Republican party, of which he has ever since been an active and efficient member. He is a gentleman of superior business capacity, having accumulated a handsome competency, and is one of the most useful men in the House.

Mr. Ferris was married, in 1840, to Miss Narcessa W. Sprague, daughter of Asa Sprague, by whom he has four children, and is a man of liberal religious views.

## PEREZ H. FIELD.

MR. FIELD is one of the most quiet and industrious men in the House. He is not a brilliant star of the first magnitude, and seldom if ever participates in the discussions of that body, but his sound judgment, good common-sense, and general intelligence, nevertheless render him a useful legislator. Wherever he is known, and especially in the village of Geneva, where he is now a successful merchant, he sustains the reputation of a high-minded and honorable gentleman.

Mr. Field is a Republican in politics, of the more conservative stamp. He is one of those who voted for the proposition in the House, sending Commissioners to Washington, in compliance with the Virginia resolutions, and has supported on all other occasions whatever he has deemed best calculated to restore peace and tranquillity to the country, in the present perilous and distressing crisis. This is his first prominent appearance in public life; but the qualifications for a representative position, already exhibited by him in the discharge of his official duties, are not inferior to those of many of his companions in the House who have had far more experience than he in that respect.

## MARTIN FINCH.

MR. FINCH was a member of the Assembly of 1860, where he was a prominent member of the Judiciary Committee, and is now, as he was then, both personally and politically, one of the most quiet, useful, and popular men in either branch of the Legislature. He is a gentleman of more than ordinary ability and intelligence, and occupies a deservedly high position in both public and private life, throughout the entire section of the State where he resides.

Mr. Finch is a native of the town of Jay, Essex county, N. Y., where he was born on the 21st of June, 1811. He is of English and Irish descent. Both his father and mother died at Black Brook, Clinton county, N. Y., the former on the 8th of Oct., 1854, at the age of seventy-nine, and the latter about the year 1848, at the age of about sixty-five. He received a classical education, being a graduate of Williams College, Mass., and having studied law, was duly admitted to the bar in 1842. Since then he has had quite an extensive and lucrative practice, at Keesville, Essex county, where he resides, and has succeeded, by his legal skill and ability, in acquiring considerable reputation in his profession. He has always been strongly averse to occupying any political position, but besides holding some unimportant town offices, has, with the exception of two years, been Supervisor of his town since 1847, and still occupies that position. He was formerly an old line Henry Clay Whig, and adhered firmly to that party until its dissolution in 1854, when his conservative nationality on all the great questions of the day at once led him into the ranks of the American organization, where he still occupies a firm and unyielding position, although now acting with the Republicans. He is not a talking representative, seldom participating in the discussions of the House, but is none the less efficient and influential in the discharge of all his duties.

Mr. Finch was married, in 1843, to Miss Caroline Jackson, a native of Chesterfield, Essex county, N. Y., and belongs to the Congregational Church.

---

## FROTHINGHAM FISH.

MR. FISH is a native of the town of Glen, Montgomery county, New York, and is in the fortieth year of his age. He is of Holland extraction, and is apparently in no wise deficient in the usual prominent characteristics of that stock. This is not his first appearance in public life. He has held various town offices in his native county, where he has always resided, and in 1849 became somewhat distinguished as a member of the Assembly. His business has always been that of the practice of the law, and he is said to occupy a very respectable position in his profession in Montgomery county.

Politically Mr. Fish was formerly a Whig. He adhered firmly to that ancient organization until it ceased to exist, and then became a Republican, to the principles and policy of which party he is still closely attached. He is not one of the rabid Abolition John Brown school of politicians, and, in the present threatening aspect of our national affairs, has generally, by his votes in the House, shown a disposition to do whatever appears best calculated to restore peace and quiet to the country. Nevertheless he is always unwilling to unnecessarily sacrifice the best interests of his party, and is usually one of the first to spring to his feet in the House when anything affecting its integrity and well-being is thrust in upon the deliberations of that body. He is also fluent and facile on all other questions, and is one of the most frequent and persistent, though not perhaps the most eloquent talkers, in either branch of the Legislature.

## GEORGE H. FISHER.

MR. FISHER was a member of the Assembly in 1860, and this is, therefore, his second term of service in that body. He was Chairman of the Committee on Petitions of Aliens, and a member of the Committee on Joint Library, during that session, and was the author of the well-known bill removing the disabilities of resident aliens and empowering them to acquire, hold, and convey real estate, which he introduced, upon the suggestion of the Governor in his Annual Message. He is a young gentleman of superior qualities, both of head and heart, and has proven himself a quiet and unpretending, though faithful and industrious, legislator.

Mr. Fisher was born on the 7th of May, 1832, at Oswego, Oswego county, N. Y., and is, therefore, one of the youngest men in the House. He is of English descent, and his paternal ancestors, who settled in Franklin, Mass., came from England as early as 1636. His father, George Fisher, who has been living in the city of New York during the past three years, settled in Oswego county, in 1816, shortly after it became a county, and was for many years one of the most successful lawyers in that section of the State. His mother, whose maiden name was Elizabeth P. Huntington, is still living, at about the age of fifty-five.

Mr. Fisher was educated at Harvard University, where he graduated in 1852, with one of the first honors of his class. After leaving college, he entered the law office of Johnson & Sessions, at Syracuse, where he pursued his legal studies until 1854, when he was admitted to the bar at Utica. He subsequently passed some time at the law school, at Cambridge, and in 1855 opened an office in the city of New York. Since then he has been engaged in the practice of his profession in that city, Brooklyn, and Williamsburgh, in the latter of which places he now resides. He has held the office of Notary Public, and was chosen a member of the House in the fall of 1859 from a Democratic district. He took but little interest in politics until the repeal of the Missouri Compromise, when he was among the first to enlist in the organization of the Republican party. Since then he has been an active and consistent supporter of the principles and measures of that party, and was two years a member of the Republican General Committee of Kings county.

Mr. Fisher was married, on the 25th of December, 1857, to Miss Emma, daughter of the late James H. Chichester, a New York merchant, and attends the Universalist Church.

## STEPHEN W. FULLERTON, Jun.

Mr. Fullerton was born in the town of Minisink, Orange county, New York, and is about twenty-seven years of age. He is of Irish extraction. His father, Daniel Fullerton, who was a member of the Legislature in 1850, is still living, and his mother, whose maiden name was Abigail Carpenter, died in 1840.

Mr. Fullerton received a common school and academical education. He was originally a telegraph operator, and subsequently occupied the position of station agent for the New York and Erie Railroad, for three years, at Goshen, Orange county. Meanwhile, he studied law, and in the fall of 1858, entered the law office of his uncle, S. W. Fullerton, who was a member of the Assembly in 1857 and '58. He was admitted to the bar in the winter of 1859, and since then has been engaged in the practice of his profession in the village of Newburgh, where he now resides. His present office is the first to which he was ever elected, and he has always been a staunch Republican of the uncompromising school, having cast his first vote for Col. Fremont in 1856. He is a good speaker, having a fine voice and considerable fluency of language, and usually participates in the more important discussions of the House. He is kind, clever, and agreeable in his intercourse with members, usually leaving a good impression upon the minds of all with whom he comes in contact, and is said to enjoy a high degree of personal popularity wherever he is known.

Mr. Fullerton is still single, and attends the Episcopal Church.

## JOHN FULTON.

Mr. Fulton is a native of the city of Albany, and is forty-six years of age. He is of pure Irish descent, and in early life, received a good, substantial business education. His place of residence is Waterford, Saratoga county, where he is now largely engaged in the manufacture of flour, besides having a line of freight barges on the Hudson river and canals, and where he has been for the last fifteen years connected in the milling business with the Hon. John House, who represented his district in the Assembly in 1821. He has had the offices of Assessor, Commissioner, and Supervisor, in the town in which he lives, and is at present a member of the Board of Education. He was a member of the Assembly a year ago, where he honestly and efficiently discharged his duties both on the floor of the House and as a member of the Committee on Canals, and was re-elected at the late election by about three hundred majority, although his county gave a Republican majority of fifteen hundred.

In politics, Mr. Fulton has always been an old line Conservative National Democrat of the Jackson school, although representing a Republican district in the Legislature. He is a gentleman of good, sound, practical common sense, with an intuitive knowledge of men and things largely developed ; and although one of the most quiet and unpretending men in the House, carries great weight and influence with him wherever he is found acting. He appears to understand and appreciate perfectly the wants and best interests of his constituents as well as of the whole State, and is always prompt and efficient in the discharge of his official duties.

Mr. Fulton's present wife was Miss Ann E., daughter of Capt. Samuel Goodspeed, one of the early settlers of Troy, and attends the Episcopal Church.

# STEPHEN ST. JOHN GARDNER.

MR. GARDNER is a native of Lumberland, Sullivan county, N. Y. He is a son of the Hon. James K. Gardner, who died at Barryville, in that county, on the 30th of June, 1860, at the age of fifty-four, and who was a man of high standing and influence wherever he was known throughout his entire lifetime.

Mr. Gardner has been successfully engaged in .the mercantile trade, near Barryville, for some time, and is said to be one of the most popular and influential men in that neighborhood. Politically he has always been a Democrat of the National Conservative school, but never held any very prominent public position until his election to the present House from a hitherto Republican county. He is, however, one of the substantial men in the Legislature, and is always prompt and industrious in the discharge of his official duties.

# JAY GIBBONS.

MR. GIBBONS ranks favorably among the youngest members of the House, and is a young gentleman of more than ordinary promise. He is a native of the town of Westerlo, Albany county, N. Y., where he was born on the 25th of March, 1833. He is of pure English descent, and his paternal grandfather, John Gibbons, who was born in Dutchess county, was one of the first settlers of Albany county, where he was always prominently known. Both his parents are still living, his father, Alfred Gibbons, having attained the age of sixty-one, and his mother, whose maiden name was Dorcas Sweet, being about the same age.

Mr. Gibbons received an academical education in his native county, and has always been employed in farming in his native place, where he has always resided. He has generally taken quite an active part in the local politics of his own immediate neighborhood, but his present position, to which he was chosen by upwards of seven hundred majority, is the first political office he ever held. In politics he has always been firmly attached to the present principles and policy of the Democratic party, and is particularly averse to sectionalism and fanaticism at either extreme of the Union. He is both personally and politically popular wherever he is known, and sustains a very respectable position in the House, being honest and industrious in the discharge of the duties devolving upon him. Mr. Gibbons was married on the 10th of June, 1856, to Miss Emily Lockwood, and attends the Methodist Episcopal Church.

## JOHN HARDY.

MR. HARDY is a native of the city of New York, where he was born in 1835, and is, therefore, one of the youngest men in the House. He is of pure, unadulterated Scotch descent. His father, William Hardy, is still living, at the age of fifty-one, and his mother, whose maiden name was Jane Glen, died in 1849, at the age of forty-six.

Mr. Hardy was educated in the public schools of his native city. He entered the New York Free Academy at its first organization, and graduated in the first class in 1853, having received what was considered a thorough collegiate education. He subsequently passed some four years in that institution as tutor, and was then a clerk in the Navy Agent's Office. Since then he has been engaged in the study of the law, for which he was educated. This is his first prominent appearance in public life, but the ability and judgment already shown by him in the discharge of his duties in the House have placed him in a rank, among his legislative peers, of which many older heads in the Legislature might well feel proud. Unassuming modesty, and a quiet, unpretending fulfilment of the obligations of the trust confided to him, are his chief characteristics ; and whether in the Assembly Chamber, or in the common walks of life, he is always the same good-natured, clever, agreeable, and companionable representative of the Democratic masses.

Politically Mr. Hardy has always been an unswerving Democrat of the olden school. All his political teachings were learned at the feet of such men as ex-Governor Marcy, Edwin Croswell, and Silas Wright. During the last Presidential Canvass he was an ardent and enthusiastic supporter of Mr. Douglass, and now looks upon a united Democracy as the only salvation of the country in the present distracted state of public affairs. His attachment to the Union of the States is strong and abiding, but he is strongly in favor of the preservation of the equal rights of all sections of the country, and believes that upon such a basis alone can the people be saved from ultimate civil war with all its attendant horrors.

Mr. Hardy is still single, and is a believer in the Christian religion. His personal appearance is quite prepossessing, and he is personally, at least, one of the most popular young men at Albany this winter.

## PETER HILL.

MR. HILL is a modern Cincinnatus, having abandoned the cultivation of the soil for the more responsible position of a public servant. His course, too, in the House seems to prove that he has not mistaken his place, for although, perhaps, the most quiet man at the Capitol, there are but few, if any, among his legislative companions, who are more honest, faithful, and conscientious in the discharge of their public duties.

Mr. Hill was born on the 31st of January, 1803, in the town of Cambridge, Washington county, N.Y. His father, James Hill, who was of English and Scotch descent, and who was several times a member of the Legislature in the days of Tompkins and Clinton, was a native of Ireland; and his mother, Nancy Thomas, whose father served as a Captain in the Revolutionary War, was born in Rhode Island. Both his parents died in the town of

Cambridge—his father in the fifty-fifth year of his age, and his mother at the ripe old age of eighty-four.

Mr. Hill was educated in the common schools of his native town. He was brought up on a farm, and has always been successfully engaged in the cultivation of the soil. He has held the office of Supervisor in Jackson township, where he now resides, besides some other unimportant town offices, and has been a Loan Commissioner during the past six years. Politically he was formerly a Whig, of the Clintonian stamp, adhering closely to the principles and policy of that party until it abandoned its organization, when he became a Republican. Mr. Hill belongs to the United Presbyterian Church.

## ROBERT C. HUTCHINGS.

MR. HUTCHINGS is one of the most promising young men in either branch of the Legislature. He is a native of the city of New York, and is only twenty-four years of age. He is descended from Knickerbocker and Puritan stock, his mother being one of the same family to which the Grinnells and Peabodies belonged in New England. His father, Edward W. Hutchings, a gentleman of high respectability and influence, is also still living, and is about fifty years of age.

Mr. Hutchings was educated at Princeton College, New Jersey, where he graduated in the class of 1857. After leaving college he passed some eighteen months in the study of the civil law in Paris, and was a correspondent for one of the principal New York papers from that city during the first Italian war. Returning to the United States, in September, 1859, he entered an advanced class in the Columbia College law school, where he graduated in May, 1860, taking the valedictory, which was the only honor awarded. He was subsequently admitted to the bar, and since then has been successfully engaged in the practice of his profession. The district from which he was elected to his present position, was represented in 1859 by the Hon. George Opdyke, and in 1860 by Theodore B. Voorhees; but notwithstanding two other Democratic candidates ran—one Mozart and the other Breckenridge—and a Republican, Mr. H. being the Tammany candidate, he was successful by a very large vote, running some twelve hundred in advance of his ticket.

Mr. Hutchings is a ready and eloquent speaker, and is one of the most accomplished writers in the Legislature. He has been for some time a leading contributor to several prominent papers, and has attained considerable reputation in the literary world as the translator of several important French works. Although calm, quiet, and unassuming in his public conduct, he has many friends in the legislative circle, and has already shown himself every way worthy of the confidence and esteem of his constituents, whom he represents truly and faithfully.

Mr. Hutchings is a young gentleman of pleasant exterior, and is calculated to make friends of all with whom he comes in contact. In person he is of about medium height, with an elegantly formed body, and has dark intelligent blue eyes, glossy black hair and moustache, and a smooth, good-natured face.

---

## FRANCIS A. HYATT.

MR. HYATT was born on the 5th of August, 1828, at Ridgefield, Connecticut. He is descended from English stock, and his ancestors were among the twenty-six original purchasers of that township, where his uncle, the Hon. John Hyatt, now resides. His father, Aaron S. Hyatt, is still living, at the age of fifty-seven; but his mother, whose maiden name was Electa Keeler, died on the 24th of September, 1830, at the age of twenty-four. His present mother, to whom he is indebted for a mother's care from helpless childhood, is a daughter of the Rev. Aaron Sanford, late of Redding, Connecticut.

Mr. Hyatt received a common English education, and is a practical and successful farmer. He has been twice Clerk of the town in which he resides, and is now an acting Justice of the Peace. Until 1855 he was always a Democrat of the Barnburner stamp, but since that time has been uncompromisingly attached to the principles and measures of the Republican party. He possesses considerable legislative ability, is conscientious and attentive in the fulfilment of the obligations of his present position, and has secured the respect and esteem of his representative associates by his unpretending course in the House.

Mr. Hyatt was married oh the 22d of October, 1850, to Miss Elizabeth M. Robinson, and attends the Methodist Episcopal Church.

## GEORGE HYLAND.

MR. HYLAND is a native of Ireland, where he was born in 1805. His parents emigrated from Sligo to Toronto in 1816, and engaged in farming. He served his time at the hatting business at the latter place, and in 1824 came to the State of New York, working at Albany, and various other places, until 1829, when he permanently located at Dansville, Livingston county—his present place of residence—which had then a population of only some three hundred, but which, through the enterprise of such men as Mr. Hyland, soon became the first village in the county in point of population and commercial importance.

Mr. Hyland is emphatically a self-made man. Thrown upon his own resources in early life, without friends or education, he applied himself vigorously to his calling, devoting all his spare moments to the acquisition of knowledge, that he might perform well the business he had undertaken. Such was the success attendant upon his efforts that in a few years from the time of establishing himself in Dansville, he became one of the leading merchants and manufacturers in the county.

In politics Mr. Hyland is a staunch Republican of the Whig school, and this is his first appearance in public life. He is now in the full vigor of manhood, possessing an ardent desire to benefit his constituents and the State, and has not failed to become one of the reliable legislators of 1861. Though no stickler for theory in religion, he has always been firmly attached to the Episcopal Church.

## WILLIAM JOHNSON.

MR. JOHNSON is one of the substantial and influential men of the House. His unpretending manner, and utter distaste for anything like parade and ostentation, hide his real moral and intellectual worth, as it were, " under a bushel ;" but nevertheless, these very qualities, together with the quiet evidence he has already unconsciously given of his ability, have marked him high among the leading men in both branches of the Legislature.

Mr. Johnson is a native of the good old Bay State, and is about thirty-seven years of age. He is of pure unmixed English descent. His father, David Johnson, died in August, 1825, in Herkimer county, N. Y.; and his mother, whose maiden name was Olive Stodard, is still living at the advanced age of sixty-three.

Mr. Johnson came to New York, while he was a mere infant, with his parents, who took up their residence in Herkimer county. He received a common school education, and was subsequently engaged some five years in the mercantile trade. From 1849 until 1856, he followed jobbing as a contractor on the canals, and is now engaged in the manufacture of woollen goods at

Seneca Falls, where he resides. In politics he has always been a staunch line Democrat, of the old-fashioned school, and although not a boisterous ranting politician, has never failed to fully discharge all his party obligations. This is his first prominent appearance in public life; nevertheless he possesses no ordinary degree of representative ability, and has been found faithful and efficient in the discharge of all his official duties.

Mr. Johnson was married, in June, 1855, to Angeline, daughter of the Hon. Jacob P. Chamberlain, and attends the Episcopal Church.

## JAY JARVIS JONES.

Mr. Jones is one of the youngest, most gentlemanly, popular, and intelligent men in either the Senate or Assembly. He was born on the 15th of January, 1837, in Harlem, or the Twelfth Ward, in the city of New York, and is of pure American descent; his parents, who are still living, tracing their ancestry as far back as the third generation in this country. Some of his ancestors, on his paternal side, were distinguished soldiers in the war of the Revolution; and his father, Edmund Jones, who served as a private in the war of 1812, was held as a prisoner on three different British frigates, and was confined in prison some eight months in England.

Mr. Jones was educated, partially, by a private tutor, and at a boarding school, where he was instructed in the usual branch of English, and the rudiments of the

French and German languages. He commenced active life on the 9th of October, 1852, as a clerk with the firm of Martin & Lawson, importers of silks and ribbons, in his native city, where he remained until he became a partner in the firm of Edmund Jones & Co., stationers and printers, at 26 John street, in which business he is still engaged. He has never belonged to any political organization but the old Democratic party, and never held any public office until his election to the present Legislature. He is a very clever and agreeable young gentleman, having the respect and good opinion of all the members of the House, and performs the functions of his office to the very letter without giving offence to any one.

## WILLIAM J. C. KENNY.

DR. KENNY is a native of the Thirteenth Ward in the City of New York, and is thirty-five years of age. He is descended from pure unadulterated Irish stock, and is by no means ashamed of the blood which flows in his veins. He graduated in St. Mary's College, in the City of Baltimore, in 1841, and then went into the office of the late Dr. Whittaker, with whom he remained as his assistant up to the time of his death. He then graduated in the New York Medical College, in 1856, and after practising about a year, was obliged to abandon his profession in consequence of ill health. Since then he has been engaged in the post-office department in his native city.

Dr. Kenny has always been a member of the Democratic party, and believes in the regularity of Tammany Hall. He was the candidate for his present position, at the last election, of that branch of his party, and although bitterly opposed by four other Democratic candidates before the people, was triumphantly elected over his Republican opponent by a small majority. He never occupied any public position until his promotion to a seat in the present House, but is nevertheless well qualified to discharge properly the duties of his office. He is a young gentleman of kind, clever, and agreeable manners, and commands the entire respect and consideration of all his Democratic friends.

## MARQUIS L. KENYON.

MR. KENYON is a native of the town of Brownville, Jefferson county, New York, where he was born on the 15th of September, 1817. He is descended from genuine American stock. His father, Samuel Kenyon, is still living, at the advanced age of about seventy-eight, and his mother, whose maiden name was Susan Cross, died some twenty-eight years ago.

Mr. Kenyon, like most successful American boys, was educated in the common schools of his native place. In early life he worked on a farm and was engaged in stage driving, and is now proprietor of an extensive line of stages at Rome, Oneida county, where he has resided since 1839. Politically he has always been an old-fashioned conservative Democrat, of the Gen. Jackson school, voting for Gen. Cass in 1848, and is now one of the most influential men in his party in the district which he represents. He never held any important public position previous to his election to the present Legislature, but has nevertheless shown himself a good legislator and a most capital man—one who will never disgrace any position whose duties require the exercise of good common sense, untiring industry, and strict integrity of character.

## FRANCIS KERNAN.

MR. KERNAN is the acknowledged leader of the Democratic party in the lower branch of the Legislature. His distinguished legal ability and his superior standing as a high-minded, honorable, and intelligent gentleman have, by universal consent among his political friends, secured him this distinction. He was the Democratic candidate for Speaker of the House, at the opening of the present session of the Legislature, and received the vote of every Democrat in that body for that position. Although this is his first appearance in the Legislative halls of the State, he has already exhibited a degree of representative tact and ability which has secured him the confidence of the great majority of the members of the body to which he belongs. As a speaker, he is eloquent and choice in the use of language, clear and concise in his statements, and logical in the management of his argument. He usually participates in the discussions of the House, but never enters the arena of debate without putting on his armor, and the lance he tilts is always pretty sure to impale his antagonist.

Mr. Kernan is a native of Wayne, Steuben county, New York, where he was born on the 14th of January, 1816, and is, therefore, forty-five years of age. He is of pure Irish extraction ; both his parents, who are still living, having been born in Ireland. He was educated to the law, and is now engaged in the practice of his profession in the city of Utica, where he resides. He was brought forward as a candidate for the Assembly at the last election, with great unanimity, by the united Democracy of his district, which the year previous gave his opponent a large majority, and was triumphantly elected by nearly four hundred majority, running far in advance of the rest of the Democratic ticket. The only prominent public position he ever held, previous to assuming the duties of his present office, was that of Reporter of the Court of Appeals, which he successfully occupied from 1854 until 1857. There are but few men indeed in either branch of the Legislature who have as intelligent and comprehensive views of our present national difficulties as he, and scarcely any, perhaps, who are more earnest than he in his desire to bring about some plan of accommodation by which the Union may yet be saved.

Mr. Kernan is a Catholic in religion, and stands deservedly high in all the social relations of private life.

## LOAMMI KINNEY.

MR. KINNEY is one of the most quiet and respectable men in Cortland county, and sustains the same reputation in the body of which he is now a member. He is well liked at Albany, and makes a good Representative.

Mr. Kinney is of English and Irish descent, and is a native of Homer, Cortland county, New York, where he now resides. His father, Abel Kinney, died in 1840, at the age of sixty-six, and his mother, the wife of Joshua G. Palmer, is now living at Canastatoe, in the seventy-seventh year of her age. Mr. Kinney was educated in the common schools of his native place, and is a practical mechanic. In politics he has always been identified with the Republican party since its first organization, and is strongly opposed to the further extension of slavery.

Mr. Kinney was married on the 4th of October, 1837, to Miss Parmelia Sumner, and attends the Congregational Church.

## WILLIAM R. KNAPP.

MR. KNAPP is one of the substantial, common-sense Democrats of the House, and quietly wields a strong influence among all his legislative associates. He was the American candidate for the Assembly, in his district, in 1856, but was defeated by his Democratic opponent. As long as the American party maintained its organization, he was ardently attached to its principles and measures ; but when the question of slavery became the great issue in the politics of the country, his conservatism at once led him again into the ranks of the Democracy. No man, probably, cherishes a more intense hatred of sectionalism, whether it be in the North or South, and although a states' rights man in whatever field he may be called upon to do battle, he will always, no doubt, be found gallantly sustaining the stars and stripes of his common country.

Mr. Knapp was born on the 27th of April, 1819, at Haverstraw, Rockland county, New York. His paternal grandfather, Libeus Knapp, served with distinction in the Continental army, and was present at the surrender of Cornwallis, at Yorktown. His father, Robert Knapp, who died in 1858, was a Colonel in the war of 1812, where he proved himself a faithful and efficient soldier.

Mr. Knapp received a common English education, and was a captain of river craft some fifteen years. He has also been extensively engaged in the brick business, and is now quietly living upon his farm, on the banks of the Hudson, at his native place. He has been five years Supervisor in Rockland county, and was four years Chairman of the Board, discharging his duties, at all times, in the most satisfactory manner. He is honest and attentive in the discharge of his legislative duties, and is not one of those whom the lobby would be likely to approach.

Mr. Knapp was married, in 1844, to Miss Charlotte Rosse, and is a member of the Methodist Church, as is also his wife.

## JOHN LAMBRECHT.

MR. LAMBRECHT is one of the Representatives in the House of the city of New York, where he is engaged in the casting business. He is a native of Bavaria, Germany, where he was born on the 10th of April, 1826, and came to the United States in 1839. His father, Francis Lambrecht, died in 1850, at the advanced age of eighty-one, and his mother, whose maiden name was Catharine Germaine, died in 1827.

Mr. Lambrecht was educated in the common schools of the city of New York. He worked some time at the carpenter's business, prior to his present employment, and has always been quite successful in life. In politics he was formerly a Whig, but was one among the first to enlist in the Republican movement at the organization of that party. He is generally active and influential in the politics of the Metropolitan city, and was chosen to his present position by a complimentary vote. Thus far, he has been prompt and faithful in the discharge of his duties, and will doubtless prove himself a capable Representative before the termination of his legislative labors.

Mr. Lambrecht was married, in 1852, to Miss Jane Seinsoth, who is a native of Newburgh, Orange county, N. Y., and belongs to the Roman Catholic Church.

## JABEZ S. L'AMOREAUX.

MR. L'AMOREAUX is a farmer, residing at Clyde, Wayne county, N. Y., and was chosen to his present position by upwards of seven hundred majority. He has always been more or less active in politics in his own immediate neighborhood, but never held any prominent public position until he came to Albany. His standing at home is respectable, and somewhat influential; and although not very well calculated to acquire any special distinction in a representative capacity, he is said to enjoy the entire confidence of his constituents. Politically he is a Republican, of woolly-head antecedents, and is one of those who, with Gov. Andrew, believe that "John Brown was right."

## HENRY LANSING.

MR. LANSING is a native of the city of Albany, where he was born on the 14th of January, 1832, and where he has always resided. He is of pure, unmixed Holland extraction, and is a son of Henry D. Lansing, one of the most highly respectable and influential men in the county of Albany. His mother, whose maiden name was Gertrude Hinman, is also still living at an advanced age.

Mr. Lansing was educated at the Albany Academy, and has always been successfully engaged in the mer-

cantile business. He was a member of the Common
Council from the Sixth Ward, in the city of Albany,
during the years 1856 and '57, and was triumphantly
elected to his present position, at the last election, by a
handsome majority, over the Hon. Robert H. Pruyn,
one of the most popular men in the district. In politics, he was formerly a Whig, of the Clay and Webster school, adhering firmly to that party as long as it
retained its organization, after which he became an
American. He has always been bitterly and of principle opposed to the principles and measures of the
Republican party, and although still claiming to be an
American, is always ready and anxious to act with the
Democracy in successful opposition to that party. As
a member of the House he is very quiet and unassuming,
professing no qualifications whatever as a speaker ; but
is nevertheless one of the most attentive and efficient
men of that body.

Mr. Lansing was married, in 1854, to Miss Fanny A.
Wood, and attends the Dutch Reformed Church.

## SAMUEL LASHER.

Mr. Lasher is a quiet man, but an industrious and
faithful representative. He brings with him to the discharge of his public duties the experience of a successful
business man, and sustains a very respectable position in
the body to which he now belongs.

Mr. Lasher was born, in 1808, in Germantown, Columbia County, N. Y., where he still resides. His paternal grandfather emigrated to this country from Germany, and settled on the same farm upon which Mr. Lasher, like his father before him, is now living. Bastian C. and Philip G. Lasher, both of whom were relatives of his, formerly represented the same locality in the Legislature, and were favorably known for their industry, economy, thrift, and good common sense. His father Peter B. Lasher, died in July, 1849, at the advanced age of eighty-three, and his mother died in December, 1859, at the ripe old age of ninety-two.

Mr. Lasher received a good common school education, and has always been successfully engaged in agriculture and business pursuits. Politically he was formerly a Whig, and was one among the first to enlist in the organization of the Republican party. He has always been a close observer of the ordinary course of political events in the country, but never cared to assume the responsibilities of office until his election to his present position.

Mr. Lasher was married some years ago to the daughter of George Kronkright, and belongs to the Lutheran Church.

# SAMUEL E. LEWIS.

Mr. Lewis is a native of the town of Preston, Chenango county, N. Y., where he was born in 1819, and where he now resides. His paternal ancestors were from Wales, and both his parents were born in Rhode Island, whence they came to this State at a very early period. His father, Clark Lewis, died in 1853, at the advanced age of seventy-five, and his mother died in 1855, at the age of seventy.

Mr. Lewis passed some time at the Oxford Academy, but was educated chiefly in the common schools of his native place. He has always been engaged in agricultural pursuits, with the exception of some two years, when he kept an hotel in Oxford. In 1851 he occupied the position of Supervisor in his native town, and was chosen a Justice of the Peace in 1859. He was re-elected Supervisor in 1860, still holding the office, and was President of the Agricultural Society of Oxford and the adjoining towns in the same year. Politically he was always a staunch Whig as long as that party retained its organization, and then became a Republican, after having served a short time in the ranks of the American organization. He is a popular man at home, and sustains a respectable position as a member at Albany.

Mr. Lewis has been twice married. His first wife was Miss Marietta, daughter of Simon Turner, and his second Miss Lydia, daughter of the late Capt. Lyman Smith. He is not a church member, but belongs to the First Universalist Society of Oxford.

## WILLIAM LEWIS.

Mr. Lewis is a native of Utica, Oneida county, N. Y., where he was born on the 7th of November, 1812. He is of Welsh descent. His father, William Lewis, died in the city of New Orleans, in the year 1820, at the age of thirty-two ; and his mother, whose maiden name was Eleanor Roberts, is still living, at the advanced age of sixty-eight.

Mr. Lewis was educated in the common schools of the town of Steuben, in his native county, where he has always since been a resident. He was reared a farmer, and has always been chiefly engaged in the cultivation of the soil. During the early portion of his life he taught school some thirteen winters, and has held the office of Superintendent of Common Schools. He also held the office of Supervisor some six years, his first election taking place in 1847, and has been twenty years a Justice of the Peace. In politics he was formerly a Whig, but was among the first to enlist in the Republican movement after the repeal of the Missouri Compromise. He is a gentleman of superior personal and political popularity in the community where he resides, and was chosen a member of the House by a flattering majority.

Mr. Lewis has been twice married, and has been living with his second wife some twenty years. He has had ten children, seven of whom are living, and attends the Congregational Church, of which his wife and eldest daughter are members.

# BENJAMIN H. LONG.

MR. LONG is one of the youngest men in the House, having been born in the town of Tonawanda, Erie county, N. Y., on the 15th of October, 1832. His great-grandparents emigrated to this country from Switzerland about the year 1700, and settled in Cumberland county, Pennsylvania. His father, Benjamin Long, died at Tonawanda on the 29th of September, 1859, at the age of seventy-five; and his mother, whose maiden name was Mary Hershey, is still living, at the age of sixty-seven.

After a year's preparatory study, Mr. Long entered Dane Law School, at Cambridge, Mass., where he graduated in August, 1856. He then entered the law office of William H. Green, at Buffalo, and was admitted to the bar in November, 1857. Since then he has been engaged in the practice of his profession at Tonawanda, where he now resides. In 1858 and '59 he was a trustee of that village, and in March, 1860, was chosen its President—a position which he still holds. These were the only offices he held previous to his election to the present Legislature. Until November, 1859, he was always an enthusiastic American, of the National Conservative stamp, but since that time he has been acting with the Democratic party. He is one of the most promising young men in the House, and by his frank, generous, and affable manner has secured the respect and esteem of all his legislative companions.

Mr. Long was married on the 17th of January, 1859,

to Mrs. Almira Josselyn, widow of the late Amasa Josselyn, of Buffalo, and usually attends the Presbyterian Church.

---

## ORRIN B. LORD.

MR. LORD was born on the 9th of November, 1813, in Hamilton, Madison county, N. Y., where he has always resided. He is supposed to be of pure English descent. His father, William Lord, who was a member of the Assembly, and who was an officer in the war of 1812, drawing a pension until the time of his death, died on the 6th of November, 1855, at the age of seventy-one; and his mother, whose maiden name was Claresa Brainard, died on the 20th of June, 1834, at the age of forty-nine.

Mr. Lord was educated in the common schools of his native place, and has always been chiefly engaged in farming. He has always taken an active and deep interest in agricultural societies, and has frequently delivered addresses on the subject of agriculture, for which he has been highly applauded. He has held various town offices, including that of Justice of the Peace, which he occupied from the 1st of January, 1847, till the 1st of January, 1855. He again assumed that position on the 1st of January, 1859, and still holds the place, having always been found faithful and capable in the discharge of all its duties. In politics he was formerly a Democrat of the Barnburner school, and has been a Republican since the first organization of that

10*

party. He was chosen to his present position by a majority of about two thousand, running far ahead of his ticket in his own town, and is one of the most quiet and attentive men in the House.

Mr. Lord was married, on the 28th of October, 1838, to Miss Palmyra Sheldon, and since in Albany has been attending the Unitarian Church—that of the Rev. Dr. Mayo.

## ROBERT LOUGHRAN.

DR. LOUGHRAN is one of the youngest members of the House, having been born at Hamden, Delaware county, New York, on the 1st of July, 1835. He is of Irish and Scotch descent. His father, William Loughran, died at Windham, Greene county, in 1853, in the sixty-eighth year of his age, and his mother is still living at the advanced age of sixty-seven.

Dr. Loughran was educated at the Delhi Academy, in his native county. After leaving school he engaged in the manufacturing business, at Windham, Greene county, where his parents had removed, and remained so employed until he had accumulated money enough to carry him safely through the study of medicine, which he commenced in the office of W. G. and A. B. DeWitt, at Saugerties, Ulster county, New York. Here he remained the usual length of time required of medical students, and then entered the Albany Medical College, from which he graduated in 1857, after attending two courses of lectures. He then returned to Saugerties, where he now resides, and associated himself in the practice of his profession with the gentlemen in whose office he had studied, and with whom he is still engaged in practice. He never held any public position until his promotion to the body of which he is now a member, and has always been a genuine Republican, having cast his first vote for Colonel Fremont, in 1856, and his last for Mr. Lincoln, in 1860. He is not a brilliant representative, but possesses what is far better—that ability, industry, and promptness in the discharge of his official duties which cannot fail to secure the unqualified approbation of his constituents.

Dr. Loughran is still single, and attends the Dutch Reformed Church.

## WILLIAM J. McDERMOTT.

DR. McDERMOTT is a native of Portland, Maine, where he was born on the 5th of May, 1830. He is of Irish descent, and some of his paternal ancestors held prominent positions in the British Government. His parents are still living. When very young he was placed under the care of J. Patterson, LL.D., Principal of the Grammar school in St. John's, New Brunswick, where he remained six years. He then entered the Seminary in Fredericktown, New Brunswick. In 1846, he was sent to Paris, and entered the College Charlemagne, where he remained until 1848. On his return he entered the medical department of the University of New York, and graduated in 1852. In the winter of 1853, he again visited Germany and France, and attended a course of lectures in the Ecole de Medecine and Hôtel Dieu, in Paris. Returning to the United States, he commenced the practice of his profession in the town of Westchester, Westchester county, where he now resides, and continued to practise with increasing success, until recently, when he joined his father, Francis McDermott, in the city of New York, in the manufacturing firm of F. McDermott & Company, now F. McDermott & Son.

Dr. McDermott never held any political office until his election to the body of which he is now a member. Formerly he was an uncompromising Democrat, with some American proclivities, and ran for his present position against the Haskin candidate, whom he defeated by nine hundred and forty majority, at the same time defeating the Republican candidate by a small majority. He is a quiet man in the House, and is said by his friends to be a faithful representative.

Dr. McDermott was married some years ago to Miss S. V. Thompson, of Rhinebeck, Dutchess county, and sustains a high position in all the social relations of private life.

## HENRY McFADDEN.

MR. McFADDEN was a member of the Legislature of 1860, and occupied a position on the Standing Committee on State Prisons. There was nothing distinguishing, however, in his career during that session, and he has been returned more in consequence of the numerical strength of his party than any particular fitness on his part for the seat he occupies.

Mr. McFadden was born in Argyle, Washington county, New York, and is sixty-two years of age. He has always led the life of an industrious and respectable farmer, never having been known among his immediate neighbors for anything very remarkable, and is now a resident of Beekmantown, Clinton county, where he has been living for some years. In politics he is a Republican of the strictest sect, being thoroughly tinctured with strong Abolition views on the subject of slavery, and is understood to be utterly opposed, in the present condition of our national affairs, to any compromise involving the sacrifice of a single plank in the Chicago platform, by which he has sworn as his political Bible.

## ALONZO MACOMBER.

Mr. Macomber was born in the town of Chesterfield, Essex county, New York, on the 28th of July, 1806, and is, therefore, nearly fifty-six years of age. He is supposed to be of Scotch descent. His education was such only as the common schools of a new county would afford, and he has always been engaged in agricultural and mercantile pursuits. He has been a Justice of the Sessions, besides having been Census Marshal in 1855, and is now a Justice of the Peace, which office he has held during the past ten years.

Politically Mr. Macomber was formerly a Whig, and since the organization of the Republican party he has been one of its most active and influential supporters in Schenectady county, where he now resides. He is not a brilliant man, making no professions whatever either as a speaker or writer, but nevertheless discharges his duties in a manner that cannot fail to secure him the approbation of the great mass of his constituents.

## JOHN MARKELL.

MR. MARKELL is a native of Manheim Centre, Herkimer county, New York, where he was born on the 2d of September, 1796, and where he now resides. He is of German descent, and his parents, who were married in 1790, were both born in the town of Palatine, Montgomery county. His father, Jacob Markell, who was once a prominent member of Congress, died on the 26th of November, 1852, at the ripe old age of eighty-two; and his mother, whose maiden name was Elizabeth Snell, died on the 13th of December, in the same year, and at very nearly the same age.

Mr. Markell was educated at the Fairfield Academy, in his native county. After leaving school, he was placed in a store as clerk, and having passed the last year of his clerkship in the city of New York, returned home and went to work on his father's farm. Here he remained until his marriage to Miss Irene Clark, of Lenox, Madison county, in April, 1823, when he engaged in farming for himself. He followed this occupation until 1828, when he rented his farm, and turned his attention to mercantile pursuits. He then remained so occupied until 1831, when he sold out his stock of goods and again returned to his farm, upon which he has always since resided. In politics, he was always a Whig, until the disruption of that party, when he became an ardent Republican. He has been Postmaster where he now resides for twenty-eight years, faithfully discharging the duties of the position, and held the office of Supervisor during five successive years from 1847.

Mr. Markell's first wife having died in June, 1841, he was again married in 1842, to Miss Caroline Sherwood, who died in July, 1858. He is now single, and is a member of the Reformed Dutch Church.

## LEVI T. MARSHALL.

MR. MARSHALL was born on the 6th of February, 1808, in the town of Vernon, Oneida county, N. Y., where he now resides. He is the third son of Levi Marshall and Mary Gridley, both of whom were of New England ancestry, and who emigrated from Litchfield county, Connecticut, to the town of Vernon, as early as 1798, which was before the organization of the town, the neighborhood being then known as the "Whitestown country." Here his father, with three brothers, entered land for farming purposes at that period, but the latter becoming tired of a pioneer life, subsequently returned to their native homes. The former, however, continued to remain with his family on his first settlement, and successfully followed farming and hotel-keeping on what was then called the great Genesee road, and afterwards the Seneca turnpike, until 1818, when he died at the age of forty-six. His widow survived him thirty-seven years, and died at the advanced age of seventy-nine.

Being only ten years of age at the death of his father, Mr. Marshall received the benefits only of a common school, concluding his education at the Hamilton Academy. He was reared a farmer, and has always been successfully engaged in that occupation. In 1835, he was elected Justice of the Peace, holding the office, by re-election, to the present time, and in 1841 held the position of Supervisor. Meanwhile he became quite prominent in military affairs, having gradually arisen to the rank of Brigadier-General, under Gov. Seward, in 1839. He was prominent in the first organization of the Oneida County Agricultural Society, of which he was seven years Secretary, and subsequently President. Politically, he was formerly a Henry Clay Whig, but, in the language of the *Oswego Commercial Times*, " there lives not in the State now a *sounder* Republican or a more worthy man." He is a gentleman of high standing and influence wherever he is known, and is honest, upright, and faithful in the discharge of all his legislative duties.

Mr. Marshall was married on the 11th of April, 1832, to Miss Mary Ann, daughter of John Smith, late of Vernon, and niece of Hon. Perry Smith, formerly U. S.

Senator from Connecticut. He is a member of no church, but contributes liberally to religious purposes, and regularly attends divine service.

---

## LUCIUS S. MAY.

MR. MAY has had considerable legislative experience, having been twice before a member of the House, and is now one of the leading men on the Republican side of that body. There is nothing particularly marked in his character, but the quiet, unpretending, and efficient manner in which he discharges his duties has not failed to secure him the respect and good-will of his fellow members.

Mr. May is a native of Union village, Washington county, N. Y., where he was born in 1819. He is descended from the Pilgrim Fathers. Both his parents were from New England, and his paternal and maternal grandfathers were both gallant soldiers in the struggle for American independence. His father, Ellis May, died on the 31st of August, 1852, at the age of seventy-nine; and his mother, whose maiden name was Mary Wells, died on the 27th of February, 1859, at the advanced age of eighty.

Mr. May received an academical education, and in 1834 located in Belmont, Allegany county, where he now resides. He has always been chiefly engaged in the mercantile trade, and in agricultural pursuits, and is a gentleman of acknowledged superior business capacity wherever he is known. He has been several times elected Supervisor of the town in which he resides, and in 1853 and '55 was a member of the same branch of the Legislature to which he now belongs. In politics he was formerly a Whig, and was one among the first to enlist in the establishment of the Republican party.

Mr. May was married, on the 18th of January, 1848, to Miss Jane Acer, of Pittsford, N. Y.; and attends the Presbyterian Church.

## ABRAM V. MEKEEL.

Mr. Mekeel is one of the finest looking and most clever and agreeable gentlemen in the House. He is descended from Quaker stock, and is now about thirty-seven years of age. He hails from Schuyler county, where he is now successfully engaged in farming, and is a relative of the Hon. Isaac D. Mekeel, who represented that county in the Assembly, in 1859, and who was one of the most popular men in that body during that session.

Mr. Mekeel received an ordinary business education, and has always devoted himself almost exclusively to the cultivation of the soil. Politically he was formerly a Whig of the most conservative stamp; but like thousands of others, was easily blown from the time-honored landmarks of a former generation by the political whirlwind which succeeded the repeal of the Missouri Compromise in 1854. As a representative he is very quiet and unassuming in the discharge of all his duties, and is perhaps distinguished more by that happiest of all faculties than anything else—the faculty of quietly disguising his real ability to a far better advantage than he could publicly exercise it.

# EDWIN A. MERRITT.

Mr. Merritt was born on the 26th of February, 1828, in the town of Sudbury, Rutland county, Vermont. He sprang from unmixed English and Scotch ancestry, and is proud of the blood which flows in his veins. His paternal grandfather was a gallant soldier in the Revolution, serving with distinction, as a volunteer, during the war, and took a prominent and active part in the battle of Bunker Hill. His father, Noadiah Merritt, who was a native of Massachusetts, died on the 1st of January, 1854, at the age of seventy-two; and his mother, whose maiden name was Relief Parker, is still living, in the seventieth year of her age.

Mr. Merritt lived four years in Westport, Essex co., N. Y. He then went to St. Lawrence county, and has been residing in the town of Pierpont since 1842. He was educated principally at a common school, but was a student, during a portion of several terms, at the St. Lawrence Academy, at Potsdam, St. Lawrence county. He then worked on a farm until he was twenty-two years of age, and after spending two years at the carpenter and joiner's trade, became a surveyor and civil engineer, in which he is still engaged. He was elected Supervisor of the town of Pierpont in 1854, holding that position some three years, and in 1857 was appointed Clerk of the Board of Supervisors of St. Lawrence county, which office he still occupies.

He was a member of the last House, and occupied a position on the Standing Committees on Insurance Companies and Engrossed Bills. He was re-elected at the last election, by a large majority, and is now, as he was then, one of the most active members of that body.

He was originally a Democrat, of the Soft-shell stamp, . and, after serving some time in the ranks of the American party, became a Republican.

Mr. Merritt was married, on the 5th of May, 1858, to Miss Eliza Rich, a lady of superior worth and intelligence in every respect.

---

# DAVID MONTAGUE.

Mr. Montague is a native of Paulet, Rutland county, Vermont. He was born on the 7th of July, 1795, and is, therefore, upwards of sixty-five years of age. His ancestors were from England, and both his parents, who are now dead, were natives of Massachusetts.

Mr. Montague received a common English education, and during the winter season has been engaged in teaching for upwards of thirty years, devoting his time, meanwhile, during the summer season, to agricultural pursuits. He has held various town offices, including those of Superintendent of the Poor, and Supervisor, and in every position in which he has been called upon to serve the people is said to have been faithful and conscientious in the discharge of all his duties. He is a gentleman of exemplary habits, cool, calm, and dispassionate in everything he does, and has a peculiar faculty of minding his own business, which secures him constantly the good opinion of almost everybody.

## MARQUIS D. MOORE.

MR. MOORE was born in the town of Chesterfield, Essex county, N. Y., and is about forty years of age. He is of English and French descent. His father, Marquis D. Moore, died in that town, in 1812, and his mother died, when he was only about thirteen years of age.

Through the generosity of two elder sisters, Mr. Moore received a limited education, and his career through life has been that of an eminently successful business-man. He was for some time engaged in elastic roofing and the manufacture of chemical oil, and is now said to be occupied as an extensive builder. He is an active and influential politician in the county of Kings, where he now resides, frequently representing his ward or district in State and County Conventions, and was chosen a Member of the Assembly of 1859, by five hundred majority. He occupied a place on the Standing Committees on Incorporation of Cities and Villages during the session of that year; and was a useful and influential Member of the House. He was formerly a Whig, adhering closely to that party till it abandoned its organization, when he became an American, although acting with the Republicans since his first election in the fall of 1848. He is industrious and efficient in the discharge of his official duties, and has shown himself an excellent representative.

Mr. Moore was married in 1835, to Miss Jane E. Lester, of Albany, who is now dead, and in 1849, married Miss Jane E. Howard, of Saratoga county. He attends the Presbyterian Church, and stands well in the community where he resides.

## LEWIS H. MORGAN.

Mr. Morgan is one of the most active and ambitious men in the Legislature. The difficulty, however, with him is, that he lacks the ability to enable him successfully to gratify his ambition. His efforts are always consistent, there being seldom a question before the House upon which he does not thoroughly ventilate himself; but the more he struggles the less progress he seems to make. He is like a person upon a boggy foundation, gradually descending with every struggle for a better footing; and he is now already so far within the filthy depths, that not even a pair of stilts could scarcely save him. Meanwhile, he is too independent ever to conciliate many very warm friends in his difficulties, and unless he very materially modifies his plan of operations he will never ascend high enough in the scale of honorable distinction to gratify the aspirations of either himself or his friends. Were he to follow the example of those of the same calibre as himself, by remaining quiet in the House, he would stand much better in the estimation of his associates; but his persistent determination to thrust himself forward on all occasions upon the deliberations of that body has rendered him completely ridiculous in the eyes of all.

## AUSTIN MYERS.

Captain Myers was a Member of the last Legislature, and as such, received a large share of their abuse and hostility resulting from the defeat of the Pro Rata Freight Bill, and the bill tolling railroads; and the passage of George Law's Monster Gridiron Bill. A secret organization was formed in his district to prevent his re-election last fall; but it did not succeed, and after receiving the nomination of his Convention almost unanimously, he was again triumphantly elected. The contest, however, was one of the severest ever known in the State. His opponents, headed by Mr. Greeley and the *Tribune*, charged him with gross corruption in his last winter's career; but he successfully defended himself before the people, declaring emphatically that he never received and never expected to receive, either directly or indirectly, any compensation for any vote given by him in the Legislature; and that he had no interest in any grant, or privilege, or right conferred by any act of the last Legislature.

Captain Myers was born on the 6th of July, 1815, in Saratoga county, N. Y. He is of German extraction, his ancestors having come from Baden, during the Revolution. They were zealous Whigs, and took an active part against Great Britain. The Captain has fully carried out the virtues which he inherited. His father, Samuel Myers, was an energetic, persevering man, and although suffering losses enough to discourage any ordinary person, he started business anew in the city of New York. Having been left a widow, by his death, in 1816, Mrs. Myers, a strong-minded, brave, true-hearted woman, removed to Ballston Springs, where she married Gideon Luther.

At the age of fifteen, Captain Myers, with the approbation of his mother, came to Albany, to work at the saddle and harness business, and in September, 1833, married Miss Maria Jane Van Alstyne, the daughter of an Albany county farmer. One daughter has been the result of this marriage, who is now the wife of William P. Sabey, of Syracuse. Immediately upon his marriage, the Captain emigrated to Syracuse, where he arrived safely with only eighteen pence in his pocket, and not an acquaintance at that point. He, however, obtained work promptly, and cleared one hundred dollars the first year. He then set up for himself in the village of Jordan, and purchased, in addition, a public house, where he demonstrated that he was fully able to "keep a hotel." In 1836, he sold his property, and went back to Syracuse, where he again engaged in the saddle and harness business, which he successfully prosecuted until 1840, when he disposed of his entire stock, worth several thousand dollars, and being an enthusiastic Whig, agreed to take his pay when Harrison was elected President. With the funds thus obtained, he purchased several packet-boats; became captain of one, and placed the others in charge of friends. For ten years he steered his own craft, literally and figuratively, gaining the reputation of being the best captain on the canal. The railroad competition, however, destroyed his profits, and he transferred his capital to the transportation business, in which he has fifty thousand dollars now invested. He is also a stockholder and director in the Syracuse and Oswego Railroad, the Chicago, Iowa, and Nebraska Railroad, the Mount Vernon Railroad, in Illinois; also in the Mechanics' Bank, and the Bank of Syracuse. He is also proprietor of the Myers block, and the Courier block, and of other real estate, to the value of one hundred thousand dollars.

Captain Myers was formerly a Whig, and although now a thorough-going steadfast member of the Republican party, is not an aspirant for political distinction. He is one of the most popular men in the Legislature, and discharges his duties honestly and faithfully, to the best interests of his constituents.

11

## JOSEPH NESBITT.

MR. NESBITT is a native of the State of New Jersey, and is forty-five years of age. He is of Irish and American descent, and was reared in the city of New York, where he is now doing business. His father, Robert Nesbitt, died some years ago, as did also his mother, whose maiden name was Eliza Webb, and who was a descendant of Admiral Blake, who came to America at the settlement of Jamestown, Virginia.

Mr. Nesbitt was educated in the common schools of the city of New York, and served an apprenticeship at the book-binding business. He has always been a Democrat of the National Conservative stamp, and has always sustained an honorable and influential position in the ranks of his party. He is, both privately and politically, one of the most popular men in his district, and by his straightforward, quiet, industrious, and unpretending course in the House, has secured the good opinion of all his legislative associates—both Democrats and Republicans.

Mr. Nesbitt was married some years since to Miss Mary Ann, daughter of Jacob Fenn, of Connecticut, and is a gentleman of irreproachable standing wherever he is personally known.

# NELSON J. NORTON.

Mr. Norton was born in Great Valley, Cattaraugus county, N. Y., on the 30th of March, 1820. He is of English descent. Both his parents, Ira Norton and Lucy Perkins, came to this State from Connecticut, and are still living in Cattaraugus county, at the advanced age of seventy-six.

Mr. Norton was educated in the common schools of his native county, which were then in a very imperfect condition. He was reared on a farm, devoting a portion of his time during the winter to teaching, and subsequently occupied the post of a clerk in a store some ten years. He then engaged in the mercantile trade, on his own responsibility, some time, and has since then been successfully devoting himself to farming. In 1848, he was appointed Postmaster under General Taylor, but was afterwards removed on the accession of Mr. Fillmore to power. He was an unsuccessful candidate for the Assembly in 1852, and now holds the offices of Assessor and Supervisor in the town in which he resides.

Mr. Norton was always an old-fashioned Whig until the dissolution of that party, when he became what he now is—a staunch and unyielding Republican. He was a prominent delegate in the last Whig Convention ever held in his county, and was one among the first to enlist in the inauguration of the Republican movement.

Mr. Norton was married, in February, 1847, to Miss Mary E. Parker, of Wyoming county, and attends the Presbyterian Church.

## N. HOLMES ODELL.

MR. ODELL is now serving his second term in the Assembly, having been a member of that body in 1860. He was one of the most quiet and yet efficient men in the House during the session of that year, and occupied a prominent position in the Committee on Ways and Means. His conduct on all measures of either a local or general character, was always distinguished by a fearless and straightforward denunciation of everything of a corrupt or doubtful nature; and no one was found more unyielding than he in his opposition to the New York City Railroad Bills, which were passed over the vetoes of the Governor, and which were generally supposed to have been tainted with more or less corruption. His course on these, and all other measures on which he was called upon to act, was strongly approved by his constituents—his re-election to the present House by a majority of nearly seven hundred being unmistakable proof of that fact.

Mr. Odell was born on the 10th of October, 1828, near Tarrytown, Westchester county, N. Y. He is of Welsh and Dutch descent, and some of his ancestors were active participants in the Revolutionary War. His father, Jonathan L. Odell, who has been a successful steamboat captain on the North river for a period of thirty years, is still living, at an advanced age, as is also his mother, whose maiden name was Jane Tompkins.

Mr. Odell was educated at the Paulding Institute, at

Tarrytown. After graduating, he engaged in the mercantile trade, at the same time passing a few years in steamboating between Albany and New York, and is now doing business under the firm name of Odell & Clark, at the Tarrytown depôt. He has occupied various town offices, including that of Justice of the Peace, which he held some four years, and in every position to which the people have called him, has discharged his duties honestly, faithfully, and with entire success. He was formerly an old-line Whig, of the Henry Clay school, and was elected to the Legislature of 1860 by a union of Democrats and Americans. Since the dissolution of the Whig party, he has always acted with the American party ; but he looks upon the Democratic party as eminently national, having a permanent organization in every State in the Union, and is always ready, if necessary, to co-operate with that party in securing the defeat of the extreme sectionalism into which, he claims, the Republican party has now hopelessly degenerated. He wields a strong influence among the Democratic members of the present House, and was Chairman of the Democratic Caucus at the opening of the present session.

Mr. Odell is still single. He is an Episcopalian, and attends Christ Church, at Tarrytown, in which the late Washington Irving officiated for many years as Warden, and the Rev. Dr. Creighton as Rector.

# FRANKLIN PHILBRICK.

MR. PHILBRICK is a native of Onondaga county, N. Y., and was born on the 15th of August, 1819. He is of English and partially of Irish descent. His parents are both dead; his father, Jonathan Philbrick, having died in Cattaraugus county on the 14th of November, 1857, at the age of eighty-one, and his mother in Onondaga county on the 5th of September, 1856, at the age of seventy-one.

Mr. Philbrick received his education chiefly in the common schools of his native county. At the age of seventeen he engaged in school-teaching, which he followed during the winter for ten years, devoting himself during the summer to agricultural pursuits. In the fall of 1846 he removed into Cattaraugus county, where he pursued the mercantile trade some three years, since which time he has been farming. He was elected a Justice of the Peace in 1848, in Dayton, Cattaraugus county, and was chosen Supervisor in 1854 and '56, in the same town. In 1859 he removed into the town of Persia, where he now resides, and where he was elected a Justice of the Peace in 1860. He never failed to act with the old Whig party while it retained its organization, and is now an enthusiastic Republican, strongly opposed to the further extension of slavery. He is a gentleman of fine appearance, looking not a great deal unlike the Hon. Howell Cobb, of Georgia, and seldom fails to attract the attention of strangers as he calmly sits among his peers in the Assembly chamber.

Mr. Philbrick was married, on the 5th of October, 1847, to Miss A. Nichols, and is a member of the Episcopal Methodist Church. He is, both personally and politically, one of the most popular men in his district.

---

## GEORGE S. PIERCE.

MR. PIERCE is a native of Dutchess county, N. Y., and from the records of the Senate and Assembly, of each of which bodies he has hitherto been a member, it appears that he is now thirty-eight years of age. During his earlier years he presented all the strong points of character which he has since displayed, and having been reared upon a farm, there were few young men who could accomplish more in the field than he before he had attained the age of seventeen. His father having died when he had reached this age, he set about preparing for college, and, in 1840, entered "Old Yale," where he graduated in 1843. It was here that he acquired that ardent devotion to politics, and that ability as a speaker and legislator, for which he is now so well known. He did not follow very closely the collegiate course of instruction, however, while at college, and spent most of his time in the investigation of mooted questions, and in the discussions of the societies connected with the institution. After leaving college he spent a season at the Cambridge Law School, under the

charge of the late Judge Story and the present Senator
Sumner.

In 1854 Mr. Pierce returned to his native county, and
during the autumn of that year stumped that and the
adjoining counties for the Democracy with considerable
success. The next fall he was elected to the Assembly
for Dutchess county, by a majority of one vote, in a
poll of over ten thousand, and even this was doubtful,
so that his seat was fiercely contested. After six weeks
of controversy, however, he was sustained also in the
House by one vote, and thus became the associate with
such men as the late Governor Young; Judge Harris,
of Albany; Alvah Worden, of Cayuga; Judge Hall, of
the Northern District of New York; Judge Chatfield,
late of the U. S. Court of Minnesota; Judge Wells, of
California; Col. Crain, of Herkimer; and Samuel J.
Tilden, of New York, who were then members of the
House, and among whom he immediately took a high
standing, although the youngest man in that body. At
the close of the session, he was appointed upon a committee to inquire into alleged frauds upon the canals,
and passed the ensuing summer in such investigation.

Mr. Pierce was now admitted to the bar of the Supreme Court, but having married in the meantime, and
purchased a farm in Ulster county, where he now resides,
on the banks of the Hudson, opposite Hyde Park, he
returned to his old vocation. He has since represented
the Ulster district in the Senate, when the present Governor was a member of that body, and occupied the
important position of Chairman of the Canal Committee

His having belonged to the Barnburner section of the Democratic party easily accounts for his subsequent transition to the Republican ranks upon the repeal of the Missouri Compromise.

---

## HENRY A. PRENDERGAST.

MR. PRENDERGAST was born in the town of Ripley, Chautauqua county, N. Y., in the year 1821, and is therefore about forty years of age. His ancestors were among the earliest settlers of Western New York, and one of them was a representative in the Legislature from Niagara county as early as 1816. On his paternal side he is descended from Irish stock, and in the early anti-rent difficulties on Philip's patent, in Dutchess county, his great-grandfather, who was a native of Tipperary, Ireland, is mentioned in the Historical Collections of the State as the " Big Thunder " of that time. His maternal ancestors were real Vermonters, and his maternal great-grandfather, Capt. Abell, was a gallant soldier in the American Revolution.

Mr. Prendergast was educated at Union College, Schenectady, where he graduated in 1842. After leaving college he commenced the study of law, but before completing his studies his health became impaired, and he engaged in farming, for a time combining the cultivation of the soil, sporting, and literature, with a restoration of health. He subsequently retired to a farm of his own, in his native town, where he has always since

11*

been chiefly engaged in agricultural and mercantile pursuits. He was formerly a Whig, but always refused to enter public life until the politics of his county were changed by the sudden uprising of the American party. In the fall of 1855 he therefore accepted the nomination for the Assembly, with about one thousand American majority against him, but was triumphantly elected. He was the Republican candidate for Speaker at the opening of the following session of the Legislature, but was defeated, and was again elected to the House in the fall of the same year. He was Chairman of Committee of Ways and Means during the session of 1857, and was again one of the leading men of his party at Albany.

Mr. Prendergast is a gentleman of ability, and stands high in the body of which he is again a member. He is a good speaker, of the nervous sanguine temperament, and is one of the most active and influential men in either branch of the Legislature.

---

## ANDREW J. PROVOST.

Mr. Provost is one of the youngest and most popular men in the House, and discharges his duties with promptness and ability. He is a native of the city of New York, where he was born on the 2d of April, 1834. His ancestors were French, and came to America about the year 1635. His father, David Provost, is still living, at about the age of fifty-eight, but his mother died in April, 1855, at about the age of fifty-five.

Mr. Provost graduated at Williston Seminary, at East Hampton, Mass., and although fully prepared for college, determined to engage in mercantile pursuits, which he subsequently abandoned in favor of the law. He accordingly, in 1851, entered the law office of Messrs. Crane & Cornell, in the city of New York, where he remained until 1855, when he was admitted to the bar. Since then he has been engaged in the practice of his profession, and is now the senior member of Provost, Fisher, & Daily, in Williamsburgh. Mr. Fisher, one of his partners, was a member of the last, as he is now a member of the present House, and like his colleague in the law, is honest and faithful in the discharge of his official duties. Politically, however, they occupy different platforms, Mr. Fisher being a consistent Republican, while Mr. Provost has always been an unswerving Democrat, of the old Jeffersonian school. Mr. Provost sustains a high social position wherever he is known, and is one of the most popular young men in the Assembly.

Mr. Provost was married on the 4th of June, 1856, to Miss Harriett, daughter of Judge Obadiah Titus, of Dutchess county, who was a member of Congress in 1832. He attends the Reformed Dutch Church, of which his wife is a member.

## GIDEON RANDALL.

MR. RANDALL is the representative in the Assembly of Orleans county. He resides near East Kendall, in that county, and is said to be one of the most popular men in that section of the State. In politics he was formerly a Whig, but since the inauguration of the Republican movement he has been one among its most earnest and uncompromising supporters. He is one of the quiet men of the House, though his pleasant, sociable, free-hearted, and energetic disposition has secured him many friends in that body. He is rarely absent from his post in the discharge of his official duties, and has always been found faithful to the true interests of his constituents. He was chosen to his present position by a majority of over fifteen hundred.

## VICTOR M. RICE.

MR. RICE is, probably, the largest and most substantial-looking man in the House. He is almost a giant in stature, with great muscular power, and a broad chest and sledge-hammer arm and fist; and by his personal appearance alone, to say nothing of the other good qualities with which nature has blessed him, is well calculated to conciliate friends wherever he goes. He is a gentleman of extremely affable, sociable, and pleasing disposition, and by his industry, integrity, and active business habits, has become one of the most valuable members in either branch of the Legislature. No motives of policy, expediency, or interest—no regard for individuals or localities, and no mere personal friendships, can ever make him swerve one hair's-breadth from his line of duty; and he is not only honest and faithful himself, but he would be the last man to allow party friends to steal, by winking at schemes of public plunder, as has been too often the practice at Albany.

Mr. Rice was born on the 5th of April, 1818, in the village of Mayville, Chautauqua county, N. Y. He is of Welsh and English descent. His father, William Rice, who was a member of the Legislature about twenty years ago, from Chautauqua county, and who is now sixty-nine years of age, is, at present, a resident of Waupaca, Wisconsin; but his mother, whose maiden name was Rachel Waldo, died in 1857, at the age of sixty-four. Both his parents were natives of Washington county.

Mr. Rice was educated at Allegheny College, in Crawford county, Pa., where he graduated with credit in September, 1841. After leaving college, he taught some eight months, when he entered the Clerk's office in Chautauqua county, and commenced the study of the law with the late William Smith. He remained here till June, 1843, when he went to Buffalo, where he has always since resided, and where, in the fall of the same year, he took charge of the Buffalo High School. He then had charge of this institution some three years, after which he passed some time as editor of the *Cataract*, which subsequently became the *Western Temperance*

*Standard.* He was employed in the public schools of the city of Buffalo from 1848 until January, 1854, during the latter three years of which time he was City Superintendent of Schools. In the spring of 1854, he was elected State Superintendent of Public Instruction, which he held until 1857, acquitting himself in the discharge of the duties of the position with credit to himself and entire satisfaction to the people. In politics he was formerly a Whig, and is now a leading Republican.

Mr. Rice was married, in 1846, to Miss Maria Louisa Winter, and occupies a high position in all the social relations of private life.

## CHARLES RICHARDSON.

Mr. RICHARDSON is a native of the town of Fairfax, Franklin county, Vermont, and was born on the 5th of October, 1814. His parents were both New Englanders; and his mother, whose name, before marriage, was Lucinda Taylor, and who was left a poor widow in 1816, with three small children, is still living, at the advanced age of seventy-two.

On the 6th of July, 1822, Mr. Richardson removed, with his mother, to Morristown, New York, on the shores of Black Lake, where she still resides, a widow, never having married the second time. In 1832, he finished his education, which was confined to the customary English branches, at the St. Lawrence Academy, in Jefferson county, and besides teaching some seven years, has since then always been an energetic and successful farmer. 'Prior to the organization of the Republican party, he was identified with the Whigs, and has filled various town offices, including that of Justice of the Peace, which he occupied from 1840 until '56, and that of Superintendent of Common Schools, which he held from 1844 until '52. He was, also, elected Supervisor in 1857, and still occupies that position.

He was a Member of the Assembly in 1860, and served during that session on the Standing Committee on Agriculture. He is a quiet and industrious member of the House, and has been found honest and faithful in the discharge of his public duties.

Mr. Richardson was married, on the 22d of January, 1837, to Miss Susannah Raught, and chiefly attends the Universalist Church.

## MARTIN ROBERTS.

Mr. Roberts is of English descent, and was born at Eaton, Madison county, N. Y., on the 10th of September, 1807. His father, Martin Roberts, after serving under a commission in the war of 1812, removed with his family to Pittsford, now Henrietta, in 1814—a pioneer in a new country, clearing and improving a large farm, upon which he continued to reside until his death, on the 28th of February, 1829, at the age of forty-nine.

His wife, the mother of the subject of this sketch, whose maiden name was Anna Heminway, died on the 12th of October, 1849, in the seventy-sixth year of her age, at Antwerp, Van Buren county, Michigan, while visiting her daughter, the wife of the Hon. Morgan L. Fitch.

Mr. Roberts was educated at Monroe Academy, in Henrietta, with a view to agricultural pursuits, in which he has always since been engaged, on the old homestead, where he still resides. He was appointed by Gov. Marcy a Captain in the 220th Regiment of Infantry, New York Militia, on the 21st of January, 1833. In 1835 he was elected Inspector of Common Schools, and the following year Commissioner of Highways, and has been five times re-elected to the latter office, holding it at the present time. In 1859, he was chosen a member of the Board of Managers of the Monroe County Agricultural Society, for a term of three years. In politics, he was originally a Democrat, and supported Jackson and Van Buren at the time of their election to the Presidency. He afterwards acted with the Freesoil or Liberty party, and supported Mr. Birney in 1844; Mr. Van Buren in 1848; and Mr. Hale in 1852. He has been a member of the Republican party from its first organization.

Mr. Roberts was married on the 25th of March, 1830, to Miss Frances A., daughter of Capt. Jonathan Whipples, of Pittsford, Monroe county, and usually attends the Congregational Church.

# LUCIUS ROBINSON.

MR. ROBINSON was a Member of the Assembly in 1860, to which he was chosen by a large majority, and was one of the strongest and most influential men in that body. As a leading member of the Judiciary Committee, he was always found prompt and faithful in the discharge of all his duties; and his course upon the floor of the House was alike creditable to himself and satisfactory to his constituents. He was, consequently, returned again at the last election by an increased majority, and lacked only a few votes of receiving the nomination for Speaker at the opening of the present session in the Republican caucus. It is generally conceded that he is, intellectually at least, the strongest man in the present House. He is a good speaker, but is not a frequent talker, and entitles himself as much by his diligence and industry, as by his abilities, to the confidence of the constituency he represents.

Mr. Robinson is a native of Windham, Greene county, N. Y., and was born on the 4th of November, 1810. He is a lineal descendant of the Rev. John Robinson, from whose church the Plymouth Colony sprang. His father, Eli P. Robinson, was a farmer in the town of Windham, and was among its first settlers, having emigrated from Connecticut very early in life. He was also a captain of militia during the whole of the war of 1812, and served at Sackett's Harbor and on Long Island.

Mr. Robinson was educated at the Delaware Academy, at Delhi, Delaware connty, N. Y. He first studied law with Gen. Root, and subsequently with the Hon. Amasa J. Parker, and was admitted to the bar in 1832. He then commenced the practice of the law at Catskill, Greene county, N. Y., in 1833, and during the years 1837, '38, and '39, was District Attorney of that county. In 1839 he removed to the city of New York. In 1843, he was appointed Master in Chancery by Gov. Bouck, and was re-appointed by Gov. Wright in 1846, holding the position until the Court of Chancery ceased to exist. He continued in the successful practice of his profession in New York until 1855, when, his health failing in consequence of excessive labor, he retired to the county of Chemung, where he has always since been a resident, and where he occupies a deservedly high position. In politics he was always a Democrat of the Silas Wright and Freesoil school, until the formation of the Republican party, and since then has been one of its most strenuous and unyielding supporters, of the National, Conservative stamp. He is a strong compromise man in our present national difficulties, and no one in the Legislature has done more than he to restore peace and quiet to the country.

Mr. Robinson was married, in 1833, to Miss Eunice Osborn, of Windham, and enjoys a high degree of personal as well as political popularity.

## MASON SALISBURY, 2d.

Mr. Salisbury was born on the 9th June, 1810, in the town of Sunderland, Bennington County, Vermont. He is descended from New England stock, his grandparents having been natives of Connecticut and Massachusetts. His father, Reuben Salisbury, was born on the 15th of September, 1776, in Shaftsbury, Bennington county, where he resided until about the age of twenty-one, when he married Miriam Streater, the mother of the subject of this sketch. Having been married, they continued to reside in Shaftsbury, subsequently at Hoosick, N. Y., and at Sunderland, until October, 1822, when they removed to Richland, now Sandy Creek, Oswego County, N. Y., where his wife died in 1851, at the age of seventy-three. About two years afterwards, Mr. Lewis's father was again married, and lived with his second wife until the 11th of June, 1856, when he died in the eightieth year of his age. He had held various civil offices during his lifetime, and was quite a prominent military man, having held a commission in the war of 1812.

Mr. Salisbury received a common English education in his native place and at Sandy Creek, where he now resides. He was brought up principally to farming, and since the age of twenty has been successfully engaged in milling; also, in 1838, he held the office of Town Clerk in Oswell, Oswego county; in 1839, that of Supervisor in the same town; and in 1840 removed to Sandy Creek. He was elected Justice of the Peace at the latter place in 1845, and still occupies that position. Previous to the organization of the Republican party, he belonged to the old Whig organization, and has always taken more or less part in politics.

Mr. Salisbury was married on the 10th of June, 1833, at the village of Delhi, Delaware county, N. Y., to Miss Mary Olmstead, and attends the Baptist Church.

---

# RICHARD K. SANFORD.

MR. SANFORD was born in Volney, Oswego county, N. Y., on the 25th of July, 1822. His father was Kingsbury E. Sanford, a native of Hartford, Connecticut. He resided during his early life in Warren, Herkimer county, and removed to Oswego county, in 1816. He married Miss Sophia Falley, at Oswego Falls, about the year 1820, and the subject of this sketch was their first child.

Mr. Sanford entered Hamilton College in 1839, and graduated in 1843, taking one of the highest honors of his class. He became a Teacher at Middlebury Academy, in Wyoming county, and at other institutions, remaining so engaged until about 1855, when he settled upon a farm in Volney. In 1858, he abandoned his farm and purchased the *Fulton Patriot and Gazette*, and has been since that time its editor. Unexpectedly to himself, he was last fall nominated for the position he now occupies, and was elected by an unprecedented majority. In politics he was formerly a radical Democrat, and voted for Hale and Julian in 1852. In 1854, he united with the Republican party. Although a political editor, he has but little taste for the usual appliances of partisanship, preferring to wage a contest of principle to winning an ephemeral triumph by the intrigues and tricks of the caucus.

Mr. Sanford was married, in 1848, to Miss Lucy A. Carrier, by whom he had two children, and who died in May, 1859, after a protracted illness and insanity. He is a member of the Presbyterian Church in the village of Fulton, where he resides, and sustains an excellent social position.

## CHARLES J. SAXE.

Mr. Saxe is the oldest of four brothers, whose aggregate height is twenty-four feet, and one of whom is John G. Saxe, the celebrated poet. He is a native of the Green Mountain State, where he was born on the 25th of March, 1814. He is of German descent on his father's side, and English on his mother's. His father, the Hon. Peter Saxe, who was a brother of the wife of Colonel J. B. Scovell, of Cambria, N. Y., died at that place on the 27th of May, 1839, at the age of fifty-nine; and his mother, whose maiden name was Elizabeth Jewett, is still living, at the age of seventy-one.

Mr. Saxe was educated at his native place, Highgate, Franklin county, Vermont, and at St. Albans, in that State, and pursued an academical course. When a boy he followed farming and merchandizing in his father's store. He also assisted in his father's grist and saw-mill, and was for fifteen years a merchant in his native place and at St. Albans. He came direct to New York from Vermont in March, 1851, and located at Troy, where he has since, as the senior partner of the firm of Saxe & Avery, been the most extensive wholesale lumber commission merchant at that place. From the age of sixteen until he was twenty-six years old, he was Surveyor of his native county, and from 1835 until 1840 was Postmaster at Saxe's Mills. He was also several years Trustee of the U. S. Deposit Fund at St. Albans, and occasionally held the office of Justice of the Peace. He is now Vice-President of the Market Bank of Troy, and occupies a high position in that city. In politics he has never faltered in his devotion to the principles and policy of the old Democratic party, and ranks high among the members of that party, as well as among his political opponents in the present House.

Mr. Saxe was married on the 22d of February, 1843, to Miss Susan Maria Baker, grand-daughter of Judge Hammond, late of Pittsford, Vermont, who died in 1847. He then, on the 22d of February, 1853, married his present wife, Miss Ellen, daughter of the Hon. Thomas Griggs, of Massachusetts, and belongs to the Methodist Episcopal Church.

# OLIVER P. SCOVELL.

MR. SCOVELL is a native of Orwell, Rutland, now Addison county, Vermont, where he was born on the 24th of March, 1820. His paternal ancestors were genuine Yankees, and his maternal German, the latter having belonged to the Royal Family of Saxe-Gotha, Germany, from which Prince Albert, of England, and all the Saxes of this country—including John G. Saxe, the famous poet—are descended. His father, Josiah B. Scovell, died in December, 1855, at Cambria, Niagara county, N. Y., in the seventy-third year of his age; and his mother died at the same place, in March, 1859, at the same age.

Mr. Scovell came to the State of New York in 1836, taking up his residence at Cambria, Niagara county, and received a good business education at the Lewiston Academy. On becoming of age, he worked two years in clearing up a new farm in Eaton county, Michigan, after which he served two years as a clerk in a store and post-office in Orleans county in this State. He was then engaged some six years in the canal forwarding business in the city of New York, and was subsequently employed as the agent of the Rutland and Burlington Railroad in Boston. He was then the travelling agent for a short time of the Albany and Rutland Railroad, and is now engaged in farming at Lewiston, Niagara county, where he resides. In politics he was formerly a Whig, of the woolly-head school, and is now an enthusiastic and thoroughgoing Republican. He enjoys a high degree of personal popularity wherever he is known, and though among the most quiet men in the House, is regarded as a gentleman of sound judgment and more than ordinary ability.

Mr. Scovell was married, on the 22d of November, 1846, to Miss Elizabeth E., only daughter of Leonard and Nancy A. Shepard. He was again married on the 1st of May, 1855, to Miss Elizabeth E., eldest daughter of Philo and Eliza Jewett, of Middlebury, Vermont, and is an elder in the Presbyterian Church.

## JOHN J. SHAW.

Mr. Shaw was a member of the Assembly in 1859, and occupied a position, during the session of that year, on the Standing Committee on Commerce and Navigation. He is a giddy-headed, well-dressed young man, of very ordinary ability—one of those who are constantly so swollen and inflated with the gas of glory and self-conceit, that the whole universe is scarcely large enough for them to turn around in, and who tread upon other folks' corns with the same unconcern that a jackass dances among chickens. His occupation in life has very properly been that of merchandizing, and it is impossible to disguise the fact, that he is far better calculated to figure successfully with a yardstick in one hand, and a piece of dry-goods in the other, than he is to shine in the Legislative Halls of the State.

Mr. Shaw is a native of the city of New York, and is

about twenty-eight years of age. He is descended from pure Anglo-Saxon stock, and is the son of James Shaw, who is a gentleman of standing and influence wherever he is known. He was educated in his native city, where he has always been engaged in the mercantile trade. Politically he was originally a Whig, and since the organization of the Republican party has been one among the most unyielding supporters of its principles and policy. He is said to be a young man of some personal popularity in the circle in which he moves; and this, perhaps, is the only qualification he possesses for the position with which his constituents have intrusted him.

## GILBERT SHERER.

MR. SHERER is a quiet, industrious farmer, residing at Penn Yan, Yates county, and was chosen a member of the Assembly by over six hundred majority. He was formerly a Whig, of the Seward school, and was one among the first to enlist in the organization of the Republican party. He is a practical, self-made man, of ordinary ability, and is distinguished in the House more by his quiet, unassuming manner, than any very brilliant discharge of his representative duties.

# HORATIO N. SHERWOOD.

MR. SHERWOOD is a clever, agreeable, and intelligent gentleman, and stands well as a member of the Assembly. He is not a star of the first magnitude, but nevertheless shines with an intensity of brilliancy which is not very far surpassed by that of some of the larger bodies in our legislative constellation.

Mr. Sherwood is of genuine American descent, and was born in the city of New York, where he now resides. His father, Willet Sherwood, who was a gentleman of high respectability and influence, died in January, 1836, in Greenwich, Connecticut, at the age of forty-nine ; and his mother died in August, 1858, at the age of sixty-one. Mr. Sherwood was educated in his native city, with a view to mercantile pursuits, and was nine years engaged in the wholesale dry-goods business. He was afterwards engaged in the grocery trade some two or three years. In 1855 he was Assistant Deputy Register of the city of New York, and occupied the position of Deputy Collector of Assessments from 1856 until 1858. He was formerly a straightforward and uncompromising Whig, and has been a staunch Republican since the organization of that party.

Mr. Sherwood was married, on the 30th of January, 1858, to Miss Elizabeth A., only daughter of Capt. Moody D. and Elizabeth Cook, of Newburyport, Mass.

## JOSIAH SHULL.

Mr. Shull was born on the 5th of January, 1820, in the town of Danube, Herkimer county, New York, and is of German descent. His maternal great-grandfather, Jacob G. Klock, was a Revolutionary soldier, and stood prominently forth during his lifetime as a County Judge, and member of both branches of the Legislature, from 1778 until 1787. His paternal grandfather, John Jose Scholl, who came to the State of New York in 1769, also took part in the Revolutionary struggle, holding the position of ensign, and was at the battle of Oriskany when General Herkimer was wounded. Mr. Shull's father, Jacob Schull, died in Danube, on the 19th of January, 1859, at the age of sixty-six; and his mother, whose maiden name was Anna Klock, is still living, at the age of sixty-two.

Mr. Shull received his education at the Fairfield and Herkimer Academies, devoting most of his time to mathematics, and was educated with a view to farming and surveying. He successfully followed these occupations until some five years ago, since which time he has devoted himself chiefly to engineering. He held the office of Town Superintendent in his native town, during the years 1847, '48, '49, and '50, and was elected to his present position by a flattering majority. He was always a Whig of the strictest sect until 1855, when he became a Republican. He is one of the most quiet, agreeable, and useful men in the present House.

Mr. Shull was married, on the 26th of January, 1843,

to Miss Sarah M. daughter of Thomas Stafford, and attends the Universalist and Reformed Dutch Church.

## HIRAM SMITH, 2D.

MR. SMITH is a native of the town of Hanover, Chautauqua county, New York, and was born on the 25th of October, 1819. His mother, who died in April, 1852, was a native of the State of New York, and his father, Rodney B. Smith, who is still living, at the advanced age of sixty-two, was born in Massachusetts.

Mr. Smith attended the common schools of his native county until 1836, when he passed some two years at the Fredonia Academy. He was educated for no particular calling, and during the past sixteen years has been extensively engaged in the mercantile, milling, and distilling business. He has, from time to time, been Town Clerk of his native town, where he still resides, and has been Supervisor during five successive years. He was a member of the last House, and during that session was a member of the Standing Committee on Internal Affairs of Towns and Counties, and the Select Committees on a Pro-Rata Freight Law, and the Rights of Persons to Personal and Civil Liberty in this State. He was always a Democrat, of the radical school, voting for Mr. Van Buren for the Presidency in 1848, and in 1856 became thoroughly identified with the Republican party. Mr. Smith was married, on the 10th of September, 1844, to Melissa P. Love, of the town of Hanover, and confines himself, in his attendance upon divine worship, to no particular church or denomination. He was re-elected to his present position by a largely increased majority, and is one of the most popular men in his district.

## HENRY P. SMITH.

Mr. Smith is a native of the town of Bolton, Warren county, New York, and is about forty years of age. He is a cousin of the Hon. Perry Smith, formerly United States Senator from Connecticut, and is descended from genuine Yankee stock, both his parents having been born in Connecticut. His father, Isaac Smith, who removed to Michigan in 1832, died in that State on the 16th of September, 1840, at the age of sixty-nine; and his mother, whose maiden name was Phebe Platt, died in the village of Lockport, on the 14th of October, 1841, at the age of sixty-eight.

Mr. Smith was educated in Niagara county, where his father located in 1819, when the former was only eight years of age. Having obtained a good business education, he embarked in the mercantile trade in 1836, and two years afterwards also engaged in the lumber business, which he has always since successfully followed. He never held any prominent public position until his election to the present House, and has never aimed higher than to be simply and emphatically a business man, an aim in which he has been eminently successful. In politics he was formerly a strong Whig, of the Silver

Grey school, voting for Mr. Fillmore for the Presidency in 1856, and subsequently acted with the American party; but in the last Presidential contest he supported Mr. Lincoln, and is now a conservative Republican. He is a gentleman of great personal and political popularity in the district where he resides, and is perhaps the only man who could, under the circumstances, have defeated his opponent for the Assembly. He is perfectly honest, upright, and faithful in the discharge of the duties of his new position, and his sound judgment and strong common sense render him one of the most substantial and influential men in either branch of the Legislature.

Mr. Smith was married on the 6th of May, 1841, to Miss Christiana, daughter of the late Benjamin Long, and is a member of the Presbyterian Church.

## JEFFREY SMITH.

Mr. Smith is one of the oldest men in the House, having been born on the 15th of May, 1801, in that part of Chemung county which was then Newtown, Tioga county, N. Y. His paternal ancestors were English, and his mother's family were of French and German extraction. His father, Caleb Smith, died on the 13th of January, 1839, at the age of seventy-six, and his mother died on the 15th of March, 1841, at the age of seventy-four.

Mr. Smith was educated in the common schools of Steuben county, where he now resides. He was reared a farmer, and has always been engaged in the cultivation of the soil. From 1828 until 1853 he held various town offices, including that of Supervisor, and in 1844 was a member of the Legislature. In 1832 he was appointed Adjutant of the 232d Regiment, and in 1834 was chosen Major. He held the latter position about a year, when he was elected Colonel of the same regiment, holding the place some four years, and then resigned. In politics he was always a Democrat, of the Jeffersonian and Jackson school, and was a Barnburner in 1847. He supported Mr. Van Buren for the Presidency in 1848, and Mr. Hale for the same office in 1852. In 1856 he was an enthusiastic advocate of Col. Fremont, and in the late Presidential contest voted for Mr. Lincoln. He has always been a persistent stickler for principle in politics, as in everything else, and has never been known to permit party discipline to infringe upon his political principles. He is very quiet and industrious in the discharge of his duties as a member of the House, and is well liked by all his legislative associates.

Mr. Smith was married in 1825, and is a member of the Presbyterian branch of the church.

---

## SEYMORE E. SMITH.

Mr. Smith is a native of the State of New York, and is supposed to be of true Anglo-Saxon descent. When quite young he removed with his parents into one of the Western States, but owing to the dangerous prevalency of fever and ague in the neighborhood in which they had settled, the family subsequently returned to this State.

Mr. Smith received an ordinary English education, and has always been engaged in teaching during the winter season, and in agricultural pursuits during the summer months. He has always been more or less of a politician in the town in which he resides, but was never called upon to serve the people in any official capacity until his election to the present Legislature. His politics are of the extreme Republican or Abolition school, and he is strongly opposed to the alleged right of secession, believing that although the just rights of all governments derive their authority from the consent of the governed, yet the only effectual mode of preserving the Union is to bring into requisition the bayonet and the sword.

## JAMES SUMNER, JUN.

Mr. Sumner is a practical farmer, and a fair representative. It is perhaps unnecessary, however, to state that this is his first prominent appearance in public life. Although a gentleman of respectability, his qualifications are not such as to justify the people of his neighborhood in intrusting him with any very important position ; and his present distinction as a member of the Legislature is owing more, doubtless, to the numerical strength of his party than to any peculiar force of his own. Nevertheless he is a man of strict integrity, upright and honorable in all his dealings, and has not failed to secure the personal friendship of any of his legislative companions with whom he has, as yet, come in contact.

## STEPHEN TABER.

MR. TABER was born at Dover, Dutchess county, N. Y., on the 7th of March, 1821. His father, Thomas Taber, an honest and energetic farmer, is still living, at the advanced age of seventy-five; and his mother, whose maiden name was Phebe Titus, died in 1824, at comparatively an early age.

Mr. Taber received an academical education, and has always been successfully engaged in farming. He was a member of the Assembly a year ago, and occupied a prominent position on the Standing Committee on Railroads. He is one of the solid men of the House, and although modest and unassuming to an unusual degree, possesses qualities which fit him well for a legislative position. He is a plain, practical man—one of the people, and is highly conservative in his views on all great questions of a State or National character. He has always been a straightforward, consistent Democrat, of the more conservative class, and there are but few men in the section of the State where he resides who wield a greater influence among their political friends. No one, however, has been less ambitious of political preferment, and he has always contented him-

12*

self with quietly pursuing his occupation, as an honest and industrious farmer.

Mr. Taber was married in 1845 to Miss Rosetta Townsend, and belongs to the Quaker church. He stands high in all the social relations of life, and is, both personally and politically, one of the most popular men in Queens county, where he now resides.

---

## JOHN D. TOWNSEND.

MR. TOWNSEND is a son of the late John R. Townsend, of the City of New York, and is one of the same family to which the Townsends of the City of Albany belong. He is a native of the City of New York, and is now twenty-six years of age. He is descended from pure English stock.

Mr. Townsend was educated at Columbia College, and studied law with ex-President Fillmore, who was then the senior partner of the firm of Fillmore and Sprague, in the City of Buffalo. He was admitted to the bar some two years ago, and has since then been successfully engaged in the practice of his profession. In politics he has always been a national conservative Democrat, although voting, on one occasion, for Mr. Fillmore on personal considerations, and bids fair to attain a prominent rank among the leading spirits of his party. He is attentive and industrious in the discharge of the duties of his position as a member of the House, and acquits himself in a manner which can scarcely fail to secure him the unqualified approbation of the constituents he has the honor to represent.

## BENJAMIN TURNER, JUN.

MR. TURNER was born on the 20th of December, 1815, in the then town of Marbletown, now the town of Olive, Ulster county, New York. He is of pure English descent, and is a brother of the Rev. William E. Turner, quite a prominent minister in the Dutch Reformed Church. His father, Benjamin Turner, is still living at the advanced age of seventy-four, but his mother died on the 15th March, 1858, at the good old age of seventy-seven. Both his father and paternal grandfather emigrated to Ulster county from New Milford, Connecticut, as early as 1791.

Mr. Turner was educated in the common schools of his native place, where he now resides. He was reared on a farm, and was engaged in teaching and agricultural pursuits until 1840, when he devoted his time almost exclusively to farming until 1848. He was then employed in the mercantile trade until 1855, when he abandoned it, and devoted himself entirely to the practice of the law, for which he had previously prepared himself, and in which he is still chiefly engaged. He has held various unimportant town offices, including that of Justice of the Peace, which he successfully filled some four years. Politically he was originally a Whig, and is now an uncompromising Republican. He has shown much more than ordinary ability in the House, and although one of the most quiet and unostentatious men in that body, is honest and capable in the faithful discharge of all his official duties.

Mr. Turner was married, on the 15th of November, 1840, to Miss Laura Ann, daughter of James Morten, of Massachusetts, and a sister of Dr. W. T. G. Morten, and belongs to the Methodist Church.

## JAMES H. TUTHILL.

Mr. Tuthill is a gentleman of ability and influence, and occupies a good position in the House. He is always at his post in the discharge of his duties, and usually participates in the more important debates in that body.

Mr. Tuthill is descended from English stock, and was born at Wading River, Long Island, on the 19th of February, 1826. He is a son of Nathaniel Tuthill, who, together with his mother, died at Greenport some years since. He was educated at Williams College, Massachusetts, from which he graduated in 1846, and is now engaged in the practice of the law as one of the firm of Miller & Tuthill, at Riverhead, Long Island. Previous to the organization of the Republican party he was always a zealous, consistent Whig, and is now a Republican.

Mr. Tuthill was married in 1850, and attends the Congregational Church. He occupies a high social position in the community in which he lives, and enjoys a high degree of personal popularity at Albany.

---

## GEORGE W. VARIAN.

MR. VARIAN is a native of the City of New York, where he now resides, and is fifty-one years of age. He is of French and German extraction, and has been one of the most successful business men in the Metropolitan City. Although always a staunch, unyielding Democrat, of the old Gen. Jackson school, he never filled any very prominent public position until his election to the Legislature of 1860, where he occupied an influential position on the Standing Committee on Banks, and on the Select Committee on Petitions, asking for the passage of a Pro Rata Freight law to be applied to railroads. He is, doubtless, one of the most substantial and influential men in the House, and although very quiet and unpretending in the discharge of his duties, has already shown himself a capable and efficient representative.

## DAVID J. WAGER.

MR. WAGER is a native of Leroy, Jefferson county, New York, where he was born on the 16th of May, 1812. He is of German extraction, and both of his parents were natives of Rensselaer county. His mother died at the age of seventy, on the 15th of December, 1857, in Philadelphia, Jefferson county, where he now resides.

Mr. Wager received an academical education, and has always been engaged in the practice of the law. He held the office of County Judge for four years, from January, 1856, and in 1859 was re-elected to the same position, where he is now serving his second term. He belonged to the Democratic party from 1833 until 1848, when he voted for Mr. Van Buren for the Presidency. In 1855 he united with the Republican party, to which he still belongs. He entertains strong anti-slavery views, and by his course, thus far, in the House, has exhibited a determined opposition to anything like humiliating concessions to the South in the present difficulty with the North.

Mr. Wager was married, on the 27th of November, 1851, to Miss Sophronia Bodman, of Theresa, and is a member of the Presbyterian Church.

# WILLIAM WALSH.

MR. WALSH was the youngest man in the last Legislature, and is one of the youngest and most clever young men in the present. He was born in the parish of Caharconlish, Ireland, on the 1st of December, 1836, and is, therefore, only twenty-four years of age. He came to America in 1839, with his parents, who are still living, and took up his residence in the city of New York, where he has always since resided. He was educated in the public schools of that city, and was chiefly engaged in mechanical pursuits until 1857, after which he followed the liquor trade, until his election to his present position.

Mr. Walsh has always been a Democrat of the National Conservative stamp, as is also his father, who, before leaving the fatherland, belonged to the Repealers of the O'Connell school. He occupies a popular position in the local politics of the district in which he resides, and is proud of the Democratic constituency which he has the honor to represent in the popular branch of the Legislature. He is a young man of some ability, attending closely to the discharge of the duties with which he has been intrusted at Albany, and deserves very great credit for having attained his present distinction at so young an age, through his own industry and perseverance. He is perfectly plain, unpretending, and strictly democratic in all his public and private habits, and is personally one of the most popular men in the New York Delegation, this winter, at Albany.

Mr. Walsh was married, in May, 1857, to Miss Martin, daughter of Charles Martin, of the county of Sligo, Ireland, and attends the Roman Catholic Church.

---

## DANIEL WATERBURY.

MR. WATERBURY was born in 1828, in the town of Franklin, Delaware county, New York. His father, Rev. Daniel Waterbury, who graduated at Union College, and was for many years an eminent, beloved, and respected Presbyterian clergyman in Andes, Franklin, and Delhi, Delaware county, and who was chiefly instrumental in the establishment of the Delaware Literary Institute, died at Warsaw, Wyoming county, on the 22d of December, 1838, at the age of forty-five; and his mother, whose maiden name was Mary Lewis Grant, and who was a most estimable woman, died on the 3d of July, 1838, at the age of forty-two.

Mr. Waterbury, being left an orphan at the age of ten, with his brothers and sisters, was reared and educated by his maternal uncle, Col. Asa Grant, a brother of Major Arvey Grant, and an extensive farmer, who enacted a prominent part in the war of 1812, and in the Legislature of 1822 and 1823, and who died in 1853, leaving his property to the subject of this sketch, together with his brothers and sister, having no children of his own.

Mr. Waterbury's grandparents, Daniel Waterbury, who successfully bore the American flag through several engagements in the Revolutionary struggle, and who died a Revolutionary pensioner, and Mary Stevens Waterbury, were both natives of Connecticut. His maternal grandparents, John Grant and Mary Lewis, were also natives of New England—the former of Connecticut, the latter of Rhode Island—and, like his grandparents, settled in Delaware county. His great-grandfather Stevens was killed by the British and Tories in the attack on Danbury, Connecticut. His great-grandfathers, Lewis and Grant, were both magistrates and captains of trained bands, previous to the Revolution, holding their commissions, still preserved, from George II. He had seven great-uncles, all of whom were officers in the Revolution. Dr. Robert L. Waterbury, physician and scientific lecturer, of New York city, and Prof. E. P. Waterbury, of the Albany Academy, are both his brothers. His sister married Col. G. D. Wheeler.

Mr. Waterbury received his early education in a common district school, afterwards attending at different times the Delaware Literary Institute, and Delhi and Fergusonville Academies, and graduated at the State Normal School in 1848. After spending some time in teaching, mostly in the city of Hudson, he graduated, with honor, at Union College, in the class of 1854, and is a member of the Phi Beta Kappa Society. He then graduated at the Poughkeepsie Law School, and having been admitted to the bar, commenced the practice of his profession in New York city. In 1857, on the death of the widow of Col. Grant, his uncle and former guardian, he returned to his native county, where he has since been engaged in legal and agricultural pursuits. He was chosen magistrate in the winter of 1860, and in the fall of the same year was, without his solicitation, and when absent from home, nominated for the position he now occupies in the House. He has been identified with the Republican party since its first organization, and is the first straight-out Republican ever elected from his district. He is unmarried, and attends the Presbyterian Church.

## STEPHEN V. R. WATSON.

MR. WATSON was born in June, 1817, in the town of Rensselaerville, Albany county, N. Y., and is of English descent. He is a son of Rufus Watson, who, together with his mother, died in Rensselaerville some years since. His education was confined to the common schools of his native place, and he commenced active life as a clerk in the city of New York. He subsequently was engaged some ten years in the mercantile trade in the city of Albany, and in 1846, embarked in the real estate business in the city of Buffalo, where he now resides. He has also, since then, been engaged in various railroad enterprises, and sustains the reputation wherever he is known of a shrewd, competent business man.

Mr. Watson never held any prominent official position until his election to the present House, but he is nevertheless looked upon by all his legislative associates as one of the most valuable men in that body. Politically he was originally a Whig, and since the organization of the Republican movement has been a member of that party. He is a gentleman of conceded merit in the community in which he lives, and is at present President of the Buffalo Street Railroad, Vice-President of the Erie County Savings Bank, and Receiver of the Lake Navigation Company.

Mr. Watson was married in July, 1848, to his present wife, Miss Charlotte, daughter of P. C. Sherman, Esq., of Buffalo, and attends the Episcopal church.

## SAMUEL T. WEBSTER.

MR. WEBSTER is a native of the city of Boston, where he was born on the 7th of November, 1820. He is descended from good old Revolutionary stock, and his parents, who were married in 1818, came to the city of New York in the year 1823. His father, Samuel M. Webster, who was a gentleman of superior character and influence, died in 1834, at the age of thirty-five; and his mother, whose maiden name was Sarah Warren Bacon, a daughter of Capt. Joseph Bacon, of Roxbury, Massachusetts, is still living at the advanced age of sixty-two.

Mr. Webster attended the public schools in the city of New York, until the age of fourteen, when, at his father's death, he became an apprentice at the silversmith's trade. Subsequently, he became a painter, which he followed successfully until January, 1852, when he received the appointment of first clerk in the Bureau of Streets, under the Hon. Henry Arcularius, Commissioner of Streets and Lamps, and the present popular member from the Sixteenth District—a position which he still occupies, and in which he introduced the present admirable method of keeping the public accounts in that branch of the city Government. In politics he has always been a bold, fearless, and uncompromising Democrat, of the broad, national, conservative school, and is one among the most ardent friends and admirers of Fernando Wood. During the past four or five years he has represented, in part, the Tenth Ward, in the Democratic Republican General Committee of Tammany Hall, and had the distinguished honor of being chosen Secretary of that body in 1856 and '57. He was also one of the Secretaries of the Joint Committee, at the time of the consolidation of the Small and Savage Committees, and ranks high among the better class of politicians in the city of New York. He was a member of the Assembly, a year ago, and was one among the most popular and influential men in that body. He was uncompromisingly opposed to all the New York City Railroad bills, and all other similar schemes, including the Sunday Laws, relating to that city, and introduced and pushed through the House the bill providing against the erection of unsafe buildings. There was no one, perhaps, who surpassed him in the efficiency and fidelity with which he discharged all his duties in that body, and the largely increased majority by which he has been returned as a member clearly shows the unqualified approbation with which his constituents received his entire course.

He is a gentleman of fine social and intellectual qualities, enjoying a high degree of personal and political popularity both at home and abroad, and is again one of the most useful men in the Legislature.

Mr. Webster was married, in May, 1846, to Miss Sarah Warren, daughter of John Smith, of Scarborough, Maine, and although attending no particular church, is a Universalist in sentiment and belief.

## BENJAMIN R. WELLS.

Mr. Wells is a very quiet and industrious man, and has proven himself a good representative. He is a practical farmer, residing at North Chili, Monroe county, and was chosen to his present position by a majority of upwards of twelve hundred. In politics, he is consistent and unyielding, always contending to the "bitter end" for pure Republican principles, and is seldom, if ever, found setting aside his political sentiments for the sake of mere expediency. His reputation in the community in which he resides is that of a high-minded and honorable gentleman, and he is one of those persons who always make friends wherever they may go.

## WILLIAM J. WHEELER.

MR. WHEELER is a very quiet and industrious member of the House. He never participates in the discussions of that body, having a natural diffidence which always prevents him from speaking, but his sound, practical common sense and good judgment render him an invaluable man and a good representative. In politics, he was formerly a Whig, subsequently acting with the American party, and since taking his seat in the Legislature has co-operated with the Democrats in their opposition to Republicanism. He is a gentleman of high standing and influence in the community in which he resides, and enjoys a high degree of personal and political popularity wherever he is known.

## MATTHEW WIARD.

MR. WIARD is the only gentleman in the Legislature of whom the author has failed entirely to obtain any authentic information. Those who know him best, therefore, will appreciate in what is here said of him the necessity of reliable *data* in biographical sketching.

Mr. Wiard was born on the island of Japan, in the last century. It is said he never had any parents at all, and there are those who assert that, like another distinguished individual, of whom we read in Uncle Tom's Cabin, he was not born at all, having just naturally sprung spontaneously into existence. Of his descent, nothing has ever been said, it being also involved in mysterious doubt. He never passed through College, but knows more than any other ten men combined in the Legislature. He owns the entire State of New York, which he took possession of immediately upon his arrival in America, and now occupies the highest position in the civilized world at Albany. His political views are strongly anti-slavery, and he has subsisted chiefly on niggers since the establishment of the Republican party, having a special abhorence of the entire race of fire-eaters. He is down on the doctrine of secession, and in favor of hanging every man south of Mason and Dixon's line who will not swear eternal allegiance to the American Eagle, and has, doubtless, a stronger solution of gunpowder in his veins than any other man in the Assembly.

## CHRISTIAN B. WOODRUFF.

MR. WOODRUFF is a native of the city of New York, where he now resides, and is thirty-two years of age. He was a member of the House in 1859, pursuing a quiet and industrious course in that body as a member of the Standing Committee on Privileges and Elections, and was re-elected to the Assembly of 1860, where he served as a member of the Standing Committees on Militia, and Erection and Division of Towns and Counties, and a member of the Select Committee on so much of the Governor's Message as related to the Excise Law.

Mr. Woodruff has always been firmly and consistently attached to the Democratic party, and wields a pretty strong political influence throughout the district which he represents. He is a young gentleman of superior personal qualifications, the attachments of his friends and associates being strong and unyielding, and he is said to be among the most faithful and energetic in the discharge of the duties of his present position.

## GEORGE W. WRIGHT.

Mr. Wright was born in Pokeepsie, Dutchess county, N. Y., on the 22d of November, 1802. He is of pure English descent. His father, who was from Litchfield county, Connecticut, died in that place about the year 1830, at the age of sixty; and his mother, whose maiden name was Mary Rice, and who came from Clarendon, Rutland county, Vermont, died in Kingston, Ulster county, N. Y., on the 1st of June, 1812, at the age of thirty-two.

Mr. Wright went into Vermont as early as 1812, and located himself in Western New York in 1826, where he remained until 1828, since which time he has been a resident of Genesee county. He received a common English education in Vermont, and having served an apprenticeship at the clothier's trade, worked at that business some ten or twelve years. He is now engaged in the mercantile trade, in which he has been successfully employed for thirty years. In the town of Pembroke, where he now resides, he has held the offices of Town Clerk, Justice of the Peace, and Supervisor, and in every position to which he was promoted was found faithful and honest in the discharge of his official duties. He cast his first vote for Mr. Crawford for President in 1824, and was always identified with the old Democratic party until 1840. He then joined the Whig party, to which he belonged until it abandoned its organization, when he became a Republican.

Mr. Wright was married, in 1829, to Miss Eliza C., daughter of U. P. B. Monroe, of Batavia, Genesee county, and cherishes a partiality for the Universalist denomination.

## DANIEL YOUNG.

Mr. Young was born at Kingston, Ulster county, N. Y., in the year 1822. His lineage embraces the Saxon, Celt, Teuton, and Frank, his father being of English and Irish extraction, and his mother of French and German. His father, Dr. John Young, who was a prominent physician of extensive practice in Ulster county, died three years ago, at the age of sixty-eight; and his mother, whose maiden name was Margaret DeWitt, is still living, at the age of fifty-seven.

Mr. Young received a preparatory education at the Academy, in his native place, and at the age of sixteen entered the United States Military Academy at West Point, with the intention of becoming a soldier. Here he remained until the completion of his eighteenth year,

13

when he was attacked by a disease of the lungs, which prostrated him for many months, threatening a fatal termination, and compelling him to resign his position. He then entered the store of an apothecary, with the expectation of becoming a druggist. He continued in this business until 1844, when he became Postmaster at Kingston. At present, he is a conductor on the Hudson River Railroad—a position in which he has secured the unbounded confidence of the officers of that company, and the reputation of being a favorite with the travelling public. In politics he has always been an unflinching, uncompromising Democrat, of the adamantine school, and as a politician asks no quarter and makes no concessions. He was chosen to his present position from the district represented in the Assembly during the past two years by the Hon. Frederick A. Conkling, and as an evidence of his great personal popularity, it may be stated that although the nominee of Mozart Hall, he was enthusiastically supported by the entire Democratic party, and was elected by a majority of seven hundred in a strong Republican district. It is needless to say that the b'hoys went for him to a man. He is a gentleman of kind and courteous manners, good-natured, and jolly almost to a fault, and although inexperienced in legislative routine, has already succeeded, by his energy, address, and sterling common sense, in making his mark as a representative of the Democratic masses.

Mr. Young was married, in 1845, to Miss Maria Louisa Masters, of Ulster county, who has been dead for nearly twelve years. Although not a professor of religion, he attends the exercises of the Methodist Episcopal Church.

# ALPHABETICAL LIST

OF

# MEMBERS OF THE ASSEMBLY,

*With the Districts and Counties they represent, Post-office address, and Politics.*

HON. DEWITT C. LITTLEJOHN, *Speaker*, Oswego co., Rep.

| Dis. | Assemblymen. | Counties. | P. O. Address. | Pol. |
|---|---|---|---|---|
| 2 | Ainsworth, Stephen H., | Ontario, | West Bloomfield, | R. |
| 5 | Andrus, Lucius C., | Kings, | Brooklyn, | R. |
| 1 | Andrus, William, | Franklin, | Malone, | R. |
| 1 | Angel, Wilkes, | Allegany, | Angelica, | R. |
| 2 | Anthony, Smith, | Cayuga, | Fleming, | R. |
| 16 | Arcularius, Henry, | New York, | New York, | D. |
| 3 | Bailey, Harvey, | Jefferson, | Lafargeville, | R. |
| 1 | Baldwin, Edmund, | Lewis, | Turin, | R. |
| 2 | Ball, L. Chandler, | Rensselaer, | Hoosick Falls, | R. |
| 1 | Barber, Cero F., | Tioga, | Spencer, | R. |
| 2 | Barnes, Milton, | Orange, | Edenville, | D. |
| 1 | Bedell, Gilbert, | Greene, | Coxsackie, | D. |
| 2 | Benedict, Lewis, Jr., | Albany, | Albany, | R. |
| 1 | Benton, Heman, | Cayuga, | Ira, | R. |
| 2 | Bergen, Alexander J. | Suffolk, | Islip, | D. |
| 3 | Bingham, Anson, | Rensselaer, | Nassau, | R. |
| 13 | Birdsall, Charles E., | New York, | New York, | R. |
| 2 | Bolles, Frederick A., | Otsego, | Unadilla, | R. |
| 1 | Brewster, Charles T., | Putnam, | Cold Spring, | R. |
| 1 | Bryan, Daniel B., | Steuben, | Sonora, | R. |
| 1 | Buckbee, Joseph, | Schoharie, | Esperance, | D. |
| 1 | Burr, James H., | Fulton & Hamilton, | Gloversville, | R. |

| Dis. | Assemblymen. | Counties. | P. O. Address. | Pol. |
|---|---|---|---|---|
| 1 | Burt, Friend H., | Broome, | Millburn | R. |
| 1 | Callahan, John, | New York, | New York, | D. |
| 3 | Camp, Benjamin F., | Westchester, | Somers, | R. |
| 1 | Carter, Thomas, | Chenango, | Pitcher, | R. |
| 2 | Catlin, Nicholas M., | Washington, | Kingsbury, | R. |
| 3 | Chapman, Abner, | Onondaga, | South Onondaga, | R. |
| 3 | Chittenden, Clark S., | St. Lawrence, | Hopkinton, | R. |
| 2 | Collin, Norton S., | Columbia, | Hillsdale, | R. |
| 3 | Comstock, Nathan, | Kings, | Brooklyn, | R. |
| 2 | Corning, Joseph W., | Wayne, | Palmyra, | R. |
| 10 | Cozans, Luke F., | New York, | New York, | D. |
| 8 | Craft, Andrew, | New York, | New York, | R. |
| 4 | Darcy, James, | Kings, | Brooklyn, | D. |
| 3 | Davis, Redman S., | Steuben, | Greenwood, | R. |
| 1 | Doolittle, John J., | Wyoming, | Weathersfield Springs | R. |
| 1 | Dutcher, John B., | Dutchess, | Wing's Station, | R. |
| 1 | Dwight, Jeremiah W. | Tompkins, | Dryden, | R. |
| 1 | Ellingwood, N. Dane, | Richmond, | Exchange Place, | D. |
| 1 | Emerick, Jeremiah, | Onondaga, | Baldwinsville, | R. |
| 2 | Farnum, Samuel J., | Dutchess, | Poughkeepsie, | R. |
| 1 | Faxon, Walter A., | Warren, | Chestertown, | R. |
| 1 | Ferrey, Elijah E., | Otsego, | Schenevas, | R. |
| 4 | Ferris, Zebulon, | Erie, | East Hamburgh, | R. |
| 1 | Field, Perez H., | Ontario, | Geneva, | R. |
| 1 | Finch, Martin, | Essex, | Keeseville, | R. |
| 1 | Fish, Frothingham, | Montgomery, | Fultonville, | R. |
| 7 | Fisher, George H., | Kings, | Williamsburgh, | R. |
| 1 | Fullerton, Steph. W., Jr., | Orange, | Newburgh, | R. |
| 1 | Fulton, John, | Saratoga, | Waterford, | D. |
| 1 | Gardner, Step. St. John, | Sullivan, | Barryville, | D. |
| 1 | Gibbons, Jay, | Albany, | Dormansville, | D. |
| 11 | Hardy, John, | New York, | New York, | D. |
| 1 | Hill, Peter, | Washington, | Coila, | R. |
| 14 | Hutchings, Robert C., | New York, | New York, | D. |
| 2 | Hyatt, Francis A., | Madison, | Fenner, | R. |
| 2 | Hyland, George, | Livingston, | Dansville, | R. |

| Dis. | Assemblymen. | Counties. | P. O. Address. | Pol. |
|---|---|---|---|---|
| 1 | Johnson, William, | Seneca, | Seneca Falls, | D. |
| 17 | Jones, Jay Jarvis, | New York, | New York, | D. |
| 4 | Kenny, Wm. J. C., | New York, | New York, | D. |
| 3 | Kenyon, Marquis L., | Oneida, | Rome, | D. |
| 1 | Kernan, Francis, | Oneida, | Utica, | D. |
| 1 | Kinney, Loammi. | Cortland, | Homer, | R. |
| 1 | Knapp, William R., | Rockland, | Haverstraw, | D. |
| 12 | Lambrecht, John, | New York, | New York, | R. |
| 1 | L'Amoreaux, Jabez S., | Wayne, | Clyde, | R. |
| 3 | Lansing, Henry, | Albany, | Albany, | A. |
| 1 | Lasher, Samuel, | Columbia, | Germantown, | R. |
| 2 | Lewis, Samuel E., | Chenango, | Oxford, | R. |
| 4 | Lewis, William, | Oneida. | Remsen, | R. |
| 3 | Long, Benjamin H., | Erie, | Tonawanda, | D. |
| 1 | Lord, Orin B., | Madison, | Poolville, | R. |
| 1 | Loughran, Robert, | Ulster, | Saugerties. | R. |
| 1 | McDermott, William J., | Westchester, | Westchester, | D. |
| 1 | McFadden, Henry, | Clinton, | Beekmantown, | R. |
| 1 | Macomber, Alonzo, | Schenectady, | Quaker street, | R. |
| 1 | Markell, John, | Herkimer, | Manheim Centre, | R. |
| 2 | Marshall, Levi T., | Oneida, | Vernon Centre, | R. |
| 2 | May, Lucius S., | Allegany, | Belmont, | R. |
| 1 | Mekeel, Abram V., | Schuyler, | Seersburgh, | R. |
| 2 | Merritt, Edwin A., | St. Lawrence, | Pierpont, | R. |
| 1 | Montague, David, | Jefferson, | Sackett's Harbor, | R. |
| 2 | Moore, Marquis D., | Kings, | Brooklyn, | R. |
| 2 | Morgan, Lewis H., | Monroe, | Rochester, | R. |
| 2 | Myres, Austin, | Onondaga, | Syracuse, | R. |
| 6 | Nesbitt, Joseph, | Kings, | Williamsburgh, | D. |
| 1 | Norton, Nelson I., | Cattaraugus, | Hinsdale, | R. |
| 2 | Odell, N. Holmes, | Westchester, | Tarrytown, | D. |
| 2 | Philbrick, Franklin, | Cattaraugus, | Gowanda, | R. |
| 2 | Pierce, George T., | Ulster, | Esopus, | R. |
| 1 | 'Prendergast, Henry A., | Chautauqua, | Quincy, | R. |
| 1 | Provost, Andrew J., | Kings, | Williamsburgh, | D. |

13*

| Dis. | Assemblymen. | Counties. | P. O. Address. | Pol. |
|---|---|---|---|---|
| 1 | Randall, Gideon, | Orleans, | Kendall, | R. |
| 2 | Rice, Victor M., | Erie, | Buffalo, | R. |
| 1 | Richardson, Charles, | St. Lawrence, | Morristown, | R. |
| 2 | Roberts, Martin, | Monroe, | Henrietta, | R. |
| 1 | Robinson, Lucius, | Chemung, | Elmira, | R. |
| 3 | Salisbury, Mason, | Oswego, | Sandy Creek, | R. |
| 2 | Sanford, Richard K., | Fulton, | Oswego, | R. |
| 1 | Saxe, Charles J., | Troy, | Rensselaer, | D. |
| 2 | Scovell, Oliver P., | Lewiston, | Niagara, | R. |
| 5 | Shaw, John J., | New York, | New York, | R. |
| 1 | Sherer, Gilbert, | Penn Yan, | Yates, | R. |
| 9 | Sherwood, Horatio N., | New York, | New York, | R. |
| 2 | Shull, Josiah, | Mohawk, | Herkimer, | R. |
| 2 | Smith, Hiram, 2d, | Smith's Mills, | Chautauqua, | R. |
| 1 | Smith, Henry P. | Tonawanda, | Niagara, | R. |
| 2 | Smith, Jeffrey, | Woodhull, | Steuben, | R. |
| 1 | Smith, Seymour E., | Masonville, | Delaware, | R. |
| 2 | Sumner, James, Jr., | Whiteside'aCorn'rs, | Saratoga, | R. |
| 1 | Taber, Stephen, | Roslyn, | Queens, | D. |
| 2 | Townsend, John D., | Astoria, | Queens, | D. |
| 3 | Turner, Benjamin, Jr., | Olive Bridge, | Ulster, | R. |
| 1 | Tuthill, James H., | Suffolk, | Riverhead, | R. |
| 15 | Varian, George W. | New York, | New York, | D. |
| 2 | Wager, David J., | Jefferson, | Philadelphia, | R. |
| 2 | Walsh, William, | New York, | New York, | D. |
| 2 | Waterbury, Daniel, | Delaware, | Margaretville, | R. |
| 1 | Watson, Stephen V. R., | Erie, | Buffalo, | R. |
| 6 | Webster, Samuel T., | New York, | New York, | D. |
| 3 | Wells, Benjamin R., | Monroe, | North Chili, | R. |
| 4 | Wheeler, William J., | Albany, | Cohoes, | D. |
| 1 | Wiard, Matthew, | Livingston, | East Avon, | R. |
| 3 | Woodruff, Christian B., | New York, | New York, | D. |
| 1 | Wright, George W., | Genesee, | East Pembroke, | R. |
| 7 | Young, Daniel, | New York, | Huds.R.R.Dpt,N.Y, | D. |

# ASSEMBLY STANDING COMMITTEES.

*Ways and Means.*—Robinson, Angel, Ferry, Pierce, Kernan, Odell, Woodruff.

*Commerce and Navigation.*—Moore, Shaw, Ferris, Mekeel, Johnson.

*Canals.*—Watson, Myres, Sanford, Shull, Barber, Fulton, Johnson.

*Railroads.*—May, Dutcher, W. Andrus, Kenyon, Varian.

*Banks.*—Camp, H. P. Smith, Field, Varian, Lansing.

*Insurance Companies.*—Benedict, L. C. Andrus, Craft, Birdsall, Saxe.

*Two-Thirds and Three-Fifths Bills.*—Fullerton, Tuthill, Bailey, Townsend, Ellingwood.

*Colleges, Academies, and Common Schools.*—Rice, Merritt, Wager, Tuthill, Jones.

*Grievances.*—Collier, Baldwin, Montague, Buckbee, Bedell.

*Privileges and Elections.*—Finch, Fisher, Birdsall, Saxe, Odell.

*Petitions of Aliens.*—Morgan, Fullerton, Chapman, Provost, Knapp.

*Erection and Division of Towns and Counties.*—Richardson, Doolittle, Brewster, Darcy, Young.

*Claims.*—Fish, Emerick, J. Smith, Lord, Taber.

*Internal Affairs of Towns and Counties.*—Dwight, Wells, Catlin, Burr, Walsh.

*Medical Societies and Colleges.*—Loughran, Lambrecht, Chapman, McDermott, Kenny.

*State Charitable Institutions.*—L. C. Andrus, Burt, Davis, Arcularius, Young.

*Incorporation of Cities and Villages.*—Prendergast, Fisher, Ball, Sherwood, Angel, Woodruff, Hardy.

*Manufacture of Salt.*—Myres, Ferris, Benton, Sanford, Bergen.

*Trade and Manufactures.*—Salisbury, Hyland, Burt, Callahan, Arcularius.

*State Prisons.*—Farnum, Anthony, McFadden, Cozans, McDermott.

*Engrossed Bills.*—Wright, Hyatt, Markell, S. E. Smith, Long.

*Militia and Public Defence.*—Pierce, Bolles, Bryan, Macomber, Webster.

*Roads and Bridges.*—H. Smith, L'Amoreaux, Hyatt, Faxon, Gardner.

*Public Lands.*—Chittenden, Norton, Carter, Darcy, Wheeler.

*Indian Affairs.*—Merritt, Scovell, Lasher, S. E. Lewis, Bergen.

*Charitable and Religious Societies.*—Kinney, Philbrick, Turner, Sherer, Provost.

*Agriculture.*—Marshall, Sumner, Ainsworth, Barnes, Gibbons.

*Public Printing.*—Shaw, W. Lewis, Roberts, Webster, Nesbitt.

*Expenditures in the Executive Department.*—Macomber, Hill, Wiard, Barnes, Long.

*Judiciary.*—Bingham, Finch, Corning, Waterbury, Comstock, Kernan, Hutchings.

*Joint Library.*—Ball, Morgan, Randall, Townsend, Jones.

*Expenditures of the House.*—Anthony, Randall, Wiard, Wright, Fulton.

# STATE OFFICERS,

## AND CLERKS IN THE DEPARTMENTS, WITH THEIR SALARIES.

### EXECUTIVE DEPARTMENT.

| Name. | Office. | Salary. |
|---|---|---|
| E. D. Morgan | Governor | $4,000 |
| Robert Campbell | Lieut.-Governor | $6 a day. |
| Lockwood L. Doty | Private Secretary | 2,000 |
| John H. Linsly | Chief Clerk | 2,000 |

### STATE DEPARTMENT.

| Name. | Office. | Salary. |
|---|---|---|
| David R. Floyd Jones | Secretary of State | $2,500 |
| Henry P. Wilcox | Dep. Secretary of State | 1,700 |
| A. N. Wakefield | Chief Clerk | 1,000 |
| Diedrich Willus, Jr. | Clerk | 1,000 |
| Jonathan H. Burdick | " | 1,000 |
| David B. McNeil, Jr. | " | 1,000 |
| Robert Bamber | " | 1,000 |
| John Sharts | " | 1,000 |

### COMPTROLLER'S DEPARTMENT.

| Name. | Office. | Salary. |
|---|---|---|
| Robert Denniston | Comptroller | $2,500 |
| Philip Phelps | Dep. Comptroller | 2,000 |
| Peter Keyser | Acct. and Transfer Officer | 1,750 |
| Brace Millerd | Chief Tax Clerk | 1,200 |
| Henry B. Burr | Clerk | 900 |
| Augustus Dennison | " | 900 |
| Henry Evans | " | 900 |

| Name. | Office. | Salary. |
|-------|--------|--------|
| Francis G. Fine | Clerk | 900 |
| Henry Gallien | " | 900 |
| I. McMurdy | " | 900 |
| A. G. Murray | " | 900 |
| Edmund Sloan | " | 900 |
| Arthur B. Wood | " | 900 |

## TREASURER'S DEPARTMENT.

| Name. | Office. | Salary. |
|-------|--------|--------|
| Philip Dorsheimer | Treasurer | $2,500 |
| Joseph Stringham | Dep. Treasurer | 1,500 |
| George A. Stannard | Clerk | 1,000 |
| Louis Duemplemann | " | 1,000 |
| Charles H. Payne | " | 1,000 |

## ATTORNEY-GENERAL'S DEPARTMENT.

| Name. | Office. | Salary. |
|-------|--------|--------|
| Charles G. Myers | Attorney-General | $2,500 |
| Stephen H. Hammond | Dep. Attorney-General | 1,500 |
| George R. Myers | Clerk | 800 |
| Matthew Hendrickson | Messenger | 250 |

## STATE ENGINEER AND SURVEYOR'S DEPARTMENT.

| Name. | Office. | Salary. |
|-------|--------|--------|
| Van R. Richmond | State Engineer and Surveyor | $2,500 |
| George R. Perkins | Dep State Eng. and Surv.. | 2,000 |
| B. S. Van Rensselaer | Land Department | 900 |
| J. Wesley Smith | Engineer Clerk | 750 |
| Henry A. Petrie | Railroad Clerk | 750 |

# OFFICERS OF THE SENATE.

| Name. | Office. | County. |
|---|---|---|
| James Terwilliger | Clerk | Onondaga. |
| Charles G. Fairman | Journal Clerk | Chemung. |
| Asahel N. Cole | Assistant Clerk | Allegany. |
| Lauren L. Rose | Deputy Clerk | Wayne. |
| Geo. W. Palmer | Engrossing Clerk | Chautauqua. |
| Ira Bowen | Librarian | Cortland. |
| D. E. Wilds | Assistant Librarian | Oswego. |
| James C. Clark | Sergeant-at-Arms | Warren. |
| George H. Knapp | Postmaster | Dutchess. |
| Peter Kilmer | Doorkeeper | Schoharie. |
| Charles Johnson | 1st Assistant Doorkeeper | Herkimer. |
| John H. France | 2d " " | Ulster. |
| Casper Walter | 3d " " | Monroe. |
| Wm. Gamble | Assistant Postmaster | Steuben. |
| Caleb S. Babcock | Assist't Sergeant-at-Arms | Westchester. |
| Nathaniel Goodwin | Keeper Senate Chamber | Albany. |
| Joseph Garlinghouse | Janitor | Cayuga. |

# REPORTERS.

| Name. | Paper. |
|---|---|
| T. S. Gillett | Albany Evening Journal. |
| D. A. Manning | Albany Atlas and Argus. |
| Wm. H. Bogart | N. Y. Courier and Enquirer. |
| John F. Cleveland | N. Y Daily Tribune. |
| Douglas A. Levien | Associated Press. |
| James McFarland | Albany Evening Standard. |
| W. M. Gillespie | New York Sun. |
| J. C. Cuyler | Albany Express. |
| Chellis D. Swain | Albany Statesman. |
| James M. Baker | N. Y. Daily News. |
| Jos. R. Dixon | Cortland County Republican. |
| John F. McQuade | Utica Telegraph. |
| Spence Spencer | American Citizen. |
| W. E. Kisselburgh | Troy Daily Times. |

# OFFICERS OF THE ASSEMBLY.

| Name. | Office. | County. |
|---|---|---|
| Hanson A. Risley | Clerk | Chautauqua. |
| C. M. Scholefield | Assistant Clerk | Oneida. |
| C. S. Underwood | Journal Clerk | Cayuga. |
| Henry V. Colt | Engrossing Clerk | Livingston. |
| P. D. Ludington | Deputy Clerk | Sullivan. |
| M. J. Farrell | Librarian | Chautauqua. |
| R. U. Owens | Assistant Librarian | Oneida. |
| C. D. Easton | Sergeant-at-Arms | Montgomery. |
| T. Miller | Assistant Sergeant-at-Arms | Essex. |
| Geo. C. Dennis | Doorkeeper | Washington. |
| H. Henderson | 1st Assistant Doorkeeper | Erie. |
| S. Wilson | 2d " " | St. Lawrence. |
| A. H. Stoutenburgh | Doorkeeper, Ladies' Gallery | New York. |
| George A. Gifford | " Middle Outer Door | Rensselaer. |
| Wm. B. Cornwell | " North Outer Door | Wayne |
| H. N. Davis | " Gent's Gallery | Westchester. |
| B. Kirk | " Cloak Room | Delaware. |
| Ithamer Smith | Postmaster | Alleghany. |
| J. F. Ripley | Janitor and Keeper of Assembly Chamber | Wyoming. |

---

# REPORTERS.

| Name. | Paper. |
|---|---|
| William Richardson | Albany Evening Journal. |
| D. A. Levien | Atlas and Argus, and Associated Press. |
| W. W. Perkins | Albany Republican Statesman. |
| J. B. Stonehouse | Elmira Daily Advertiser. |
| H. J. Hastings | Albany Knickerbocker. |
| R. M. Griffin | Albany Evening Standard. |
| J. B. Manning | Brooklyn Eagle. |
| J. T. Cleveland | New York Tribune. |
| Alexander Wilder | New York Evening Post. |
| J. B. Swain | New York Times. |
| Hiram Calkins | New York Herald. |
| George W. Bull | New York Commercial Advertiser. |
| James H. Ledlie | Auburn Daily Advertiser. |
| F. B. Hubbell | Troy Daily Whig. |
| D. Card | Rochester Daily Express. |
| Henry W. Faxon | Buffalo Daily Courier. |

CPSIA information can be obtained
at www.ICGtesting.com
Printed in the USA
BVHW041338270622
640732BV00001B/66